Dear Mystery Reader:

Enthusiastic. Fervent. And above all, loyal. These three words best describe Don Winslow's fast-growing legion of fans. Unfortunately for Don's many readers, however, finding books in his Neal Carey series was murder. But thanks to DEAD LETTER, those days are over. After much clamor for paperback editions of the Neal Carey series, St. Martin's Press is making it happen. For the first time, all of Don's Edgar-nominated series will be available in paperback.

A Long Walk Up the Water Slide is the exciting fourth installment in the Neal Carey series. Splitting his time between grad school and private eyeing, Neal's got what looks to be a simple mission: find Polly Paget and clean up her act before she goes on television to denounce her boss, a conservative network president, as a rapist. But as usual for Neal, no case is as easy as it looks. Along the way, Neal must contend with FBI agents, hit men, and a porn king who've all got Polly at the top of their most wanted list.

Like Elmore Leonard and Donald Westlake, Winslow is a brilliant, comical writer with appeal well beyond the mystery genre, in fact, even beyond the book world. Columbia Pictures has bought the film rights to all five Neal Carey novels and plans on developing the character for a feature film. Check out one of Don's books and find out for yourself what all the buzz is about. Enjoy!

Yours in crime,

Joe Veltre

Joe Veltre
Associate Editor
St. Martin's DEAD LETTER Paperback Mysteries

Also by Don Winslow

A Cool Breeze on the Underground
The Trail to Buddha's Mirror
Way Down on the High Lonely

a long walk up the water slide

DON WINSLOW

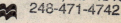
St. Martin's Paperbacks

A LONG WALK UP THE WATER SLIDE

Copyright © 1994 by Don Winslow.

Cover photograph copyright © Kaz Chiba/Photonica

Library of Congress Catalog Card Number: 94-3772

ISBN: 0-312-96617-2

Printed in the United States of America

St. Martin's Press hardcover edition published 1994
St. Martin's Paperbacks edition/July 1998

St. Martin's Paperbacks are published by St. Martin's Press, 175 Fifth
Avenue, New York, NY 10010.

10 9 8 7 6 5 4 3 2 1

To Buddy

*"Today, everyone takes part
in public executions
through the newspapers."*
—Elias Canetti, *Masse und Macht*

*"Motive? There are only three motives:
greed, lust, and greed."*
—Anonymous witness

Prologue

*H*e never should have smelled the coffee.

Neal Carey was lying in bed when the scent drifted under the door and snuck into his nose.

As he lingered in that pleasant zone between sleep and wakefulness, he savored the fact that it was Saturday morning and he didn't have to get up for anything. But the coffee smelled so good, not rushing-to-work, out-of-a-can coffee, but some of that special coffee that Karen had bought in Reno last month. Saturday-morning coffee, hazelnut or maybe Kenya AA, and he thought he detected a scent of chocolate.

If it was a custom blend, Karen must have been up early grinding it, which was unusual because she liked to sleep late on weekends. Neal pictured her shiny black hair and blue eyes and decided that maybe he'd join her in the kitchen so he could sip coffee and look at her. They could have a big breakfast and then drive out into the hills somewhere for a long hike, or maybe head out to Milkovsky ranch, borrow a couple of horses, and ride along Sandy Creek until they found a spot for a picnic. The day had the potential to be a glorious September Saturday in the northern Nevada wilderness known as the High Lonely, where for the first time in his life Neal Carey wasn't a bit lonely.

And that coffee just smelled so damn good.

Neal rolled out of bed, opened the door, and heard a voice.

That voice: the voice with all the soothing qualities of a rock scraping across a cheese grater.

"This is very nice," the voice was saying. "Your own blend?"

Neal heard Karen answer, "Half hazelnut, half macadamia."

Macadamia?

"And these muffins," the voice said, "delicious."

"Neal made them," Karen said.

Neal stood behind the bedroom door for a second, then walked through the small living room and stood in the kitchen doorway.

Karen spotted Neal first.

"Honey," she said, "look who's here."

"Hello, son," Joe Graham said.

It isn't just the voice, thought Neal. It's the smile, the sweet, cheerful, mocking smile of a rat on a landfill.

"Hello, Dad," Neal answered.

Karen gave Neal a peck on the cheek and handed him a cup of coffee.

Maybe I should give this stuff up, Neal thought. It smells like battery acid, makes my stomach hurt, and gives me a headache.

He pulled out a chair and sat down at the table.

That's where he made his big mistake. He should have gone back to bed, pulled the covers over his head, and refused to come out until Joe Graham was thirty thousand feet in the air, winging back to New York. If Neal Carey had done that, he never would have met Polly Paget, or gone to Candyland, or had to take a long walk up the water slide.

But he didn't.

He smelled the coffee.

Then he drank it.

Part One
Pollygate

Son, this job is so simple," Joe Graham said between bites of toast, "that even you could do it."

"More orange juice, Joe?" Karen asked. She hovered over Graham with a pitcher in her hand. Before that, she'd hovered over him with a plate of scrambled eggs, fried potatoes, and rye toast. Prior to that, she had just generally hovered, dispensing coffee, juice, and muffins while she made breakfast.

Neal shot her a dirty look. In the nine months they had lived together, Karen had made breakfast for him exactly once—Pop-Tarts, burned.

Neal did most of the cooking in the house.

Until Graham arrives, Neal thought, *and she turns into Aunt Bea.*

Karen returned the dirty look. Not an Aunt Bea dirty look, but a Karen Hawley "don't tread on me; I'll cook breakfast any damn time I feel like it" look.

Besides, Karen loved Joe Graham. That little leprechaun face was just so damn cute, and the artificial arm made him so vulnerable. She liked the way he respected himself and the people around him. And she knew the story of how Graham had raised Neal from an abandoned child into a pretty decent human being. Karen treated Graham like a beloved father-in-law, even though he wasn't Neal's real father and Neal wasn't her husband.

In 1980s America, Karen thought, families don't always come in square boxes.

"So what is this? Your Serpico look?" Graham asked.

He'd never seen Neal with long hair before, never mind the beard. And the worn denim shirt hanging over faded blue jeans? The kid needed a decade check.

"Sort of a disguise," Neal mumbled.

He was embarrassed. At first, the beard and hair were just that, a gesture toward disguising his identity, but then he came to like the look. Not even the look so much, he thought, but the feel: more laid-back, loosely wrapped, a nice change after he'd spent the first 27 years on his toes and wrapped tighter than the insides of a baseball.

"I like it," Karen said. She ran her fingers through his hair where it met his collar. "But maybe I should give it a trim tonight. It's looking a little shaggy."

This is nice, Graham thought. This is nice for the kid; he finally has somebody. Every other time I've come to get him, I've found him buried in a stack of books, index cards, and bad memories. Kid used to eat self-pity like it was ice cream. This time, he's with a stand-up woman who loves him so much, she doesn't take any of his crap. And he can't feel too sorry for himself; he opens his eyes in the morning and she's there.

"So do you want work?" Graham asked.

"Dad, I've been thinking . . ."

"When did that start?" Graham asked. He felt it was his duty to insult Neal.

"It's a recent development," Neal admitted. "But I've been thinking about retiring."

He'd been thinking about it real hard since the moment he squeezed the trigger and dropped a man dead in the snow. Then he disappeared into Karen Hawley's bedroom and didn't come out for weeks, hiding from the Feds, the Highway Patrol, and the local cops.

Then the funniest thing happened: nothing.

When he finally poked his head out—long hair, beard, and all—nobody cared. No cops came; no questions were asked; nobody in the little town of Austin, Nevada, said anything.

And Neal got a life.

"You're what, twenty-eight?" Graham asked.

"Working for Friends counts like dog years," Neal answered, "so I'm really one hundred and ninety-six."

Friends was shorthand for Friends of the Family, banker Ethan Kitteredge's private organization that helped his wealthier clients out of jams, which usually meant putting Neal and Graham smack in the middle of one. Neal had just gotten out of the last jam, and wasn't eager to get into another.

Besides, I'm happy, Graham, Neal thought. I get up in the morning, fix Karen her lunch, then go to my desk and work on my Smollett thesis until about noon. Then I either make lunch or walk down to Brogan's for a sandwich and a beer, then back to work until late afternoon, when I whip up dinner. Then Karen comes home and we eat, after which she usually grades homework. Then we might watch a little television before we go to bed. I like my life.

"I'm thinking about transfering my credits from Columbia," Neal said, "and finishing my degree at Nevada."

Finishing my degree: It had an unreal sound to it. He'd been trying to finish his master's degree for about six years, but work for Friends had taken him on some major detours from his goal of one day teaching English at a little college somewhere.

"Have you been getting the checks?" Graham asked.

Neal nodded. A few weeks after he'd gone underground, a package arrived at the door with a complete set of ID for a young man named Thomas Heskins. A few days after that, the checks started to come in an amount roughly equal to Neal's monthly salary as an operative for Friends of the Family.

Karen frowned at the mention of the checks, which were a

touchy subject in the house. Neal made more money sitting around the house working on "Tobias Smollett: The Image of the Outsider in the Eighteenth-Century English Novel" than Karen made working fifty-plus hours each week teaching elementary school. In typical Neal Carey fashion, he had decided to write his master's thesis before enrolling in a graduate program.

Karen Hawley loved Neal Carey deeply, but he did have a horse-and-cart problem. And now that she had a sabbatical semester, it was starting to become *her* horse-and-cart problem.

"The checks," Graham said, "were not meant to be a pension. They were sort of disability payments while you had to hide out."

Were? Neal thought. This didn't sound good.

"What are you saying, Dad?" Neal asked.

"I'm saying you can be Neal Carey again if you want."

Why would I want to do something like that? Neal thought.

"Who did you pay off?" Neal asked.

The "you" in this case being Kitteredge's bank in Providence, Rhode Island.

"The usual," Graham said. Washington politicians were about as hard to purchase as magazine subscriptions, although you did have to renew them more often. Besides, the feds didn't have much of a hard-on for this case. If someone did them a favor by disposing of a dirtbag neo-Nazi like Strekker, well, it was one less dirtbag they had to worry about. Graham couldn't prove that Neal had performed this particular service and they had never talked about it, but the last time Joe Graham had seen Neal Carey, he had been trotting out into the sagebrush with a rifle in his hands.

"Ed thinks it's time you came back to work," Graham said.

Ed was Ed Levine, manager of Friends' New York office, where Graham worked and Neal usually didn't.

"Who's missing?" Neal sighed. "Who do you want me to find?"

Because that was mostly what he did for Friends.

Graham smiled his rat-sucking-on-garbage smile and said, "That's the beauty part."

"What's the beauty part?" Neal asked. Giving in and asking was easier than letting Graham drag it out.

"You don't have to find anybody," Graham answered. "We already found her."

"Sooo . . . ?" Neal asked.

Graham grinned.

"We want you to teach her English."

"Who? Why? Where's she from?"

"Brooklyn," Graham answered.

"Which leaves who and why," Neal said.

"Are you taking the job?" asked Graham.

He wasn't going to give up anything else unless Neal was on the job.

Uh-uh, thought Neal. I say yes and then you tell me you found her in some prison in Outer Mongolia and my job is to break in, teach her English, and escape on camelback across the Soviet Union.

"I'm retired," Neal repeated.

"How much?" Karen asked Graham.

Neal raised his eyebrows at her.

"We've been talking about putting a deck on the back of the house," she explained.

Neal turned to Graham. "What is she, a witness?"

"Maybe," Graham answered.

"*Maybe?*"

Graham said, "It might depend on how good you do with her."

"Who is she," Neal asked, "Eliza Doolittle?"

Graham rubbed his artificial hand into his real palm. It was a habit he had when he got nervous or impatient.

"Are you on, or what?" Graham asked.

"Is this a mob thing?" Neal asked. Because mob witnesses were dangerous. People tended to get killed in their general vicinity. "You want me to clean up some mob bimbo who's mad because Guido slapped her around, and now she wants to tell the world about his funny friends, right?"

"Nothing like that," Graham promised.

"And where do I have to go?"

"That's the next beauty part. You don't even have to leave the house. We want to bring her here."

"Here," Neal echoed.

"Here?" Karen asked.

"Here," Graham repeated.

Neal laughed and turned to Karen. "Now how much do you want the deck?"

Graham also turned to Karen and gave her his most obsequious smile. "We think *you* would be a major asset in the cleaning-up process."

Karen poured Graham a fresh cup of coffee, sat down next to him, and put her arm around his shoulder.

"You know, Joe," she said, "when I envision this deck, I see a cedar hot tub on it."

Neal whooped with laughter.

"I like her," Graham said. "She's a vicious putz like you, but I like her."

"There's a lot to like," Neal agreed. A lot to love, he thought.

Graham said, "Okay, we're talking deck with Jacuzzi money."

"That was easy. Who is this mystery witness?" Neal asked.

Graham paused dramatically. He chewed his last bite of toast twenty-eight times and announced, "Polly Paget."

Karen's big blue eyes got bigger.

"The whole country's looking for Polly Paget," Neal said. "I should have known you had her."

Graham shrugged.

"Where is she?" Neal asked.

"Out in the car."

"You left that woman sitting out in the car?!" Karen yelled. "What do you think she is, luggage?"

"She was asleep."

Karen punched Graham in the shoulder and stormed out the kitchen door.

"Ouch," Graham said, looking a little hurt.

"One of Karen's dirty little secrets," Neal explained as he took a blueberry muffin, "is that she reads *People* magazine. Is it all true?"

"Polly Paget says it is," Graham said as he rubbed his shoulder.

Neal munched on the muffin. Graham's answer meant that he didn't know whether or not to believe what Polly Paget was saying about Jackson Landis.

2

*P*olly Paget had been a typist in the secretarial pool of Jack Landis's New York office and, according to Polly, Jack Landis had done a few laps in her end of the pool.

On its own, Neal knew this was not particularly earthshaking. Polly Paget certainly wouldn't be the first secretary who had typed twenty words an hour and had the job security of a federal employee, and she wouldn't be the last secretary who did more work on her desk than at it. What started to make Polly Paget exceptional was the fact that she claimed she had been raped.

None of which would have even made the paper, except that the alleged rapist was none other than Jackson Landis himself, the founder, president, and majority owner of the Family Cable Network. Jack was also the devoted husband of Candy Landis, with whom he cohosted the top-rated cable show in the country, "The Jack and Candy Family Hour," a program so wholesome it made "The Lawrence Welk Show" look like a Tijuana animal act.

Neal didn't know whether he believed Polly himself.

She fits the part, Neal thought.

"Disiz a cute lihul place yoo got heah," Polly said as Karen set her suitcase down in the kitchen. "Gawd, izit faw enough away from evryting, or what. Oi mean, we drove an drove an drove an drove and Oi dint see anyting, nevuh moind a mall. An joo have a batroom Oi could use? Oi have *really* gadda pee.''

Polly Paget was a walking, talking—especially talking—stereotype. Her auburn hair was *big*—teased, blow-dried, and sprayed into a huge red halo that looked like a sunset over an oil refinery. She had a handsome, long face with a wide slash of mouth and two long incisors that looked just a little like fangs and gave her a slightly predatory look. Her long, thin nose had a slight Roman curve. Neal had to admit to himself that her eyes were sexy. Framed by wide red eyebrows, her green cat eyes sparkled behind the layers of mascara, eyeliner, and fake lashes. Everything about Polly screamed *bimbo*.

And Polly Paget was tall—a good five ten, with long legs, small breasts, and wide shoulders. She looked a hell of a lot more like the wolf than the lamb.

And the clothes: Today she was dressed entirely in brand-new denim that made it look as if she'd gone shopping for her trip to the West. Lots of silver and turquoise jewelry, and bright red fingernails that were so long, she couldn't possibly type even if she wanted to.

"You got any losh?" she asked as she came out of the bathroom. "So my hands don't dry? I've got the worst problem with dry hands. They crack if I don't use enough losh. I have some in one of the other bags, but it's out in the car."

Neal winced. Polly didn't say *the* or *they;* she said *de* and *dey,* and she seemed to have a little ventriloquist hidden in her throat that made her words sound as if they were coming out of her nose. And she didn't say *car;* she said *caw.*

Karen said, "I think I have some lotion in the bedroom. I'll go get it."

"I'll go get it with you," Neal said.

In the bedroom, Karen found a plastic bottle of lotion while Neal rummaged through the chest of drawers.

"What are you looking for?" Karen asked.

"A revolver," answered Neal. "One bullet or two?"

Karen smiled and grabbed Neal's shoulders.

"Her hair is so big!" she whispered. "I've always wanted to meet a woman with big hair like that."

"But do you want her staying here for a month or more?"

Karen looked at him sharply.

"Neal, the woman was raped!"

"The woman *says* she was raped."

Karen's blue eyes got serious as she tightened her grip on his shoulders.

"Neal Carey," she said, "if a woman says she was raped, then she was raped."

Not necessarily, Neal thought.

It was a little early for a beer, but it was also a little early to be taking on a new case, so Neal popped the cap with only a trace of guilt. Brezhnev, an enormous black dog of indeterminate breed, raised his head an inch off the floor and growled until Neal left a dollar on the counter. Brogan, the owner and namesake of the grubby saloon, snored away behind the bar in the old BarcaLounger he had rescued from the county dump. Neal hadn't seen Brogan get out of that chair except to go to the john, and there were people in Austin prepared to swear, based on olfactory evidence, that he didn't always get up for that.

Brogan started snoring. His head was tilted back and something kind of yellow dribbled from the edge of his mouth.

"Is he asleep or faking it?" Graham asked.

Neal looked over at Brezhnev, who kept one narrow eye on him.

"He's asleep. They take turns when someone is in the bar. The dog won't go to sleep unless Brogan is awake."

"He can't fake out the dog?"

"Nobody can fake out that dog."

Neal opened a second bottle, hopped back over the bar, and sat down at a table next to Graham, who was busily wiping the greasy tabletop with a handkerchief.

"Isn't there a clean place in this town?" Graham complained.

"It doesn't open until dinner," Neal answered. "So what does the bank have to do with Polly Paget?"

Karen had thrown them out of the house for a while so she could "get Polly settled." Which, Neal figured, meant putting away her underwear, finding a place for her cosmetics, and pumping her for information.

"Can I have a glass?" Graham asked.

"Brogan probably has one somewhere, but I don't think you want to see it," Neal answered. You could pull fifteen years of fingerprints off one of Brogan's beer glasses.

Graham took a fresh handkerchief from his jacket pocket and wiped the mouth of the beer bottle. He took a tentative sip and said, "Jack Landis is the majority owner of the FCN network. The bank's client, Peter Hathaway, is the largest minority owner. The minority owner wants to be the majority owner. Hathaway is pissed off because he thinks that Jack is overextending. And then there's Candyland."

"Candyland." Neal chuckled. He'd heard about Candyland on "The Jack and Candy Family Hour."

Candyland was going to be an enormous "family vacation resort" on the outskirts of San Antonio—as soon as it was finished, of course. They were still several million dollars short, so Jack and Candy were selling shares to their faithful viewers. Just send in five hundred bucks for your time-share condo. Jack and Candy made this offer about every twelve seconds. They were like vice cops in a strip joint when it came to hitting you up for Candyland money.

"It's a disaster," Graham said. "They're way over budget in every category and they're running out of cash."

"Are they really going to build it?"

Graham shrugged.

"Let me guess," Neal said. "The bank has a loan on it."

"But of course," Graham answered. "And the minority owner wants to work with the bank and get it straightened out. But how do you fire the most popular couple in America?"

"Tough one," Neal answered. "Maybe if he raped his secretary . . ."

"Bingo," Graham said.

"So is Polly telling the truth?" Neal asked.

"I dunno," Graham answered.

"The cops didn't believe he raped me," Polly said to Karen. "I mean, I was balling the guy for a year, right, and then I cry rape. But honest to God, the last time it was."

Karen was helping Polly put her underwear away in the small guest room. This was no easy task. Polly had a lot of underclothes.

"Jack is no great shakes in the sack anyway, to tell you the truth," Polly continued, "but who *would* be married to 'Canned-Ice'—that's what he used to call his wife. I mean, where would he get the practice, right? So he *needed* somebody, okay, and he was, like, nice to me? So every time he came to New York, we'd go back to my place and do it . . . and do it and do it and do it . . . but I got feeling *bad* about myself. I mean, this thing was going nowhere and there was his wife on the TV talking about how they had tried to have kids but couldn't and I'm in bed with the guy watching this. He used to like to do it while they were on the TV together, which got really creepy. I mean, there they were together all sweet and lovey-dovey and there we were in bed *doing* it. Don't you think that's kind of creepy?"

"Definitely creepy," Karen said.

"Even my best friend, Gloria, thinks it's creepy, and she's looser than I am. So anyway, after a while I said, 'Jack, I'm not doing it anymore while "The Jack and Candy Family Hour" is on,' and he got mad and we broke up, but then he came back and was really sweet and everything and so I took him back and we started doing it again, but *not* during 'The Jack and Candy Family Hour.' That's on tape, not live, you know."

"I kind of figured that out," Karen said. She handed Polly a bra that looked like a postdoctoral project at MIT.

Polly held it up and said, "One of the things I'm going to do with the money is have my boobs done, because I'm thinking about trying Hollywood, and you need boobs. I mean, I have boobs, of course, but not *boobs.*"

She held her hands out to demonstrate what she had in mind. Karen winced.

"I think you look great," she said.

"*Do you?* Awwww," Polly said. "Sometimes I think I look like a cheap tramp. I think that's what the cops thought, like 'She was asking for it,' you know, but I wasn't. I told Jack it was over. I was through with him and he asked for one last time and I told him no, but he wasn't going to take no for an answer, and the son of a bitch held me down and did it and I think that's rape, don't you?"

"Yes, I do."

"So do I, but try telling that to the cops. They look at you like you're nuts or something, but we'll see who's nuts."

Probably Neal after a month of this, Karen thought.

"So you decided to sue the son of a bitch," Karen said.

"The only way to make him pay," Polly said, "and I need the money, too, seeing as how I'm out of a job and I'm a shitty secretary anyway, to tell the truth, and I'm going to have a hard time finding a job because everyone in the whole country *hates* me."

"I don't hate you," Karen said. She felt goopy for saying it, but it felt like one of things you have to say. Anyway, she meant it. She kind of liked Polly Paget.

"You know the rest," Graham said to Neal. "Polly goes to some sleazebag lawyer, whose first move is to call every tabloid in the phone book and tell them how to spell his name."

Neal remembered seeing the headlines at the checkout counter in Austin's only grocery store. I WAS RAPED, SCREAMS BIMBO. BOMBSHELL DROPS BOMBSHELL. HAPPY JACK CAUGHT IN LOVE NEST. POLLY GETS HER CRACKER. IT'S ALL A LIE, SAYS CANDY LANDIS. CANDY STANDS BY MAN. Then the networks picked it up—a more somber tone but the same voyeuristic thrust: "Family Network chief Jack Landis accused of rape by alleged longtime mistress. Financial improprieties also alleged. An unidentified board member said to be demanding an investigation."

Then Jack responded. Media rivals were trying to destroy him. Filth peddlers wanted to drag him down into the gutter with them. The usually buttoned-up Candy broke into sobs on the show—who could be so cruel to do something like this? Polly Paget was a tool. The Family Cable Network will go on. Candyland will be built! Wild applause . . . audience members wept unashamedly. It was beautiful.

Then Polly's idiot lawyer held a press conference. Polly made a statement. She looked awful on camera and sounded worse. The good gentlemen and ladies of the press shredded her during the Q and A. She came across as a hard, cold, calculating . . . bimbo. It was awful.

That, Graham told Neal, was when the minority owner called Ethan Kitteredge at the bank. Kitteredge paid off Polly's lawyer, brought in a new firm, and arranged for Polly Paget to drop out of sight.

The press went crazy. A missing Polly Paget was much better

than an all-too-present one. Delicious speculation seized the public. Where was Polly? Why had she run? Had someone threatened her? Did this prove she was lying? Where was she?

"We put a fake Polly on a plane to L.A.," Graham explained, "and drove the real Polly up to Providence. She hid out at Kitteredge's house for ten days while the lawyers grilled her. That's when we decided we needed your dubious services. So we got on a private plane, flew to Reno, and here we are."

Hiding Polly turned out to be a brilliant move. With Polly not there to open her mouth, the minority owner was able to fill the ravenous media void with stories of cost overruns, lavish expenditures, and shoddy accounting until the press, inevitably, dubbed the affair "Pollygate."

And media magic struck Polly, too. Missing, she made the delicate transition from bimbo to sex symbol. Mysterious, she became a combination of Garbo and Monroe. Casual friends sold their stories for four figures. Grainy snapshots went for more. Offers came pouring into the new law firm and went unanswered—television interviews, magazine stories, a centerfold.

It was a feeding frenzy, a media circus. The only thing missing from Pollygate was Polly.

3

"Where is she?"

Candy Landis asked this question as if she actually expected an answer.

Her husband, Jack, stood against the big floor-to-ceiling corner window she had specially built to give him views of both the River Walk and the Alamo. She thought he looked handsome standing there, his full head of hair still black, his back straight, his tummy hanging just slightly over his belt.

Charles Whiting cleared his throat and started again. "She left her New York apartment in the company of a tall, heavyset male Caucasian and entered the back of a black limousine with opaque windows."

"Opaque? What's opaque?" Jack asked.

"You can't see through them, dear," Candy Landis said.

"Opaque," Jack Landis repeated to himself. "Go ahead."

"The limousine proceeded to La Guardia Airport, where Miss Paget exited the vehicle in the company of the same male Caucasian. The subject then proceeded to a first-class counter at American Airlines—"

"What subject?"

"Miss Paget."

"So what's the subject?" Jack Landis asked. "Geometry . . . history? Are we back in junior high or something?"

"That's an FBI phrase," Candy explained. "Isn't that an FBI phrase, Chuck?"

"It's a general law-enforcement term, Mrs. Landis."

"So then what did the subject do?" Jack Landis asked as he watched a young lady with legs longer than a deer's stroll along the sidewalk.

Charles Whiting cleared his throat again. In his years with the bureau, he'd had occasion to brief the director several times and hadn't been interrupted like this. But then again, Charles cut a distinguished figure. At fifty-four, his six foot three inches were still taut and ramrod-straight. Even under his gray suit, his shoulders showed the effects of his fifty daily push-ups. There was just enough gray on his temples to give him an air of experience, and his blue eyes were clear and firm.

"The subject boarded a flight for Los Angeles," Charles said. "Then . . ." Whiting paused.

"Go ahead, Chuck," Candy Landis said.

"Well . . . that's when we lost her, ma'am."

"Lost her? Lost her!" Jack Landis yelled. "What did she do, parachute or something!"

"She was a . . . uh . . . different woman when she got off the plane, sir."

"I've felt that way after a long flight myself," Candy said.

Jack gave her a look that was meant to be withering. It wasn't.

To his disappointment, Candy looked as composed as she always did. Her heart-shaped face was freshly made up, her lipstick was perfectly painted on her thin, tight lips, and every single one of her blond hairs was in place and then sprayed into a perfect halo of shining marble. She was wearing her usual business suit: tailored jacket, midcalf skirt, a white blouse with a rounded collar and a little red bow.

She's a goddamn pretty woman, Jack thought, but she looks like a painted statue, and about as soft.

Charles Whiting jumped into the awkward silence. "When she exited the aircraft, she was not Polly Paget."

"Was she in the company of the aforementioned male Caucasian?" Landis asked acidly.

"Yes, sir."

"So they pulled a switch in this opaque limo, huh?"

"That's what we think, sir."

"Too bad we didn't think that *before* she disappeared, huh, Chuck?"

Chuck assumed that Landis meant this to be a rhetorical question and didn't answer. He'd become familiar with rhetorical questions at the bureau. The director liked them.

The next question wasn't rhetorical.

"Who's behind all this?" Candy asked.

Jack Landis turned around slowly, his hands spread out and his jaw open in mock disbelief.

"Oh, come on, boys and girls," Jack said. "We know who's behind all this, don't we? I mean, shit, it don't take Efrem Zimbalist, Jr., to figure out that Peter Hathaway tried to use this lying bimbo to get my television stations from me. She couldn't go through with it and now he's whisked her away before people find out he's behind it. Believe you me, Pollygate is over with."

"But it isn't over with, Jackson," Candy said patiently. "Restaurant receipts are down, franchise offers are down, and contributions to Candyland have just about dried up."

Jack chuckled. "Okay, but I'll bet the ratings on the show are way up, so we're making up in advertising dollars whatever we're losing on the other end."

And, Sam Houston, will you look at the bumpers on that one.

"Not even close," Candy said. She'd spent three days reviewing the figures with the comptroller. "Ratings are up, but most of our advertisers are family-oriented businesses, and they're nervous about being associated with a scandal."

"Get new advertisers, then," Jack snapped. "Get some with some *cajones.*"

Whiting winced at the vulgarity. Candy didn't blink a perfect eyelash.

"Well, hell, the woman disappeared, didn't she?" Jack asked. "Don't that just prove what I been saying all along, that she made this whole thing up?"

Candy answered, "As a matter of fact, the polls show that her credibility rating has gone up six points since she disappeared from public view."

"Up?" Jack yelled.

"Up," Candy answered. "Sixty-three percent of respondents think that it is 'more likely than not' that you slept with her—"

"I didn't."

"And twenty-four percent believe that you raped her. Consider this for a moment, dear: If these numbers reflect the opinions of the board members—"

"I'm the chairman of the damn board!"

"Perhaps not for long, dear," Candy said calmly. "If these numbers don't turn around, Peter Hathaway might be chairman of the board soon. He's already bought up forty-three per—"

"I know, I know!" Jack yelled. "What are you, Miss Percentage today? So what are we supposed to do?"

Candy answered, "What we really need is for Miss Paget to come forward and publicly admit that she lied."

"Maybe you want to bring her on the show," Jack said.

"If that's what it takes," Candy said, then added, "dear."

Jack Landis stared down at the Alamo. Christ, he thought, I know how those poor bastards must have felt. And what if it ain't Hathaway who has Polly? What if it's the Justice Department? Or worse, "60 Minutes." Goddamn, that ancient capon

Mike Wallace would just love to spend a few of those sixty minutes with Polly Paget.

And so would I, Jack thought. Speaking of low dogs, so would I.

He missed going to bed with Polly. Polly was wild in bed, just wild. She would do things . . . just do things without thought or calculation that just made him crazy. That red hair whipping around, and those crazy green eyes sparkling . . .

Not like Canned-Ice, who tried hard, Lord knows. But that was just it. Everything Candy ever did in the bedroom, you thought she read in some magazine or book or something. You could almost hear her thinking about "technique." She brought all the spontaneity of a metronome into the bedroom.

Candice Hermione Landis looked at her husband and knew what he was thinking.

Jackson Hood Landis had grown up in poverty in East Texas and was scared to death of going back to either one. Candice herself had grown up in middle-class Beaumont, where her minister father made just enough money to send her to SMU before he died of a heart attack. Her mama thought that she was definitely marrying down when Candice took the vows with a salesman like Jack Landis, but Candice loved him, so that was that.

She and Jack saved and worked hard and bought a little restaurant in San Antonio, then another, and then another, and then Jackson heard the magic word: *franchise*. It didn't seem like it was very long at all before there were Jack's Family Diners ("A Lot of Good Food for a Little of Your Money") all over the country, and suddenly Jack and Candice were rich—very rich, oil money–rich, so rich that they didn't know what to do with the money.

So they bought the television station. ("Two things Americans are always going to do," Jack said, "eat and watch TV.") Of course, Jack wasn't content with one little station in San

Antonio. He had to franchise that, too, and pretty soon they had a network. And because Jack figured that since they were a family restaurant, they ought to be a family television network, too, that's what they did. They started the Family Cable Network, television the whole family could watch.

They sold America good wholesome food and good wholesome entertainment. And then came that fateful day when they decided to host an on-the-air Christmas party to thank all the employees and the viewers. Jack and Candice appeared together and the viewing public just loved it.

Who would have thought it? All they did was host a little party together, just like they did at home. They had guests and made conversation, and Candy played "The Old Family Bible" on the piano and everyone sang, and then Jack carved the turkey and Candy served, and the letters came *pouring* in. So they did a Fourth of July on-the-air barbecue, and then Thanksgiving . . . and another Christmas, and they had advertisers lining up to buy airtime.

"The Jack and Candy Family Hour" was born. At first it appeared weekly, but by popular demand, it became a daily show—five afternoons a week, plus the holiday specials, constant reruns morning and night.

Jack was wonderful on the show. He was a great performer . . . so handsome . . . and the audiences loved him, but Candy had the brains; it became her life's work.

She programmed the guests, bringing on good family entertainers, people with inspiring stories, and experts with some useful knowledge to share. (She really liked to find some good family entertainer who had an inspirational story or some expert knowledge. She had yet to find anyone who had all three.) She especially liked singers who had once been alcoholics and got cured by God, or comedians who'd had a gambling problem but got cured by God, or just plain folks who had had something horribly wrong with them and got cured by God. Not that the show was overtly religious; they were always very careful about not specifying which particular God did all this curing—it could be either a Christian *or* a Jewish God. She also liked to have women ex-convicts on the show—especially the ones who had had kids while in prison—and then have an expert on at the same time to teach them money management and how to stay within a budget instead of stealing things.

Candy planned the menus for the kitchen segment, making sure that each and every meal was both wholesome and economical, although she did splurge a little bit on her annual "Romantic Dinner for Two When the Kids Are Spending the Night at Grandma's" segment. Mostly she specialized in "stretcher meals"—making that Sunday roast last through Tuesday, or the chili that you could eat as just chili, or chili over spaghetti, or chili on a baked potato—not, as Jack had once joked on the air, meals that you ate before you got carried out on a stretcher.

Candy gave makeup tips (she noticed that women ex-convicts either wore too much makeup, which was unattractive to men, or no makeup at all, which was also unattractive to men, although she suspected that some of these women weren't interested in attracting men at all), and weight-loss tips (a can of Budweiser and a chocolate doughnut do not a breakfast make), and even tips on how to keep the passion alive in your marriage (a filmy negligee behind a locked door doesn't necessarily make you a prostitute).

While Candy knew that some people—perhaps thousands of people—made fun of her, she also knew that her work did some good for thousands of others. There were people out there who had sought help because a show had set an example for them, there were families who had made it through the week on her tuna casserole, and there were marriages that were better off just for the fact of having sent the kids to Grandma's for the night.

"You have to find her, Chuck," Candy said. "Find Polly Paget and persuade her to come forward and tell the truth."

Chuck Whiting met her eyes and saw the pain in them. Chuck Whiting, former FBI agent, dedicated Mormon, devoted husband and father of nine, was a true believer. He believed in God, country, family, and Jack and Candy—especially Candy. Looking at Candy's blue eyes, at her firm jaw and silky skin, at the golden hair that shone like a temple, at the shimmering purity that was Candice Landis, Chuck Whiting—had he not been a true believer in God, country, and family—would have thought he was in love.

"I'll find her, Mrs. Landis," he said. He felt a lump in his throat.

"Well, you kids have a good time playing detective," Jack said. "I got a meeting to go to."

He nodded to Whiting, gave Candy a peck on the cheek, and walked out.

Charles Whiting could barely breathe. His chest was tight and he was afraid he was blushing, because Candy Landis was looking at him in a very personal way. Charles Whiting wasn't comfortable with emotional intimacy and would have been the first person to tell you so.

"Yes, Mrs. Landis?"

"He had sex with her, didn't he, Chuck?"

Charles felt dizzy. He took a deep breath and answered, "Yes ma'am. The evidence would seem to indicate that he might have."

Charles watched helplessly as Mrs. Landis lowered her eyes, looked down at the desk, and nodded. He felt even worse when she looked back up, her eyes moist.

"And do you know where she is?" she asked.

"We're close to ascertaining her location, ma'am."

Candy nodded again, then went back to perusing her data.

Somehow, she thought, I have failed, failed to keep the passion alive. And Jackson found his way to Polly Paget.

"Get me Polly Paget," Ron Scarpelli said.

Scarpelli thought this kind of simple, impossible command gave him an authoritative voice. He'd learned that at a seminar on personal power: Speak in an authoritative voice.

Walter Withers hadn't attended the seminar but recognized the brisk 80's tone. Here I am, he thought, sitting on a pornographer's black leather sofa with my knees up to my chin, sipping on his chichi designer water, trying not to stare at the legs of the six-foot-tall woman in a black dress who's his "personal assistant," and he's attempting to employ personal power techniques. It's superfluous, Mr. Scarpelli. It's your penthouse office, your view of Central Park, your magazine, and your nickel. You don't need to speak in an authoritative voice.

Withers didn't say that, though. He was fifty-six years old, five—okay, twenty pounds overweight, and owed Sammy Black ten thousand big ones plus the vig, which was growing every day. But for the first time in a long time the ball had stopped at Walter's number and he wasn't about to walk away from the table.

So he said, "Everyone in the country wants Polly Paget, Mr. Scarpelli."

"But I'm not everybody," Ron Scarpelli assured him. He looked to the personal assistant for confirmation. She formed her dark red lips into a dazzling smile.

And why not? Withers thought. He wondered how much she pulled down a year as a personal assistant.

"I don't touch her," Ron Scarpelli said, misreading Withers's thoughts. "She's married. Isn't she beautiful?"

"Yes, she is."

She looked like money. From the gloss of her black hair

pulled tightly back to the perfect pale skin, the health-club figure, the clothes.

"Recognize her?" Scarpelli asked.

"Certainly," Withers said, flipping through his mental index cards for the name. "She's Ms. Haber, your personal assistant. She escorted me in, offered me water . . ."

Walter thought wistfully of the days when one would be offered a civilized martini at any decent office in midtown.

Scarpelli beamed. "August 1980."

I can't seem to recall last Thursday and he's playing memory games from two years ago.

Withers held his palms up.

"Miss August 1980," Scarpelli urged. "The centerfold!"

She's smiling at me, Withers thought, as if she isn't the least bit embarrassed that her boss just asked me to summon up the image of her on her back displaying herself.

Withers didn't want to tell them that he had seen *Top Drawer* magazine maybe twice and it had just *depressed* him. It had been twenty years since he had gone to bed with a woman who looked anything like Ms. Haber and he knew he wasn't going to have that pleasure if he lived another twenty, which was unlikely. So looking at the pictures was like being broke and hungry and standing outside the Carnegie Deli with one's nose pressed to the window.

"Certainly," Withers said. He vaguely recalled some punch line about "not recognizing you with your clothes on" but didn't chance it.

"I want Polly Paget in my magazine," Scarpelli said, getting back to business.

"Well, that's what I thought."

"Nude."

As if he invented sex, Withers thought. Walter himself followed the school of thought that women were more alluring with their clothes on, given the right clothes. Half the erotic pleasure of romance, if memory served, was in the gradual baring of secrets, the delicate interplay of fabric and flesh, the——

"Full frontal, if possible," Ms. Haber chimed in.

"Why don't I locate the entire Ms. Paget?" Withers asked, "and let you take it from there?"

"That's funny, Walt. I like that," Scarpelli said, not laughing. Then he asked, "But what makes you think you can find her? Why should I hire you when I can buy the best private investigators in the world? Which—no offense—by the look of you, you ain't."

This is true, Withers thought. Needlessly offensive, but true. My suit is shiny and my eyes aren't, I have those little broken blood vessels in my nose, and my tie is old. But it's a tie, not a gold chain, you jumped-up little porno prince, and I bought it at Saks.

"I'm a genuine private investigator, Mr. Scarpelli," Withers answered. "I have a license, a gun, vast experience, as well as a certain je ne sais quoi. Now, certainly you can engage one of the big agencies. They have a lot of personnel and most of them look better than I do. But none of them know where Polly Paget is."

"And you do," Scarpelli said.

Actually, I don't. But I know someone who does.

Withers set his water down on the glass-topped table and stood up.

"Thank you for your time and the water," he said. "I'll take my offer elsewhere. I think Ms. Paget would be quite charming in bunny ears."

Speaking of speaking in an authoritative voice.

"Wait," Scarpelli said quickly. "Sit down, please."

"Please," Ms. Haber echoed.

Withers sat down. He pulled his old Dunhill cigarette case

from his jacket pocket. Ms. Haber quickly produced a lighter and an ashtray.

"I'll pay her half a million dollars," Scarpelli said.

Withers held out the case. Scarpelli shook his head and Ms. Haber leaned forward to light his cigarette.

"I will require a ten percent finder's fee," Withers said. "Plus expenses."

"Where is she?" Scarpelli asked.

As if I would tell you, Withers thought. As if I knew.

"And I will need some up-front cash for her," Withers continued, ignoring the question.

"I'll give you a cashier's check."

Withers shook his head.

"No?" Scarpelli asked.

"No," Withers answered. "Women like Ms. Paget are childlike. They lack the patience for delayed gratification. They understand cash."

As does Sammy Black. The last time I tried to give him a check, he made me eat it and tell him what rubber tasted like.

"Let me get this straight," Scarpelli said. "You want me to give you a bundle of cash to carry around in case you find Polly Paget? Is that it?"

"That's it. Fifty thousand would probably get her attention."

Maybe thirty would, too. Minus the vig.

"Fifty thousand dollars in cash," Scarpelli said. "What do I look like to you?"

Here it is, Withers thought. The job on the line, right here.

"A good businessman, Mr. Scarpelli," he said.

Scarpelli smiled. Ms. Haber smiled. Withers smiled.

Scarpelli got up from behind his big glasstop desk and opened the door to a walk-in closet that had about fifty suits hanging in it, twenty or thirty pairs of shoes—treed and on racks, and a few dozen shirts on wire-rack shelves. He pushed aside a gray silk double-breasted, flipped open a panel on the wall, and dialed the combination. A minute later, he came out with five packets of cash, which he tossed on Withers's lap.

"Call me Ron," Scarpelli said.

Call me a cab, Withers thought.

"Where is she?" Peter Hathaway asked with the air of a man about to be let in on a wonderful practical joke.

Ed Levine turned to Ethan Kitteredge, who almost imperceptibly shook his head.

"Do you really need to know?" Ed asked Hathaway.

Peter Hathaway kept the smile on his face but it tightened up a little. Peter Hathaway was used to getting answers, and they were usually the answers he wanted. That was one of the reasons he owned a significant portion of a television network at the age of thirty-seven. One of the other reasons was his family's wealth, and their connections. All of which had helped to bring him to this very private office in the back of an old bank in Providence, Rhode Island.

Hathaway decided to use a metaphor to make himself clear. He'd learned about metalevel communication while getting his MBA at Brown and he used it successfully with his own colleagues and associates. Metalevel communications avoided the ugliness of head-on confrontation.

So Hathaway broadened his smile, looked around the wood-paneled office with its mahogany bookcases, wooden model sailing ships, and dingy nineteenth-century nautical paintings and said, "You know, Ethan, you could stand to get some light in this office."

Ed saw Ethan Kitteredge wince at Hathaway's use of his first name and wondered just what the hell this yuppie Hathaway was talking about. Sitting there in his preppy little black sports jacket and green cord trousers, with his shiny new Haliburton briefcase at his moccasined feet, wasting Kitteredge's time when he should be out playing tennis or lacrosse or some other kid's game.

Ethan Kitteredge sat back in his chair, touched the tips of his fingers together, and smiled at Hathaway.

"This is a bank, Mr. Hathaway," Kitteredge said. "We handle people's money. In this particular office in this bank, we handle people's problems. There is nothing . . . light . . . about it."

Hathaway acknowledged the gaffe of calling Kitteredge by his first name but still felt some gratification that the bank president had picked up his metaphor. Once your co-communicator has picked up your metaphor, you have won the communication.

"That's true, Mr. Kitteredge," he said. "But you are keeping me in the dark."

"Yes," Kitteredge agreed.

Hathaway's smile was sincere. He liked winning.

"So where is she?" he asked again.

"Safely in our hands," Kitteredge answered.

Peter Hathaway dropped the metalevel.

"I'm the client, right?" he asked petulantly, brushing a shock of black hair from his forehead. "I want to know."

Kitteredge looked to Ed.

"It's like this," Ed explained. "If you knew where Polly Paget was, you might inadvertently say or do something that might lead to her discovery."

John Culver, sitting in the back of a van parked on the street outside, chuckled at the truth of this statement.

"I'm not a child! I'm not stupid!" Hathaway yelled.

Keep your voice down, Culver thought as he eased the headset away from his ears.

"Nobody said you were," Ed said. We were just thinking it,

he added to himself. "It's just that you're not a professional at this kind of thing, and we are, so why don't you let us handle it?"

Kitteredge added, "We are continuing our investigation of Mr. Landis. When that inquiry has . . . matured . . . and Miss Paget has progressed to a point where we feel she can successfully negotiate the media and the legal process, we will contact you."

Hathaway sank back into his chair and sulked.

I'm a professional, he thought. All right, the rape was sheer luck, but I was professional enough to contact Paget, bring her into our orbit, create a media sensation . . . and now this nineteenth-century throwback and his pet bear refuse to tell me where she is!

"I gave her to you!" Hathaway argued.

"Would you like her back?" Kitteredge asked.

No, Hathaway admitted to himself. I wouldn't know what to do with her. The slut is a disaster. If she opens her mouth in public one more time, Jack Landis will have the world thinking that she raped him.

"Excuse me," Peter said. "I have to visit the little boys' room."

Please, Culver thought, leave the briefcase here. I didn't go to all the trouble of breaking into your office and planting a bug in your new Haliburton for the dubious pleasure of listening to you urinate—at best.

Hathaway went into the lavatory to relieve himself and do a couple of lines. Cocaine gave him a competitive edge.

"Have you heard from Mr. Graham?" Kitteredge asked.

Ed nodded. "He got her safely to Austin, no problem."

Now why, Culver pondered, would they take her to Austin, a mere sixty miles from San Antonio?

"And do we think Ms. Paget will remain willingly in the wilds of Nevada?" asked Kitteredge.

Nevada? Austin, Nevada, Culver thought. Is there such a place?

"Seems to be."

Hathaway came back in a few moments later looking considerably refreshed.

"Where is she?" he asked simply, as if for the first time. As if he thought they'd tell him.

In Austin, Nevada, Culver thought.

4

Neal Carey watched Polly Paget eat dinner.

Neal had seen some real eating in his life. He'd seen horses eat and pigs eat. He'd seen Ed Levine eat. But he'd never seen any creature eat like Polly.

Polly ate like a hyperkinetic steam shovel in a gravel pit. She scooped slices of London broil and heaps of baked potato into her mouth and consumed them without seeming to chew or, for that matter, swallow. And as the putative digestion process continued, her hand whirled around on the plate for another go.

"More salad?" Karen asked.

"Mmmflckmmmff," answered Polly.

"I think she's asking you to pass the rolls," Neal said.

Polly smiled and nodded. Small drops of sour cream oozed from the sides of her mouth.

Karen set a roll on her plate. Polly's knife flicked out and covered it with butter.

"How do you keep your figure?" asked Karen.

"MMttbbllsmm."

"Metabolism," Neal translated.

"I got it," said Karen.

I wish I got it, Neal thought.

He was in a vile mood. Graham had left cheerfully, sticking him with Polly Paget and what seemed an impossible task: Turn this bimbo into America's sweetheart. Get her ready for a deposition, and a trial, and a trial by media. Teach her how to speak, how to answer questions, and how to not answer questions.

That last bit should be no problem, Neal thought, just get some food within reach. The big problem would be Graham's final command: Make her get her story straight.

That made Neal think that maybe Friends had some doubts.

You could interpret it two ways, Neal thought. Maybe they think she's such an airhead that she needs practice recalling the facts in some kind of order. That's the nice interpretation. The not-so-nice interpretation is that's she's lying and needs to decide which tale she wants to tell and then memorize it. In which case, they want me to pick apart inconsistencies and work on them until her story is unassailable. And the really ugly interpretation is that Friends helped set this thing up from jump street.

"So," Polly said in a rare pause between bites, "you're supposed to turn me into a real lady, is that it?" (Actually, "Yaw spozt tuh toin me intareel lady, zatih?")

"Something like that."

"Good luck. My mother couldn't do it; the nuns couldn't do it . . . Saint Anthony couldn't do it."

She paused for a laugh.

"That was a joke," she said. "Saint Anthony . . . patron saint of lost causes. I pray to him all the time."

"Really?" Karen asked.

Polly actually set down her fork. "Oh, yeah, patron saint of anything lost. He's helped me find my contacts, my keys. . . . He wouldn't help me find my birth-control pills, though, because the Pope is against birth control, you know."

"I heard that," Neal said.

"Yeah, anyways, Saint Anthony is my favorite saint."

"How did you get the name Polly?" Karen asked.

Polly shoved down some salad and answered, "I know, it

doesn't sound very Catholic, does it? I mean, I don't think there's any Saint Polly. My dad used to say before he died that he named me Polly because he'd always wanted a parrot, but he was just teasing; really, it was the movie.''

When Neal's head stopped spinning, he asked, "What movie?"

"*Pollyanna.* He liked it a bunch."

"Apparently."

She set her fork down again, rested her chin on the tops of her hands, looked at Neal, and said, "You think I'm a bimbo, don't you?"

It caught him off guard.

"No," he said.

"Say the truth," she said.

If that's what you want.

"Okay," he answered. "It's crossed my mind."

"Neal!" Karen said.

"No offense," Neal said. "My mother was a bimbo."

Polly's head snapped back and she gasped. "That's an awful thing to say about your mother! You should be ashamed, talking about your mother that way!"

Neal shrugged. "It's the truth."

"All the more reason," she said. Then she turned to Karen. "You know what I don't like about men?"

Karen took a moment to give Neal a dirty look before answering. "I have a few ideas."

"They're stupid," Polly said.

We sure are, Neal thought.

Walter Withers sat at the bar at the Blarney Stone and snuggled up to a glass of Jameson's that felt so good, he didn't mind Rourke's habitual harangue.

"This used to be a great town, you know that?" the bartender asked. "When Jimmy Wagner ran it, him and the Irish and the Italians."

Withers nodded agreeably.

It's a great town right now, he thought. I'm sitting in a nice warm dark bar with a glass of good whiskey in my hand and fifty thousand dollars in cash at my feet. And as soon as I complete my business here, I'm going to meet Gloria at the Oak Room, speaking of the days when this was a great town. A drink or two at the Oak Bar and then a taxi over to the Palm for a rare porterhouse and a glass or two of dark red.

And I wonder where Blossom Dearie is singing tonight.

"A great town," the bartender repeated. "Guy got out of line, the cops smacked him around, and that was that."

Withers nodded again. As the only customer at the bar, it was his job.

"Ah, Walt, the wife walked out again."

Withers shook his head sympathetically. "Women, huh?"

"Yeah, says she can't stand my drinking. I don't drink that much. You know that bartenders aren't drinkers, Walt. We see too much."

An opening.

"Have you seen Sammy Black, Arthur?" Walk asked. "Has he been around?"

"Just this afternoon he was in here asking about you," Rourke answered. "So I says to her, I say, 'You don't like my drinking? I don't like your eating.' She gets pissed off, packs her things, and storms off to her mother's—who's what, maybe ninety?"

Withers was almost grateful when Sammy Black walked in, even if he did have Chick Madsen with him.

"Break his wrist, Chick," Sammy ordered. Sammy was wearing a black overcoat, black sports jacket, black shirt, black shoes, probably black underwear. "A man who picks Minnesota to beat the spread on the road on Monday night deserves a broken wrist.''

Chick waddled over to Withers's stool, started to grab his wrist, then hesitated.

"Right or left, Sammy?" Chick asked.

"You right-handed or left-handed, Walter?" Sammy asked.

"The sinister hand," Withers told him.

"What?"

"Left-handed, Sammy," Withers explained.

"His left wrist," Sammy ordered.

Chick grabbed his left wrist.

"That won't be necessary," Withers said. "I have the payment in full."

"You do? Hold on. Let me tell Tinkerbell. Tink, Walter has the money," Sammy said. He paused to listen, then said, "Tink doesn't believe you, Walter. Let's all clap and say we believe.''

"I can't clap, Sammy. Chick has hold of my arm," Withers said.

"And I don't hear any snapping of bones or screams of agony, Chick," Sammy chided.

Withers said, "It's in the briefcase by my feet. Let me get it.''

"Okay, I'll play." Sammy sighed. "Let's see what's in the briefcase.''

"Unhand me, sir," Withers said.

Chick let go of his arm. Withers took a hit of the Jameson's, then reached down and picked up the briefcase. He turned on the stool so his back was to the bookie and his goon and dialed the combination. Then he opened the briefcase and set it on the bar.

Sammy Black's eyes got big the way they always did when he saw a lot of cash. Then he got mad.

"You been betting with someone else?" he asked with the

righteous indignation of a wronged spouse. "Walter, you munt, I carry you all this time and you get well with someone else? This is gratitude, Walter?"

"I didn't win this money," Withers said. "I found gainful employment."

"Very gainful, indeed, Walter," Rourke said as he looked into the briefcase.

"Now, my good sir," Withers said, "how much do I owe you?"

"As of today, it's twenty-two five," Sammy said. "Walter, do you know there's a very interesting line on Raiders-Pittsburgh tomorrow?"

Withers handed him two stacks of the cash and then counted three thousand dollars off another. He closed the briefcase, slid off the bar stool, and handed the money to Sammy.

"Keep the change," he said. "Buy yourself some clothes that don't make you look like a lounge singer at the Albany Ramada Inn."

"You're a loser, Withers," Sammy said.

"Not tonight, my good man. Not tonight."

Withers tossed Arthur a jaunty wave and strolled out the door.

"Don't bet on it," Sammy mumbled.

"The wife walked out on me again, Sammy," Arthur said.

Sammy Black just stared out the door.

"Women, huh?" answered Chick.

"The missus still believe you?" Joey Foglio asked as he stood at the urinal.

"Candice is the least of my worries," Jack Landis called out from his stall.

They were in the men's room of Big Bob's, one of Joey's restaurants. Big Bob's was a barbecue joint so basic, they didn't even have plates. They just dumped slabs of meat on sheets of butcher paper and sent you out to the long picnic tables to gorge yourself.

"There ain't no Big Bob really, is there?" Jack asked.

"You wanna see Big Bob?" Joey asked. "Come on out here!"

Joey, Harold, and the two guys guarding the door laughed. Harold was Joey's personal assistant, which usually meant the personally assisted Joey in beating up people. The two guys at the door were bodyguards, just in case any of those people came back with a resentment coupled with a gun.

Jack Landis didn't laugh, truly believing that Joey Foglio was egomaniacal enough to name an eating establishment after his own johnson—which he guessed was preferable, anyway, to naming one after somebody else's.

Joey shook himself off, zipped up, and stepped over to the sink to wash his hands.

"I got a lot of unhappy people out there, Jack," he said.

"The sausage?" Jack asked.

"I mean my subcontractors," Joey answered.

Jack hitched his pants up, took his jacket off the hanger, and put it on.

"I ain't exactly delirious with joy, either," Jack said.

He opened the door and walked over to the mirror to check his hair.

Joey Foglio came and stood beside him. It was not a comfortable feeling. Joey Foglio was a big man. He had a big broad head with a flat forehead you could sell advertising space on.

Foglio looked into the mirror and combed his own full head of silver hair straight back.

"What are we going to do?" he asked. "You ain't been paying your bills."

"Maybe it would help if your contractors would just overcharge me by, say, fifty percent instead of a hundred,'' Jack said.

"That was the deal," Joey reminded him. "You get your kickbacks."

"Not lately," Jack complained.

"Because you ain't been paying your bills," Joey said.

"Because contributions are down."

"Because you tripped over your own dick," Joey said. He put his comb back in his pocket.

Jack eased a stray strand of hair back over his ear. "Someone put her up to this. The bitch isn't smart enough to do it on her own."

"Smart or stupid," Joey said, "she's got you by the short and curlies."

Jack always thought Joey sounded stupid when he tried to talk like a Texan. He was even dressed like one today, with Tony Lama boots, brand-new jeans, piped cowboy shirt, and a vest.

A greaseball cowboy, Jack thought. Great.

"Just find her," Jack said. "Find her and pay her off."

"I'll find her," answered Joey. *"You pay her."*

"Half and half," Jack offered.

"And I get the half that eats?" Joey asked. "You play, you pay."

"I never touched her."

"Jack, Jack, Jack. You're like, what, a Baptist?"

"Yeah." What was this greaseball talking about?

"You should be a Catholic, Jack," Joe Foglio continued, "then you wouldn't be consumed by all this guilt. Look at me. Do I look like I'm consumed with guilt?"

Jack Landis had heard that the very definition of a sociopath was a person who didn't feel guilt, but he decided not to share that thought at the moment, so he said, "No."

"Because I'm a Catholic," Joe said proudly. "See, you Baptists are supposed to—what is it?—Accept Christ as your personal savior, right?"

"I guess that's the basic idea," Jack answered to get it out of the way. "Now, what are we—"

Joey continued. "See, that's a mistake, that 'personal' part. What you need is a middleman, a fixer, a priest. I go to confession every day, Jack, every day. I go to confession, I rat myself out to the priest, the priest squares it with God, then I got the whole rest of the day to chase more pussy, skim more money—whatever—and the odds are still on my side I go to heaven. I couldn't believe it when the nuns first told me about this, I thought it was so great.

"Believe me, Jack, this world was made for Catholic men. You want me to set you up with a priest? I think you gotta take a few classes, let him pour some holy water on you . . . no big deal."

Jack wondered how on earth he got to be partners with a man who was obviously insane. He had to get Joey focused on the problem of Polly Paget.

"The gravy train's derailing, Joe, you're the guy who can get it back on the track."

Talking to me like he's on TV, Joey thought. Like I'm going to buy a time-share in Candyland. Like I'm a jerk.

I'll show you a freaking train, Jackie.

"I already got a plan," Joey said.

"You do?" Jack asked. "What is it? No, I don't want to know."

"No, you don't want to know, Jack." Joey looked at Harold and they both laughed.

Jack straightened his string tie, smiled into the mirror, and steeled himself to go back out into public.

"You're the man, Joe," he said.

Harold opened the door and Jack Landis stepped out.

"And you're the jerk," Joey said softly.

The bodyguard started to laugh.

"He still doesn't get it, does he?"

Foglio shook his head. "Proves you don't need brains to make money in this country."

Landis had any brains, Foglio thought, he'd know that I knew all about him and Polly Paget almost from the first cigarette—an insurance policy against Jack Landis canceling our deal.

A sweet deal it is, too. So much easier than honest crime.

And the stupid Paget skank blows it. Because maybe this cracker bastard doesn't buy her dinner and a movie one night. Rape, my aching ass. Broad can't sell it, then complains it's been stolen. And then goes to the newspapers.

"You want me to make the call, Joe?" Harold asked.

"Yeah," Joe said. He didn't make phone calls himself, lest he someday appear on the Justice Department's Greatest Hits tapes, volume five. "Yeah, reach out."

Reach out, reach out and touch someone.

Joey Foglio left the men's room humming to himself.

5

*I*t's nice, Walter Withers thought, that there's a place you can still go to hear someone do a Hart tune and not butcher it. Or do a Hart tune at all, for that matter.

Ah, New York, New York. Sitting in a dark room, listening to a smoky piano behind a chanteuse, sipping on quality scotch with a beautiful woman at the table beside you.

All right, maybe Gloria is not exactly beautiful in the modern anemic fashion, and perhaps she is a bit . . . bed-worn . . . a woman of experience, one might say. Perhaps the blond hair comes from a bottle. So many good things do. Perhaps her makeup is a tad thick. A woman of a certain age is entitled. Perhaps she smokes incessantly. She came to maturity in the age of black-and-white films, and besides, it allows me to light her cigarettes for her. Perhaps she is a drunk. I have been buying her drinks.

To loosen her tongue, among other things.

He leaned over his glass and peered through the smoke into her eyes.

"You look lovely tonight, darling," he said.

Gloria took a demure sip of her fourth martini and said, "Let's go back to my place."

"Check, please," Withers said.

She saw his eyes light up and said, "Walter, if you think I'm giving you so much as a hand job, you're fooling yourself. It's late and I'm expecting an important phone call, if you know what I mean."

Walter knew what she meant. He paid the tab and gave the doorman a five to hail a taxi.

Gloria lived in a huge drab building on West Fifty-seventh Street. A blue plaque outside the main door claimed that Béla Bartók had once resided there.

Withers didn't particularly care for Bartók.

Her apartment was big, a testament to rent control. Withers plopped himself down in one of her old overstuffed chairs in the living room.

"You want a drink, Walter? What a dumb question," she said. She went into the kitchen, found a bottle of scotch, and poured a straight shot.

"Why are you doing this?" Withers asked as she handed him the glass.

"Does it make a difference? Look, I'm like an older sister to the kid. I love her. But she's never going to beat Jack Landis in court and she's never going to make it on her brains, so she might as well get something out of this mess."

"Posing nude for a magazine?" Withers asked.

"Marilyn Monroe . . . Jayne Mansfield . . . Mamie Van Doren . . ." she said, counting them off on her fingers. "Look what it did for them."

"These will be pretty graphic shots, I think, Gloria."

She looked at him as if he was a dope, shrugged, and said, "You sell what you have to sell."

"Apparently," he answered.

Neal snuggled up against Karen. "What do you think?" he asked.

She rearranged the blanket so that it covered both their shoulders and said, "I think she's telling the truth."

"You do?"

"You don't?"

"I don't know."

"That's your problem, Neal," she said. "You don't trust people."

"Occupational hazard," he answered.

"That's part of it," Karen said. "You really don't trust women."

Skip the rest of it, Neal thought. I've already heard it. How my father never showed up and my mother was a junkie hooker and so I never really had a chance to be a kid and learn to trust and yadda-yadda-yadda. It might be true, but I still have to get up mornings.

"I trust you," he said, "and you're a woman. Singular. You get trust combined with collective nouns and you're right. I don't trust women, and I don't trust men, for that matter."

"You trust Graham."

True, he thought.

"What about Landis?" he asked her. "He says he never touched her. Do you trust him?"

"No."

"Why not?"

"Because he's lying," Karen said.

"And you know this because she's telling the truth."

"Right."

"Try this out," he said. "Suppose they had an affair, which I agree they probably did. One night he says he wants sex; she says she doesn't. He thinks she's playing and forces the issue. To him, it was a game; to her, it was rape. Which is it?"

"Rape."

"It's not that simple," he said.

"It's just that simple," she insisted. "The difficult question is, why does Polly have to become Audrey Hepburn before she can be believed?"

"Let me remind you that just this morning all Polly Paget

was to you was a Jacuzzi on the deck," Neal said. "It doesn't make us all that different from the newspapers, the magazines, or the TV shows. We all have an economic interest in that commodity known as Polly Paget, who is now asleep on the bed in our study."

"Ouch," Karen answered. She snuggled up a little tighter. "You're right, but she's still a person, and I like her."

"So do you want her to be Polly Paget and lose or Audrey Hepburn and win?"

Karen thought about it for a few seconds, then said, "I want her to win."

So do I, Neal thought. At least I think I do. The question is, how?

Walter Withers was asleep in the chair when Gloria's phone rang.

She kicked his ankle and said, "Hey, Sam Spade, wake up."

Withers came to and looked at his watch.

Three o'clock in the morning, he thought. How long have I been out?

He heard Gloria say she'd accept the charges.

"Is that you?" Gloria said a couple of seconds later.

"Sorry I'm calling so late," Polly whispered, "but I had to wait until they went to sleep. Did I wake you up?"

"I was having a nightcap," Gloria said. She motioned Withers to stay still in his chair. "How are you? *Where* are you?"

"I'm in the middle of freaking nowhere with some English teacher and his girlfriend. She's nice, but he's kind of a grouchy nerd. He's supposed to teach me how to talk."

"Honey, that's the last thing you need." Gloria laughed.

"Talk right, I mean, so I sound like a lady."

"Well, la-di-da," Gloria said. "Who set you up with these people?"

"My lawyers. And it's supposed to be a top secret kind of

thing, so don't tell anyone. I just had to call you because I'm lonely and I'm scared."

"Scared? Sweetie, of what?" Gloria asked.

"It's just so weird. This place is so, you know, out there."

"Out where?" Gloria asked.

Yes, Withers thought. Out where?

"Austin, it's called."

Withers heard Gloria say, "You're in Texas!"

"I don't think so," Polly answered. "I think we're still in Nevada. We are, because they had a slot machine in the gas station. Gloria, I can't stay on the phone for long. I just wanted to hear your voice and tell you where I am in case something happens to me."

"Honey, why should anything happen to you?" Gloria asked.

"I gotta go, Gloria," Polly whispered.

"You have a phone number?"

"Yeah, hold on." Polly read the number off the phone. "But hang up if anyone but me answers. No one is supposed to know I'm here."

"I got it, kid," Gloria said. "Take care of yourself. I love you."

"Love you, too," Polly said.

Gloria set down the receiver and looked at Walter. He was rumpled and bleary-eyed. His old Brooks Brothers suit was wrinkled and his shirt was stained. He was an old-school gentleman in a world that didn't have much use for old-school gentlemen.

"She's in Austin, Nevada, sport," Gloria said. "Wherever that is."

Withers groped for the briefcase at his feet, set it on his lap, and fumbled with the combination lock. When he got it open, he counted out five thousand dollars and handed it to Gloria.

"Are you going to offer me a nightcap?" he asked.

"Yeah, at the Blarney Stone. You can beat closing time if you get a cab now," she said. "Put it on my tab."

Withers pulled himself out of the chair.

"It's been a lovely evening, my dear," he said.

She found a scrap of paper by the phone, wrote "Austin, Nevada" and Polly's phone number on it, and stuck it in his pocket.

"In case you forget," she said. "And Walter, take care of that money. Stay away from the bookies."

"Gloria," he said with some surprise, "you have maternal instincts."

She pushed him out the door.

When she heard the elevator door open and close, she picked up the phone.

A tired male voice answered. "It's about time."

"She's in Austin, Nevada."

"Where the hell is that?"

"How would I know? Get a map."

"Did you send your boy on his way?"

"I did my job, knuckle-dragger," Gloria snapped. "Do yours."

"Don't worry about it."

Gloria cradled the phone in her neck and poured herself a drink. "And tell your boss this settles my debt. The account is closed."

"Well, that's between you and him."

"Just tell him."

Gloria hung up the phone. She sat down on the sofa and knocked back the drink. It would be tough getting to sleep tonight, tougher than usual. Maybe she should have let Walter stay. But he was lousy in bed, lousier when he was drinking, and he was always drinking these days.

You've been going at it pretty hard yourself, kiddo, she

thought. Especially since Joey Foglio bought out your debt from Sammy Black. You knew even then that something bad was going to happen.

Chick nudged Sammy Black awake and pointed across the street at Walter Withers getting into a taxi.

"About time," Sammy said. They'd been sitting in the car on Fifty-seventh since following Withers back from the Plaza.

"You think he got lucky?" Chick smirked.

"Walter never gets lucky."

Chick smiled at him.

"What?" Sammy asked.

"Aren't you going to say, 'Follow that cab'?"

"Drive the car."

Sammy had confidence in Chick's ability to follow the cab. Helen Keller could follow Walter Withers at three in the morning. All she'd need would be directions to the Blarney Stone.

"Don't get too close," Sammy said as Chick turned left on Third Avenue, behind the cab.

"You slammed her a few times, didn't you?" Chick asked.

"Who?"

"Gloria."

"No," Sammy lied. "I wouldn't have if I could have, which I could, because she owed me a bundle."

"Why did Joey Beans want the book on her, anyway? He wanted to slam her?"

"I don't know; I didn't ask," Sammy said. "When someone big as Joey Foglio—and don't you *ever* call him Joey Beans again—reaches out all the way from Texas and wants to buy a piece of your book, you sell, not ask. Here we are."

Chick pulled the car over and they got out just as Withers finished paying the cabbie. To Sammy's relief, Withers still had the briefcase. It would be just like him to leave it sitting at Nathan's or someplace.

"Walter!" Sammy called. "Hold on! Can I have a word?"

Withers looked startled.

"I'll do you one better, Sammy," he said. "I'll give you a word and a drink."

"Not in there with Arthur 'The Mouth' Rourke," Sammy said. "We need privacy."

But Withers had beat them to the doorway.

"No problem," Sammy said.

He stepped inside. Arthur was wiping the bar with a wet rag. Withers was already on his usual stool. He was the only patron. Big surprise.

"Arthur," Sammy said. "You got to go pee."

"I don't have to pee, Sammy," Arthur said.

"Yes you do."

Dumb harp.

Arthur stopped the rag for a second and thought. It was an exhausting process.

"I guess I do got to pee," he said finally.

"Yeah, a long one, okay, Arthur?"

Arthur stepped out from behind the bar and walked into the men's room in the back.

Sammy sat on the stool next to Withers. Chick took the one on the other side.

"Now, Walter," Sammy said. "I want that money."

"I paid you your money, Sammy."

"I mean the rest of that money," Sammy said, pointing to the briefcase. "In there."

"But it doesn't belong to you."

This is a robbery, you dumb drunk, Sammy thought. Jeez, I have to draw you a picture?

"Walter," Sammy said, trying to keep his temper, "you

know and I know that you're just not capable of holding on to that money. You're going to lose it to someone, and that someone should be me rather than some stranger. After all, I've put up with a lot of shit from you. So give it to me now so I don't have to tell Chick to hurt you."

Withers considered this for what seemed like a long time. Then he said, "No."

Chick started to laugh. Sammy gave him a look threatening enough to reduce him to giggles instead.

"I'll tell you what let's do," Sammy said. "Let's pretend you made a bet with that money. And you lost. I won't even charge you the vig."

Walter Withers shook his head. He looked so confused that even Sammy had to laugh this time.

"Walter?" Sammy asked. "Walter? Are you still with us?"

Withers looked at him seriously. "The game just isn't played this way, Sammy. When I lose, I pay. But I didn't lose."

"Yeah, you did," Sammy said. "You lost, Walter."

Chick stood up and loomed over Withers.

Withers nodded slowly. Then he set the briefcase on the bar, opened it, and walked away.

Sammy and Chick stood up and leaned over the briefcase.

"Holy crow, Walter," Chick said.

Sammy grabbed the money and started to count it.

Withers turned around, pulled his revolver from his jacket, and shot Chick in the back of the head. Sammy whirled just in time to the see Withers pull the trigger into his face.

Arthur ran in at the sound of the blasts, then stood frozen in the middle of the room. Withers took the bar towel, wiped the blood off the briefcase, carried it to the far end of the bar, and sat down.

"Am I too late for last call, Arthur?" he asked calmly.

"No," Arthur answered, staring at the bodies slumped over

the bar stools. He let himself behind the bar, shook a shot of Jameson's in a glass, and slid it to Withers.

"The damnedest thing just happened, Arthur," Walt said.

"What's that, Walt?"

"Some guy just walked in here and shot Sammy Black and his goon."

Withers swallowed his whiskey and smiled mildly. Then he put a thousand dollars on the bar and walked out.

Overtime was thinking about the night he died.

It gave him a lot of pleasure. Few other men, and no one he knew, could have jumped off the Newport Bridge into the swirling currents of Narragansett Bay and survived the impact, never mind swim to shore and then walk twenty miles before morning.

To be reborn as "Overtime." He didn't even know who had given him the nickname. It had to have been one of his clients, maybe an island dictator who had hired him to eliminate a political rival, or a security chief who needed plausible deniability. Probably it was one of the dons who needed an absolutely guaranteed clean hit.

Overtime prided himself on working clean. Nobody took pride in their work anymore. It was one of the reasons the country was going downhill so fast. People were content to do sloppy work and customers were prepared to accept it.

Overtime was the proud exception. He worked quickly and cleanly: one shot, just in, just out. Professional.

Not for him the showy hit in a restaurant, spraying bullets all over the place and leaving behind pools of blood and posthumous photo opportunities. Not for him the bomb in the car with its innocent bystanders. Overtime killed only what he got paid to kill. If the client wanted innocent bystanders, the client could pay for them. No group rates, no discounts. This philosophy had made him rich——cash in his pocket, and a bank account in Grand Cayman.

What he didn't have was a woman.

Overtime was lying in his bed in an expensive hotel room in New Orleans and feeling the disquieting stirrings of lust. Not that he was going to indulge in a woman, although one phone call would have sent the cream of a very creamy crop up to his room. Comped, on the house, whatever he wanted——black, white, yellow, all of the above. Anything for Overtime.

But he never indulged in a woman when he was on the job. Women talked. Women could identify you.

Problem: sexual tension.

Analysis: said tension is a distraction.

Solution: auto-gratification.

Overtime pulled the plastic cover off a copy of *Top Drawer* magazine and flipped through the pages, looking for a sufficiently erotic photograph. Self-sufficiency was one of the foundational tenets of Overtime's life, something he shared with Ralph Waldo Emerson. It would be nice to get back to the beach and read some Emerson.

Overtime never carried the same author around with him for more than one trip. That would be a pattern, and patterns, like women, could identify you. And he hadn't jumped off that bridge to be defeated by a paperback book.

He found a picture: a tall, thin brunette with tight features and a cruel, intelligent mouth. He hated the stupid-looking blond cows that overpopulated these magazines. The brunette looked smart. She would do.

It's silly, he thought as he developed a stimulating mental image, how some men balked at killing women: such a sexist attitude. If women have the right to play, they have the right to lose. The downside potential of liberation. The Equal Last Rites Amendment.

Overtime was an equal-opportunity button man. A Title

Nine killer. The first person he had ever killed, and the last person he had ever killed for free, had been a woman. But she had been his wife, and that was personal, so it didn't count.

And a very unprofessional job it was, he thought with some chagrin. He had slashed her maybe a hundred times, maybe more. Sloppy, emotional. Messed it up so badly that he'd had to drive his car to the bridge, leave the suicide note, and do a perfect forward, twisting one-and-a-half gainer into the bay.

"Med student kills wife and self. Film at eleven."

The phone rang. He picked it up but said nothing. The voice on the other end sounded nervous.

"Uhhh, we think we got it locked."

You *think?*

"Call me when you know," Overtime said. "Where's the staging area?"

"Vegas."

Not good news. Overtime hated Vegas. There was nothing to do but gamble, and Overtime didn't gamble. Basic mathematics precluded an activity in which the odds were against you.

"Is the dog in yet?" he asked.

"He's on his way."

"I want pictures. Current ones, please."

Overtime hung up and turned his concentration back to the photograph. He needed to achieve release. Sexual tension was a distraction. Not that he had much to do but wait. Let the dog catch up to the bird. The bird worries about the dog, and doesn't think about the hunter.

Then *bang*.

One shot, just in, just out. Professional.

Release.

6

I think there are three trees," Neal said for the fiftieth time that morning.

"Oi tink dere aaw tree trees," Polly repeated for the fiftieth time.

"Three trees."

"Tree trees," Polly said. "The hell we talking about trees, anyway? Nobody's gonna ask me about one tree, never mind tree trees. They're going to ask me about *doing ih.*"

"Doing it," Neal said. "There's a *t* at the end of the word. Pronounce it. I'm begging you."

"And we never did ih in a tree," Polly said. "Ih, ih, IH!"

Neal dropped his head down on the kitchen table and moaned softly.

Six days. Count them, Lord, six days. Six days of "I think there are three trees," and "Park the car and go the party with Barbara," and "I like my bike." Five days of trying to get her to respond to a simple question with a simple answer instead of a stream-of-consciousness soliloquy that would have made James Joyce reach for a nice drink of Drano. Israel won an entire war in six days, and I can't get one woman to pronounce *it.*

Neal raised his eyes and looked up at her.

Today's costume consisted of black toreador pants, a black tube top, and enough black jewelry to dress Scarsdale in mourning for a week.

She made a face at him, lifted her bare foot onto the table, and started to paint her toenails.

Neal watched her make careful, precise strokes until he realized he was being mesmerized by her almost Zen-like concentration.

"Say it," he said.

"Take me to dinnuh," she answered without taking her eyes off her task.

"I can't take you to dinner," he said, stressing the *r*. "You'd be seen."

"I want to go out to dinnuh," she whined. "Anyways, nobody in this dog-shit town is going to recanize me."

"*Recognize*. Say it and I'll get you a magazine."

There was a slight hesitation in her stroke.

"What magazine?" she asked.

"*McCall's?*"

"*Cosmo*."

"If I can find one."

She leaned forward to check out a possible flaw in the paint job, then slowly and distinctly said, "I think there are three trees."

"You've been jerking my chain."

"I'm the one on the chain," she said. "When's Karen coming home?"

"When she's done shopping, I guess."

"Karen's my bud."

That's for sure, Neal thought. The two women were practically joined at the hip. They stayed up half the night watching junk TV and eating ice cream and corn chips. He would lie in bed listening to them giggling and whispering.

Polly put her other foot on the table.

"Time for the TV break," she said.

"No, it isn't."

"Close."

Neal straightened up in his chair. "Park the car and go to the party with Barbara."

"Pawk de caw an go tuh de pawty wit Bawburuh."

Neal whimpered.

"Once again," she said, "yaw making me say stuff I am nevuh going tuh say adenny troil! What caw? What pawty? Bawburuh who? We nevuh went to no pawties; we just went tuh bed! He'd stick his ting in me; he'd take his ting out—dat was de pawty!"

"His *ting?*" Neal asked.

She looked up from her toenails.

"You know," she said. "His ting."

"You mean his thing?"

"What do you tink I mean?" she asked, frowning.

Neal stood up and walked over to the counter.

"I don't know," he said. "His organ? His male member? His penis?"

She sniffed. "I don't say dose words."

"Well, you'd better learn."

"Be nice."

"It's not my job to be nice," Neal said.

"And a good ting, too. . . ."

"It's my job to get you ready for the trial."

She leaned way over, blew on her toenails, then said, "I'm telling Karen dose words what you said."

Neal smiled. "What words?"

"You know, like ting."

"You mean penis?"

"I mean ting."

"Penis."

"Ting!"

"Penis!"

"Ting!" Polly yelled as she stood up. "Ting! Ting! Ting!"

"Penis! Penis! Penis!" Neal yelled as Karen walked through the door with an armful of groceries.

"Diction lesson?" she asked.

"He wants me to talk dirty," Polly accused.

"Don't they always?" Karen asked. She set the grocery bags on the counter.

Neal took a deep breath and then said, slowly and distinctly, "When you give your deposition, as you will have to do . . . you cannot talk about his ting . . . or even his thing. . . ."

"Why not?" Polly asked.

Karen put her hand on Neal's arm and said, "Because they won't take you seriously. Neither would a jury. They'd laugh, and that's not the reaction you're looking for, is it?"

"No," Polly admitted.

Karen asked, "Then can you say, 'He forced himself on me'? or even, 'He forced himself into me'?"

Polly thought about this for a few seconds.

"I can say *himself*," she decided.

Karen turned to Neal. "Professor?"

"That's fine. Very dignified," Neal answered. "Thank you."

"Happy to be of service," Karen said. "Isn't it time for the TV break?"

Polly gave Neal a 'See?' look and stalked into the living room.

Karen put her arms around Neal and kissed him on the cheek.

"I love you," she said.

"But?" Neal asked.

"But you could try telling her why you want her to do something," Karen answered. "She's not stupid."

Neal made a noncommittal murmur.

"She didn't go to Columbia, and she's not pursuing a graduate degree in English literature," Karen said, "but that doesn't mean you should treat her like the slowest puppy in obedience school."

"Are you saying I'm a snob?"

"Of course you are," she answered. "But let me ask you something: You were a street kid, right?"

"Yeah."

"Where did you get your blue-blazer accent?"

Neal blushed. "Friends sent me to a tutor."

"Was he as mean to you as you are to Polly?"

Neal recalled the fussy retired Shakespearean actor in the musty old apartment on Broadway.

"Meaner, actually."

"Then you know how she feels," Karen said, "actually."

She kissed him again.

Polly's voice came shrieking from the living room, "Jack and Candy're on!"

Karen took Neal's arm.

"Come on," she said, "maybe we can get a good recipe."

Jack Landis smiled soulfully into the camera, a brave no-nonsense smile.

"I'm still here," he said.

The studio audience went nuts.

"I'm still here!" Jack repeated, enjoying the reaction. "And my accuser has disappeared. What does that tell you?"

Applause, foot stomping, cheers.

Candy sat on the sofa, out of camera range. She smiled at the studio audience.

The camera dollied in for a close-up on Jack.

"Well," he said, "the lawyers don't want me to say much more than that, so I guess it's a case of 'enough said,' huh?"

The audience chuckled appreciatively.

"So, ladies and gentlemen, without further ado . . ." Jack

said, giving his trademark opening, ". . . the lady who shares my life with me and her life with you . . . Caaandy Laaandis!"

The applause sign lighted superfluously.

Candy rose gracefully from the couch and stepped up to her mark, next to Jack's mark. The camera switched to a two-shot as Jack put his arm around her and she pecked him on the cheek. Then she turned her smart smile to the camera.

Normally, at this point the director would have switched to a close-up, but these days he was using as many two-shots of Jack and Candy as possible.

"On today's show," Candy announced, "we'll meet a man who was declared legally dead but came back to own his own business."

"And," Jack read from the monitor, "we'll talk to a U.S. senator who is fighting for you, the American family."

Candy picked it up seamlessly: "I'm going to show you how to spice up that old ground chuck, and . . ."

"I've prevailed on Candy," Jack said, "to sing one of our favorite old songs."

"All that, plus a progress report on Candyland, on today's 'Jack—"

"—and Candy—' " Jack added.

" 'Family Hour,' " they said in chorus.

The director went to a commercial.

Polly polished off a salami-and-cheese sandwich, a large bag of potato chips, seven chocolate-chip cookies, and a Diet-Pepsi before Jack and Candy even sat down to her "Red Burger Surprise."

"Where does all that food go?" Karen whispered to Neal as she looked at Polly's skinny frame.

"Right to her brain," Neal answered.

Karen elbowed him.

"By the way," Polly asked. "Is there a doctor in this town?"

"Are you sick?"

Polly shook her head. "My friend hasn't visited."

"What friend?" Karen asked, then blushed. "Ohhh . . ."
That friend.

"I think we got trouble," Joe Graham said into the phone.

He was sitting by the window of his fifteenth-floor hotel
room in the northern suburbs of San Antonio. The window
provided an interesting view of the foothill country, including
the access road to the massive construction sight known as
Candyland.

"Trouble is our business," Ed Levine answered, having
developed a sense of humor since his divorce. He had his feet
on the desk and was also looking out the window, which gave
him a picturesque view of garbage blowing across Times Square.

"I'm serious," Graham insisted.

"Okay, okay. What kind of trouble?"

"Well, for starters, I'm stuck in this room doing this surveillance, so I order room service and I get the tacos. Have you ever
tried to eat a taco with one hand?"

"Can't say I have, Joe."

"Every time you pick one it up, it shoots hot sauce out the
other end."

"Have you tried picking it up in the middle?" Levine asked.

"Yeah. Then it shoots hot sauce out both ends."

"This is trouble all right," Levine said patiently, figuring that
Graham was suffering from stakeout syndrome, the combination of boredom, cabin fever, and loneliness that compels surveillance guys to invent reasons to talk on the phone. "What
else?"

"It looks like a Teamsters picnic out here," Graham said.
"You got trucks coming and going, coming and going, coming
and going all the time."

"Uhhh, it's a construction site, Joe," Ed said. Maybe I'd better think about pulling him, he thought.

"Yeah, but when do they unload?" Joe asked. "I've seen the same truck go in, come out ten minutes later, and go right back in."

"You're taking down the plate numbers, right?"

"No, Ed, I'm drawing pictures of the trucks with my crayons. What do you think?"

Testy, Ed thought. Another prime symptom. He picked up his coffee mug and saw something usually described as a foreign object floating on the top. He picked the foreign object out with his thumb and forefinger and took a swallow of the coffee.

"What else?" he asked.

"I think I'm starting to hallucinate," Graham said.

Days of sitting by a window staring through binoculars will do that, Ed thought.

"Why is that?" he asked.

"Black limo comes up the road, guy gets out to talk to one of the truck drivers. Guess who the guy is?"

"Jimmy Hoffa?"

"No," Graham answered. "Get this, Ed. I could swear I saw Joey Beans get out of that limo."

Is this the coffee I bought this morning, Ed asked himself, or yesterday morning? And Joey Beans?

"You are hallucinating, Graham," Ed said. "Joey Beans working for Jack Landis?"

"Or vice versa," Graham observed.

"Naaah," Ed said.

Joey "Beans" Foglio had been such a loose cannon in the greater New York metropolitan area mob franchise that the old men finally gave him a career choice: accept a lateral transfer down south or be recycled in a Jersey gravel pit. Joey Beans had opted for the sun and fun of the Lone Star state, and Levine had a vague knowledge that he was working card games or something out of Houston. But Joey Beans building water slides and kiddie-car tracks?

"Something is very sick here," Graham said. "I'll send you the plate numbers, names on the trucks, all that stuff. Can you get a look at construction invoices?"

"I'll give it a shot," Ed answered. Shit, a gangster like Joey Beans hooked up with Landis? No way.

"We'd better give Neal a call," Graham said. "He's not going to be happy."

"He's never happy." Ed thought he'd try to cheer Graham up and added, "Hey, speaking of happiness, guess who went to that big tote board in the sky a few days ago?"

"Who?"

"Sammy Black."

"No shit."

"No shit," Ed said. "Sitting in a bar at closing time. Guy walks in while the bartender's taking a piss, pops Sammy and his bodyguard in the head, and walks out."

"They must be having parties all over Midtown South."

"They are. The homicide guys have a nickname for the shooter," Ed said. "Preparation H."

"Because he removed that itching burning hemorrhoid?" Graham said. Not that funny a topic, seeing as how he'd been sitting on this chair for three days.

"Listen, I'll get on this Joey Beans stuff," Ed said. "You take it easy with those tacos, okay?"

Yeah, okay, Graham thought as he hung up. He was worried. He had promised Neal there was no mob stuff, and now he thought he had seen Joey Beans. And although Ed Levine was very good at chasing paper, mob guys were pretty cute these days. It could be weeks before Ed could unravel the kind of twisted paper trail the mob was capable of leaving. And he wasn't sure that they had days, never mind weeks. There had to be a quicker way.

Graham put his binoculars away.

Sammy Black in a box, huh? Old Walt must be standing for a round somewhere.

7

Martini, please,'' Walt Withers said.

Withers didn't notice that the bartender scowled at him and didn't move an inch to fix his drink. Withers was preoccupied trying to figure out where he'd been the past few days. He had woken up hard in a Reno hotel room and gone for a drink or two and then woken up harder in a different Reno hotel room.

Thank God Gloria had left the note in his jacket pocket, he thought. In other days, Gloria would have been what is known as a good broad, but those were different times.

So Withers had solved the mystery of what he was doing in Nevada, and he wouldn't be the first private investigator in history to blow a few days on a bender. What bothered him was the money.

He was $1,327 short.

He had done the figures in his head thirty times. Five thousand had gone to Gloria for the tip, and he didn't think Scarpelli could object to that. Twenty-three thousand had gone to Sammy, and certainly Scarpelli could and would object to that. Withers was just hoping that Scarpelli would be so pleased with his smutty pictures of Polly that he'd forget about it. Or maybe he could just short Polly on the up-front money. In any case, he'd much rather owe money to Ron Scarpelli or even Polly Paget than to Sammy Black. Ron Scarpelli or Polly Paget would not break his wrists.

But what had happened to the other $1,327? He had used plastic to pay for the airline ticket and the hotels.

Oh my God, Withers thought. Could I really have drunk $1,327?

The bartender was staring at him.

"Yes?" Withers asked.

"I don't serve martinis," the bartender growled. "I don't serve martinis, or white wine, or anything with fruit in it."

Withers swore he heard a dog growl from behind the bar.

The bartender continued, "I serve beer, whiskey, and gin. What do you want?"

Feeling somewhat guilty at the possibility of having consumed in excess of a thousand dollars in alcohol, Withers answered, "Do you have coffee?"

Growling dog again. Next it will be a trumpeting pink elephant.

"Made a pot just this morning," Brogan mumbled. He stepped over to the coffeemaker, found a mug that had been washed at least once during the Reagan administration, wiped it on his shirttail, and poured it full of the greasy coffee. "Milk or sugar?"

"How old is the milk?" Withers asked.

"It has Amelia Earhart's picture on the carton."

"Black, thank you."

"Fifty cents," Brogan said.

Withers laid a five on the bar and told him to keep the change. It was time to get to work, and that meant getting in good with the locals.

"Do you have a phone I could use?" Withers asked.

"Phone booth across the street, outside the gas station," Brogan said. He took four dollars and fifty cents in quarters out of the cash register and set the change on the bar.

Withers drank his coffee under the watchful eye of the bartender and then went across the street. Except for modern additions like the gas station and the power lines, the street looked like the set of a Western. He had never been in this small a burg in his life. He didn't know they still existed.

That gave him an idea.

Luckily, the phone booth had an intact phone book, something you'd never see in New York. In a town this dinky, Withers thought, it shouldn't be too tedious or time-consuming a process to take the phone number Gloria gave me and check it against the numbers listed in the book, which will then produce an address. Yes, you have to get up pretty early in the afternoon to put one over on Walter Withers, P.I., he thought.

"She can't be pregnant," Neal said.

"Why not?" Karen asked.

"Because she can't be. It makes things too complicated."

"Don't whine."

"I'm not whining," Neal whined.

"I dunno," Polly said. "My friend is usually very prompt."

"Well, maybe your friend got a flat tire or something," Neal said irritably.

Karen looked at Neal and shrugged.

"And this is going to be the water slide," Jack Landis was saying on the television. "The biggest in the world."

"I wouldn't ride down that ting," Polly said as she looked at the videotape of the water slide at Candyland.

"Not in your delicate condition, anyway," said Neal.

"Right, Jack," said Candy. "And we're having a 'Name the Water Slide' contest. You can win an all-expenses-paid week during the grand opening of Candyland by picking the name for the water slide. Who are the judges going to be, Jack?"

"Why, you and me, Candy," Jack answered.

"Can we turn this off?" Neal asked. He had a headache that had started in his toes.

"Now, what are we looking at here, Jack?" Candy asked.

"These are the time-share condos, Candy," Jack said. "And believe it or not, we still have a few to sell, but you have to act now. Just dial one-eight hundred-CAN-DICE for a color brochure. You know, Candy, folks can buy seasonal, month-long, week-long, or even a weekend package. We have something for every size wallet, fat or thin."

"Yes," Candy picked it up, "and for those of you who aren't interested in a time-share but would still like to contribute to this wonderful family fun center, we have special discount Honored Guest coupons for when you come to visit Candyland."

"How about The Break Your Stupid Neck and Drown Ride?" Polly suggested.

"Neal," Karen said, "if she's pregnant, she's pregnant, whether you want her to be or not. Believe it or not, you can't control it."

"Do you want to ask her?" Neal asked.

"Ask her what?"

Neal stared at her.

"Ask her if she thinks that photography is an art or not," Neal said. "Ask her who the father is."

The phone rang.

"That's none of your business," Karen said.

"Oh, you don't think so?"

"No, I don't think so."

The phone rang.

"It's Jack," said Polly.

"On the phone?" Neal asked.

"The father," Polly answered.

The phone rang again.

Neal picked it up and said, "What?"

"There's a guy sniffing around," Brogan said. "I was worried he's looking for . . . your houseguest."

"How do you know . . ." Neal began. He turned his back

away from the living room and asked, "All right, what does he look like?"

"Like he's from the East."

The East, meaning New York or Moscow, which were pretty much the same to Brogan.

"Okay, I'll check it out," Neal said, then added, "Thanks."

"Let me know if you need me," Brogan said. "The shotgun is loaded and the dog's awake."

"Thanks."

Karen and Polly were hugging when Neal turned around.

"Oh, please," he said.

Karen looked over Polly's shoulder and said, "This is an important moment to a woman, Neal."

Her eyes were teary and her nose was getting red. Neal was afraid she was going to cry. The last time he'd seen Karen cry was when a mechanic told her that her jeep was going to need transmission work.

"We don't even know if she's actually pregnant yet," Neal said.

"I just feel it," Polly said.

The women hugged again.

Neal took Karen by the elbow and guided her away, saying, "Could I talk to you for a second?"

In the kitchen, he said, "That was Brogan on the phone. He's hinky because there's a stranger in the bar. And he knows about Polly."

"Neal," Karen said, "Brogan's is the only bar on a state highway for a hundred miles in either direction. Strangers go in there."

Neal smiled and said, "Paranoia is not only a character flaw; it's my business. I'm going to go check it out."

Karen sniffled before she asked, "Why don't you pick up one

of those home-pregnancy tests until we can get to the doctor?"

A doctor, Neal thought. Great. That means a receptionist, too, and maybe a nurse. Throw in a few lab technicians, some hospital orderlies. Maybe we can just save time and go on the nightly news.

He heard Jack Landis's mellifluous voice say, "Folks, we've been under attack lately. You know, there are people out there who are so afraid of our family values, they'd resort to just about anything to destroy us. And I don't know about you, but I just can't think of a better way to show them that they just ain't going to get it done than to dial one-eight hundred-CANDICE. . . ."

I'll give you a time-share, Neal thought. You can share some time in a little cell with a lonely guy named Bubba—yearly, monthly, even on weekends.

"Make her do her Shakespeare," he said to Karen.

"Aww, Neal . . ." Karen whined.

"Make her do her Shakespeare."

Neal took about three minutes to walk down the hill to Austin's Main Street, which also happened to be Route 50. A car came through at least once every four hours or so.

A rumpled-looking guy in an old suit was coming in his direction up the sidewalk. Brogan's right, Neal thought, he looks like the chairman of the English department at a New England prep school circa 1956.

And he's headed right for our place, too.

Neal stopped in front of the man.

The man looked at him curiously.

"Mr. Withers?" Neal asked.

Withers blinked a few times, then said, "I know you, don't I?"

"You're Walter Withers, right?" Neal asked.

Withers studied Neal, then his eyes brightened.

"And you are . . . at least you were . . . Joe Graham's puppy," Withers said. "I remember you."

They shook hands awkwardly, then Walter Withers's face fell.

"Oh, Lord," he said. "Is Graham working this thing? Is he looking for her, too? You're the competition, aren't you? Well, of course you wouldn't tell me, would you? Joe Graham trained you. You were trained by the best, my boy, the best."

Neal remembered a time when Walter Withers had been pretty damn good himself, back when Withers had been with one of the big agencies and they couldn't help bumping into each other on some of the larger jobs. Joe Graham had pointed Withers out to Neal as an example. Rumor was in those days that Walt Withers, Loomis-Chaffee old boy and Yale alum, had learned his craft in the CIA, then gone to the private side for the money and the New York nightlife. Back in the fifties, New York had style and so did Walt Withers. Walt had dressed exclusively from Brooks Brothers and Abercrombie, and one of Neal's enduring adolescent memories was when Mr. Withers had flipped open a Dunhill cigarette case and offered him a smoke. Neal had politely declined, admitting he needed to cut back himself. Walter Withers was a gentleman.

But the nightlife had stretched into the mornings and then became an all-day affair and the big agency dropped Walt, who started the sadly predictable descent down the ladder. His fifties style went out of style, he was woefully unsuited for undercover stuff, and the jobs that Graham threw him when he needed an extra man were mostly backup stuff. But even backup guys needed to be sober to back you up, and after a couple of no-shows, Levine put the kabosh on any freelance hiring of Walt Withers. Neal hadn't seen him for many years, and by the look of him, Walt hadn't spent many of the intervening nights drinking coffee in a church basement.

But here he was in Austin, so was Neal, and so was Polly Paget, and neither man believed in that kind of coincidence.

"Maybe we can work something out, Mr. Withers," Neal said.

"Call me Walter, please, my boy. It's Neal, isn't it?"

Neal nodded.

"Work something out. . . . Share the kill sort of a thing, I see. . . . Interesting . . ." Walter said. "Sporting of you."

I'm a sport, Mr. Withers. And you're standing here trying to figure out a way to beat me. Share the kill . . . right.

"It depends on who your client is," Withers said.

I'm not proud of this, Walt, but here we go.

"Mr. Withers . . . Walter . . . I'm just a little thirsty," Neal said. "Why don't we go in and discuss this over a drink?"

The smile returned to Walt's face.

"Joe Graham did train you well," he said.

Uh-huh. And I hope he forgives me, Neal thought as he led Withers into Brogan's.

" 'The shotgun is loaded and the dog's awake,' " Charles Whiting repeated. "What does that mean?"

John Culver shrugged. "I don't interpret them, Chief. I just record them."

"Some sort of code," Whiting said.

Probably not, Culver thought. He'd learned from tedious hours listening to drug deals go south that what it probably meant was that the shotgun was loaded and the dog was awake.

It had been a frustrating four days since Whiting and Culver had met in Reno and driven across desert and mountain to the remote town of Austin. They'd taken a room in the better one of Austin's two small motels, told the owner they were geologists, and spent their days dutifully driving around the hills and their nights dutifully planting microphones and driving around with a directional sound finder.

The good news was that Austin was very small, so if Polly was in town, they had a good chance of picking something up. The bad news was that Austin was very small, and it couldn't be long before people started asking questions.

But now they had something, thanks to Culver's hunch that in a town this small, the saloon was a good place to pick up scuttlebutt.

"Apparently," Whiting continued, "they have a warning system set up. Did you pick up the number he dialed?"

Culver replayed the tape and listened carefully to the sounds of the dialing. He shook his head.

Whiting didn't complain or question. He'd hired Culver away from the DEA because the drug guys were a lot better than the FBI technicians, who were so hung up on court orders and constitutional safeguards that they couldn't record a football game on the VCR. Your basic drug guy could and would cheerfully bug a confessional booth and get Marcel Marceau's venial sins on tape.

Whiting thought it over for a couple of minutes. If he walked over to this bar and asked questions, the bartender might make another call, and then they could train the sound finder on the phone. But this Neal person might already be in the bar and that would give away the game. There was another problem: Whom was the bartender talking about when he said that someone was in there sniffing around? Was somebody else hot on Polly's trail? And if so, who?

Whiting had an idea. It wasn't uncommon for people in

backwater towns to harbor fugitives. If there was a conspiracy in Austin to protect Polly Paget . . .

Ten minutes later, he was showing Polly's picture to the clerk at Austin's one grocery store.

"Have you seen this woman?"

The old lady behind the counter took a quick peek and said, "Every day."

It wasn't quite what Chuck had been looking for. It was a whole lot better.

"Where?" he asked, his heart quickening.

The old lady pointed behind him.

Chuck whirled around to see a newspaper rack where pictures of Polly were spread all over the color tabloids.

Back to plan A, Chuck thought.

"I have a lot of money for her," Chuck said.

The old lady smiled.

"That's interesting," she said.

"In fact," Chuck continued, "I have a lot of money for anyone who could tell me where she is."

The old woman looked around and quickly leaned over the counter until her lips were an inch from Chuck's ear, then whispered, "Can you keep this confidential?"

"You have my word," said Chuck.

"Elvis," she hissed, "is sweeping up the storeroom right now."

Chuck's face flushed as the old woman straightened up and regarded him with disdain.

"Young man," she said, "I sell a little produce, a lot of canned beans, some pop, and a few bottles of beer. I do not sell people. Now, I do know where you can *rent* a person for an hour or so, but it isn't here."

Chuck's face turned from pink to scarlet.

The old lady continued: "Is there anything else I can do for you?"

"No, ma'am."

"Then please be on your way."

Chuck went on his way.

Evelyn picked up the phone two seconds later and dialed Karen Hawley's number.

"Karen," she said when her old friend answered, "I thought I should let you know that someone just came in looking for . . . your houseguest."

"Thanks," Karen said, "Brogan called, too. Neal went down to check it out. But how did you know—never mind."

Inside the van, John Culver lowered the shotgun mike and rewound the tape. He listened for a second and gave Whiting the thumbs-up sign. This time the phone number came singing through the headset.

Within five minutes, they found Karen Hawley's address in the reverse phone book Whiting had finagled from an old buddy in the Reno field bureau. After they'd parked the van a block away from the house, Chuck Whiting called the boss again and said to get there right away.

He didn't want to do that. He hated to do that. But those were his orders, and Chuck Whiting had spent a lifetime obeying orders. It was too late to change now.

Overtime thought about the circus. Particularly, he thought about that moment when the Volkswagen pulls up next to the house on fire and fifteen clowns get out of the little car, trip all over themselves, spray each other with water, and throw buckets of confetti on the house. Then the house burns down.

He edged the curtain back into place and stepped away from the window. He sat down on the motel room's one chair, its ripped mustard yellow upholstery repaired with duct tape, and opened up a package of peanut-butter crackers. He had checked in the night before and packed his own food and drink. He'd gone out once, at about three in the morning, to check the target area. He worked out his approach and his escape and it wasn't going to be a problem.

Just in, just out.

Then he went back to his room to get some sleep and wait for the clowns.

And now they were here.

8

$\mathcal{N}$eal had to admit to himself that he was glad when Walter Withers switched to coffee after one shot and a beer. Neal had planned to get Withers soused, leave him unconscious at Brogan's, then spirit Polly out of town. But Withers drank just enough to take the edge off and now he seemed brighter and more alert than he had when Neal met him on the street.

Bad for the plan, Neal thought, but good for Walter. The problem now is how to get rid of him.

"You were about to tell me who your client is," Withers prompted.

No I wasn't, Walt.

"That might depend on who *your* client is," Neal said.

Wither's eyes twinkled. He's actually enjoying this, Neal thought.

"Ah, yes," Walt said, "which one of us is going to get undressed first? We mustn't dawdle with the seduction here, my boy. I don't think we're going to have the room to ourselves for very long."

"Are you expecting company, Walt?"

Brogan coughed rhetorically and made a show of ramming the cleaning rod down his shotgun. He nudged Brezhnev awake and the dog growled.

Withers chuckled. "We're smart, young Neal, but we're

not the only smart people in the world. If we could track Miss Paget to this barren and lonely hideaway, so can other people."

"How did you find her, Walt?"

"With brilliant detective work, Neal," Withers answered.

"A snitch."

"Of course."

Walt finished his coffee and said, "I'd love to stay and catch up on the good old days, Neal, but I have to go and make an offer to Miss Polly Paget. You will excuse me, I'm sure."

He pushed his chair out and stood up.

Brogan stood up and snapped shut the shotgun chamber.

"You're not going to have him shoot me, are you, Neal?" Withers asked.

"If I did, it would be with only the deepest regrets, Mr. Withers," Neal answered.

Withers picked up his briefcase. He looked up at the ceiling thoughtfully and then dropped his head back down and laughed. Looking straight at Neal, he said, "I've misapprehended you. You're not looking for Miss Paget; you're hiding her, aren't you?"

And doing a lousy job of it, too, Walt.

"And you brought me in here to get me drunk," Walt continued. "That betrays low character, Neal. Yours and mine, I'm afraid."

True enough, Mr. Withers.

"I haven't met very many saints in this business, Mr. Withers," Neal said.

"Joe Graham is a saint."

"Joe Graham is a saint," Neal agreed. And what would he do in this situation? I wonder. I'd love to know, seeing as how he put me in this situation.

"And I suppose while we were having friendly drinks, you've had her moved?" Withers asked.

Well, no, Walt. That's what I should have done when I first heard you were here, but I was too busy sulking about her possibly being in a family way.

Neal nodded.

Walt sat back down. The jauntiness suddenly deflated in that way chronic alcoholics have of looking either eighteen or eighty within seconds. Now he looked eighty. His skin resembled old yellow paper that could crumble at the touch, and his eyes looked tired. His next drink wouldn't be coffee.

Withers sighed and leaned across the table.

"Here's the problem, my boy," he said. "I took a chunk of the advance money to pay off a gambling debt. I'm afraid I drank some of the rest. All forgivable, really, if one comes up with the goods, but . . . you've done me in."

He spread his hands, palms up.

"Who are you working for?" Neal asked.

"I have the great honor to be in the service of *Top Drawer* magazine, which has commissioned me to persuade Miss Polly Paget to serve as onanistic inspiration to millions of adolescent boys and adolescent men. These are the depths to which I have sunk, young Neal. Even in these substrata of our often-sad profession, I fail. I fail."

He dropped his chin to the table and stared at the greasy surface of the tabletop as if it represented an eternity in purgatory.

A brilliant performance, Neal thought. Top-drawer, indeed. And if this outrageous play for sympathy doesn't work, he'll try a threat: Play ball, or I'll go to the press just out of spite. Well, one good act deserves another.

"Two bourbons, Brogan?" Neal asked.

Brogan was so taken with the scene, he poured the drinks himself and brought them over. He even forgot to demand cash up front.

"You want to take naked pictures of her?" Neal asked.

"Not personally," Withers answered. "I'm just supposed to find her, make an offer, and give her an advance."

"But they'd be in good taste, right? The pictures?"

Neal had seen *Top Drawer* magazine. Caligula would have found its photos in questionable taste.

"The lighting, I'm told, is impeccable," Withers answered. He knocked back the bourbon in one swallow. If he detected a glimmer of hope, he wasn't letting on.

"And you're not working for Jack Landis, right?"

"I'm not," Walt mumbled sadly. Then, as if it was a fresh thought, he added, "Oh my God, are you?"

"No," Neal said. He drank his whiskey slowly, thoughtfully, and then let out, "I don't know, Walter. She's not a prisoner; she can do what she wants. And it looks like she going to need money. . . ."

Withers lifted his eyes from the table. "Believe it or not, Neal, they're talking about half a million dollars."

Neal whistled softly. Then he said, "Could they do it and guarantee her privacy?"

"Her *privacy*, my boy?"

"I mean, absolutely promise not to reveal her whereabouts?"

Withers brightened, although Neal couldn't tell if it was the emerging deal or the whiskey.

"Well, after all," he said, "they're revealing everything else; I suppose they could withhold that."

Neal silently counted to ten, then said, "I'd have to be present when you talked to her."

"Not a problem, Neal. In fact, a pleasure."

"No cameras, no tapes, no wires. And I'd have to pat you down, Walt."

"I'll get naked myself if that would help, Neal."

From the Book of Joe Graham, chapter eight, verse four: When you have the trap set, let the mark pull the string.

"Okay," Neal said. "Get a room at the motel down the street. I'll talk to her and call you in the next day or so."

Withers answered, "If it's all the same to you—and no offense—I don't want you out of my sight."

Tugging at the string.

"Then—and no offense to you, Walt—get lost."

"She has maybe, what—a half-hour lead, Neal? Can that hold up if every reporter, private investigator, and curiosity seeker in America descends on this burg by cocktail hour?"

Pulling on the string with both hands.

"You wouldn't do that, would you, Walt?" Neal asked.

"I wouldn't if I had a choice, Neal, but . . ."

He let the conclusion trail. It was Neal's turn to stare at the table.

"Okay," Neal said. "Let me go get my car."

"We'll take my car. You can drive."

"Automatic or standard?"

"Automatic."

"I can't drive a standard shift," Neal explained.

Overtime watched the drunken old detective and the younger man cross the street and get into the rental car. The old sot must be Withers, Overtime thought—too drunk to drive—and the young one must be the English tutor.

He kept watching as the car turned around and headed west on Route 50—away from the target house.

Where the hell are they going? Overtime wondered. Then he had an unpleasant thought: What if they moved her while I was sleeping?

Overtime felt extremely irritated for a moment. If he had to track the bitch, it would take time, and he was getting paid by the job, not the hour. Any time he spent following the target around the country was money out of his pocket.

He let his temper run for a minute, then cooled himself off.

No, most likely the English teacher had some unexpected street smarts and was taking Withers for a ride, which meant he'd be back.

And then they'd have to move.

Overtime didn't like the timing. He'd rather wait until night and then take a window shot.

What to do, what to do? He should wait for Withers to find her, but right now he didn't think that Withers could find her if she was in his underwear. On the other hand, maybe the dipso detective had done him a favor. Two women, alone in the house, how much of a problem could it be?

Overtime packed his things and threw them in the trunk of the car.

It was time to move.

"'The quality of mercy is not strained,' " Polly said. " 'It droppeth as the gentle rain from heaven/ Upon the place beneath. It is twice blest'—what the hell does this mean?"

"Which part?" Karen asked, preoccupied.

"The whole part," Polly answered. She didn't think Karen was paying a lot of attention and it pissed her off. If she had to say this boring shit, then someone ought to be bored *with* her. Usually, it was that dweeb Neal, who actually seemed to like it, except he winced and made faces like his head hurt when she was speaking.

Karen got up from the table and wandered over to the window.

"I think it means that mercy comes freely from God," Karen answered. "Like rain."

"Everybody knows that," Polly said. She just hoped it was true. She wondered why Neal had left before the Shakespeare lesson, then wondered if it had anything to do with Joey Beans. Maybe Joey Beans isn't too pissed off. And maybe mercy falls like rain.

"You're edgy today," she said to Karen.

"I'm not edgy."

"You are," Polly insisted. "Definitely edgy."

"Do your Shakespeare."

Karen had never seen the van parked at the end of the street before. Maybe Neal's paranoia is infectious, she thought. Still and all, I wish he was back. Where are you, Neal?

Polly stood up on her chair and ahemed dramatically. Maybe she could get Karen to laugh. That's what buds do.

" 'It blesseth him that gives and him that takes,' " she intoned, waving her free hand. "I'll be Neal now."

She jumped down from the chair, sat down, and put her head in her hands.

" 'Polly,' " she said. " 'There is a *t* at the end of *thattttt*. Pronounce itttt. Say *thattttttttttt*. Please, I'm begging you . . . before I go in the bathtub and open a vein.' How come you're not laughing?"

"Maybe because I'm edgy," Karen said.

Karen eased back from the window. She didn't know whether she should pull the shades. Or whether to call Brogan's. Damn it, Neal, where are you? And who's out there?

"I think you're jealous, Karen," Polly said.

Karen sat down at the table. "Jealous of what?"

"The baby."

"Oh."

"I think maybe you want Neal to give you a baby and he won't," Polly said.

"I'm kind of hoping for a new softball glove, actually," Karen answered.

"Say the truth."

Karen couldn't help glancing out the window. The van was still there.

"The truth," she said. "All right. I think I would like to have a kid with Neal. But not quite yet. Maybe in a year or so."

"You're not getting any younger, kiddo."

"Thanks."

Karen laughed. It was true. The old biological clock was clanging, and she had finally found a man she loved who might even be a good father. No, make that a great father. Maybe she'd talk to him about it tonight . . . if the son of a bitch ever got home.

Polly got up, went to the cabinet, and got a bottle of red wine and a glass. She poured a drink for Karen and asked, "Is it true about Neal's mother being a whore?"

"I'm afraid so."

"That's terrible."

"Worse things have happened to kids," Karen answered. "All things considered, he came out of it pretty well."

And God bless Joe Graham. I wish he were here, too. Because another strange car pulled up the street.

"Polly, go into the bedroom," Karen said.

"That's all anyone ever says to me."

"Do it," Karen ordered. "Pull the blinds and shut the door."

Karen's voice left no doubt she was serious. Because the van stopped again, a limousine pulled up behind it, and a strange man was walking up the street.

Where are you, Neal?

This is a breeze, Neal thought as he sped out into the vast sagebrush country south of town. Of all the possibilities, there were a lot worse than Walter Withers representing a porno magazine.

It would be almost worth it to see Ethan Kitteredge's reaction as he saw the photos, Neal thought. Then he stopped himself from imagining what the pictures would look like.

"What's funny?" Withers asked.

"Nothing."

"You were laughing out loud."

"Was I?" Neal asked as he pictured Kitteredge pitching face-first onto his desk. "I just had a funny thought."

"This is beautiful country," Walter observed, "in a Spartan fashion."

Yes it is, Neal thought. The car was running down a dirt road in the Reese River Valley. The Toiyabe mountain range ran parallel to the left, the Shoshone Mountains farther off to their right. The landscape was a marvel of muted purples, grays, and browns, punctuated by patches of emerald green alfalfa fields. The best alfalfa in America, Neal thought proudly, because of the altitude—six thousand feet. Damn beautiful country, Walter, and you're going to get a chance to see plenty of it.

"You really tucked her away, my boy!" Withers said. "We haven't seen a single house!"

Uh-huh.

Neal took a sideways glance at Withers. A sheen of greasy sweat covered his face and his hands shook on his lap. The man had been on a wicked bender. Maybe it would have been a kindness to have gotten him drunk. It's only a matter of time, anyway.

"Do you have a bottle in here, Walter?" Neal asked.

"I'm afraid not," Withers said. He knew what Neal was thinking and the kid was right: He needed a drink. "Not to worry. I want to be stone-cold sober when I make the pitch. This could be a big break for me, Neal, my road back to the top!"

Maybe Polly wouldn't mind posing for a few dirty pictures,

Neal thought. A half million bucks buys a lot of "losh," not to mention baby lotion. Neal felt sick to his stomach. He put his foot down hard on the accelerator.

The Milkovsky Ranch was twenty hard miles south of Austin. Once you turned off the main road, you still had a good drive down to the big log ranch house, dwarfed by the enormous hay barn.

"How did you find this place?" Withers asked in amazement as they pulled into the driveway. "I didn't know this even existed anymore. It looks like something out of *Shane*."

The house sat by itself in the broad expanse of the valley. The land gradually sloped east down to the tree line along Sandy Creek and then up into the jagged, rocky peaks of the Toiyabes. Some cattle wandered in the sagebrush and a few crows perched on the barn roof, but they were the only signs of life.

Neal didn't answer the question. He turned to Withers and urged, "Look, at least let me go in first and warn her."

"That's exactly what I'm afraid of."

"Fine," Neal said with all the petulance he could muster. "Come on."

He got out of the car and slammed the door behind him. He could hear Withers's footsteps on the gravel behind him.

Neal knew the door would be unlocked even though Shelly was off at college and Steve and Peggy were running around seeing Europe. Ranchers left the houses unlocked in this country, in case anyone got stranded. It wasn't all that critical on a September day when the weather was benign, but the practice had saved more than one life on a January night. With houses sometimes ten and fifteen miles apart, most people would rather take the chance of getting robbed than having even a stranger die on the road.

Neal let himself in the back door and stepped into the kitchen. He jerked the microphone out of the shortwave radio that passed for a telephone out here. Then he opened a cabinet door under the sink and pulled out a half-full bottle of Wild Turkey and set it on the counter.

Walter Withers looked at him curiously.

"I expect that you'll behave like a gentleman in the house, Mr. Withers," Neal said. "I'll send someone out for you in the morning. Your car keys will be at Brogan's."

Withers blinked.

"You wouldn't abandon me in this wilderness, would you, my boy?"

"I wouldn't if I had a choice, but . . ."

Neal stepped out of the door and trotted to the car. He heard Withers holler, "You're a bastard, Neal Carey!"

What can I say, Mr. Withers?

"Let's get this over with," Chuck said, using an understated, matter-of-fact tone to hype the drama.

Culver yawned and picked up the mobile phone. He was used to squadrons of adrenaline-crazed DEA types—their jaws grinding and knees twitching—gripping solid-steel two-man battering rams, M-16s, and automatic pistols as they readied themselves to rush a cocaine fortress that was usually better armed than they were. Culver had Vietnam vet drug agents order him to call in a tactical air strike on a crack house, and once or twice he had actually requested one over the phone just to settle them down. So Culver wasn't too impressed with the upcoming assault on a single woman whose most desperate act to date had been to file a lawsuit.

Nevertheless, he picked up the phone and faithfully spoke the words Whiting wanted: "We're operational."

Chuck Whiting checked the knot on his tie and gripped the Bible in his hand. Although Whiting had never done a lot of undercover work—in fact, he hadn't done any—he did recall the old axiom about keeping your cover as close to the truth as possible. But he just couldn't bring himself to mock his faith by going to the door as a Mormon missionary—he had spent two happy years in Uruguay doing just that.

So he went as a Jehovah's Witness.

Karen answered the door and opened it a crack.

"Yes?" she asked.

"Ma'am," the man said politely, "do you know where you'll spend eternity?"

"Well, I sat through *The Sound of Music*," Karen told him.

The man laughed politely and said, "I'd like to come in and share a few things about the Bible that you may not know."

"Uhhhh," Karen said, trying to look over his shoulder, "the prison chaplain did a pretty good job of that, you know, before my appeal went through."

"Oh?"

This would be a good time to come home, Neal.

"Yeah," Karen said, "and sitting on death row for all those years, I had a lot of time to read and everything. . . ."

"If I could just come in and pray with you," he said.

"I don't pray well with others."

The man scratched his head and looked down. Then he leaned on the door and said, "Look, enough is enough. I'm coming in the house."

The man is big, Karen thought. If he wants to come through this door, I can't stop him.

"I don't think so," she said as she tried to close the door.

Neal was at the bottom of the hill when he realized he'd forgotten the home-pregnancy test.

He thought about skipping it. He needed to get back, call Graham, and get Polly out of there, but this pregnancy test could provide important information, either way it went. So he turned the car around and parked it outside of Brogan's.

He locked it up and went into the bar. Brogan was asleep, so Brezhnev settled for a low, threatening rumble as Neal came in. Neal set the keys on the bar and retreated.

It took him about three minutes to find what he was looking for in the store and another three minutes to get enough nerve to take it to the counter. He picked up a bottle of Coke, a package of chocolate-chip cookies, and some oven cleaner to make the pregnancy test blend in.

Evelyn arched an eyebrow at him.

"The oven's dirty," Neal said.

The eyebrow arched a little higher.

"And I'm thirsty," Neal said.

Evelyn leaned over the counter and grabbed his wrist.

"Neal Carey," she said, "you should marry that girl."

"You're right," Neal said.

He paid for his purchases and started to walk back to the house.

Karen tried to shut the door, but the the man stood his ground in the doorway.

Then another man came over the top of him and slammed the door back open. Karen was about to punch him when she saw the woman standing on the doorstep behind him.

"What are you doing here, Mrs. Landis?" Karen asked.

Candy held up her hands and said, "I want to see the cheap tart who says she's been sleeping with my husband."

Polly stepped up behind Karen and raised her hand.

Candy flushed, summoned up her nerve, and said, "My husband has a disgusting nickname for the sexual act. What is it?"

Polly looked her square in the eye and enunciated, "Jack-in-the-box."

Candy Landis looked at the teased hair, the stiletto finger-nails, the mascara, the eyeliner, and the skintight black outfit and asked the eternal question of the wronged wife: "What do you have that I don't?"

Polly looked at Candy's chiseled hair, her plain nails, her white blouse buttoned up to the neck and tied with a bow, and her tailored business suit that looked like a piece of armor.

Polly rolled her eyes and sighed. "Where to begin?"

Overtime watched this scene, put his car into a K-turn, and retreated down the street. He blessed his good fortune as he recalled one of Chairman Mao's old sayings: "All is chaos under the heavens, and the situation is excellent."

9

*L*evine pulled the plastic lid off the cardboard cup and frowned. He set the cup down on his desk and looked at the young accountant, who was taking his own coffee out of the bag.

"Does this look black to you?" Ed asked.

The accountant looked into Ed's cup and said, "No, it looks regular."

"Maybe you have the black."

The accountant took the lid off the other cup and gave Ed the bad news. "Regular."

"What did you tell the guy?"

"I told the guy one black, one regular."

"He gave you two regulars."

"Do you want me to go back?" the young accountant asked. He was afraid of Levine.

Levine was irritated. Why did deli guys invariably screw up and give you regular instead of black when it would be a lot better if they screwed up and gave you black instead of regular? You could always put the cream and sugar in, but you couldn't take it out. It didn't make sense.

"I have to get a coffeemaker," Ed said. He started to drink the coffee and the relieved accountant sat down. "This better be an onion bagel, though."

"It is. I watched him put it in the bag."

"What'd you get?"

"Plain, toasted, with butter."

Ed unwrapped his bagel and wondered why Spitz and Simon had sent him the only goy accountant in midtown. Maybe because they knew it was going to be an all-nighter. They'd better be giving me a discount on the hourly, Ed thought.

"So, what'd you bring?" Ed asked.

The accountant looked worried.

"You said a bagel and coffee," he said.

"Your research," Ed said. "What did you think, I brought you over here to eat? What do you have?"

The accountant wiped his fingers off on a napkin and reached into his briefcase.

"Mr. Spitz worked these up for you," he said.

There goes the discount, Ed thought.

"What you'll see there," the accountant said, laying a stack of papers on the desk, "is that there are about twenty companies delivering various goods and services to the Candyland construction site. We managed to track eight of them back to the source and we should have the rest in a couple of days."

Ed made himself swallow some coffee on the theory that there was still caffeine in there with the milk and sugar.

"And?" he asked, because the accountant was just sitting there looking proud of himself.

"The eight we traced go back to something called Crescent City Management in New Orleans."

Ed felt his stomach turn sour, and it wasn't the coffee. It was the knowledge that organized crime in Texas was a colony of Carmine Bascaglia's empire in New Orleans.

"Who's behind Crescent City?" Ed asked.

"A group of lawyers," the accountant answered. "It's all there in the report."

"Eat your bagel," Ed said. He started to worry. Was it

possible that the mob had the arm on Landis? Had they just muscled their way in to get the job, or were they sucking the blood out of him, as well? There'd be so many ways to do it—eight guys on a job that needed five . . . four supervisors on every electrical outlet . . . overcharges on materials . . . bill for top quality and deliver the cheap shit instead. . . .

But what was in it for Jack Landis? It didn't make sense for him to rob himself. Unless . . .

Oh shit. It was so wonderfully evil that Levine had to smile. No, it couldn't be, could it? All that money pouring through the telephone lines—just dial 1-800-CAN-DICE and make your contribution to organized crime? Get yourself a time-share in a condo that is never going to be built? Or if it is, is going to fall down on you the first time you sneeze?

Nah.

But Graham sees a lot of trucks coming and going with no time to unload, then he thinks he sees Joey Foglio get out of a limo on the site, and . . . what?

What could Joey Beans have on Jack Landis?

Oh shit.

Ed set down his coffee and reached for the phone.

There was always a lot of controversy about what to do with the San Antonio River where it made the big bend downtown. The city's important wives, who were sensitive about living in a backwater, wanted to turn it into the Venice of the West. Their businessman husbands, who were tired of pumping the water out of their store basements, wanted to pave the damn thing over and use it as a sewer.

The wives won.

The local story has it that those civic-minded ladies put on a puppet show for the city council, but a lot of cynics would tell that it was some heavy-duty string pulling at home that turned the tide, so to speak. Anyway, the city of San Antonio hired a designer named Hugman to turn their fair burg into the Venice of the West, and damned if he didn't do it.

The River Walk runs for a dozen or so blocks through the center of San Antonio like a substratum of the city. Numerous staircases take you down from the street level and twenty or so bridges can take you from one side to the other.

Down on the river itself, you can stroll either bank and wander among sidewalk cafés, restaurants, bars, shops, even bookstores. You can get about any kind of food down on the River Walk, from Tex-Mex to Mex-Mex, from French cuisine to Cajun cooking, from Italian to your old basic burger and chicken-fried steak. You can eat it indoors, outdoors, on a barge cruising the river, or carry it around with you if you want. And they've been known to serve a drink or two on the River Walk.

It isn't exactly Venice and it isn't exactly Texas, either. The River Walk is a hybrid of Spanish, Texan, French, Italian, New Orleans. You can do a lot of traveling in a short distance on the River Walk, but Jack Landis wasn't paying attention to any of it.

Jack was in a sweat.

Joey Beans was just digging into a blackened filet mignon when Jack came huffing to the table.

"Siddown before you have a heart attack," Joey said. "Relax."

That's the trouble with these Anglo types, Joey thought. They just can't relax and enjoy what life has to give to you. Here it is, a beautiful evening on the River Walk—the trees sparkling with lights, the lights reflecting off the river, a table with a view of the river and half the young pussy in San Antonio—and this crooked little businessman can't drink it in.

"A glass of red for Mr. Landis," he told Harold. The muscle-bound hunk went into the restaurant to fetch the waitress.

"Make that hemlock," Jack said as he sat down. "Guess what?"

"You went to take whiz and your dick fell off?"

Joey Beans was in a humorous mood.

"Worse," Jack said. "We found Polly. Whiting just called. I've been looking all over for you."

Joey Beans tasted a bite of his steak. It was superb.

"My beeper went off," he said as he chewed. "I had Harold call you, but you must have left."

Joey paused to scope out a leggy young blonde crossing the footbridge over the river. Joey figured she was probably headed for a night of beer drinking at the Lone Star Cafe on the other side of the river.

He jutted his chin at the woman crossing the bridge.

"Why does she want to drink beer with a cowboy when she could have champagne with Joey Foglio?" he asked. "Hey, Jack, other than the fact that your retired fed bastard didn't die in a plane crash, that's good news you found Polly, isn't it? You want a steak? I'll tell Harold to order you a steak. How do you take it?"

"I don't want any damn steak," Jack answered as soon as the blonde got out of sight. "Guess who's with Polly right now?"

"We gonna play guessing games all night, Jack?" Joey asked.

"Candice," Jack said.

Joey noticed that the poor bastard's hands were shaking.

"So?"

"SO!" Jack hissed. "So what if Polly tells her everything?"

Joey smeared some sour cream on his baked potato.

"Jack," he said, "what's she gonna say she ain't said already? That you pronged her parakeet, too?"

The waitress came with a glass of red. Joey Foglio gave her a ten-dollar bill and a "when do you get off" leer. Joey was in the mood for some strange tonight.

"So what if Candy believes her?" Jack asked.

"Jack, are you saying to me now that you did this girl?"

Jack guzzled his wine.

Joey didn't believe what he was seeing. Grown man looks like a twelve-year-old caught in the bathroom with a *National Geographic*. Guy builds an empire, two empires . . . a frigging fortune . . . and he's pissing his pants because his wife might find out he's getting some outside the house.

"Well?" he asked.

"Maybe," Jack answered.

"Maybe," Joey echoed. "So tell Candy to pay her off."

"It's not that easy," Jack said.

Joey cut another bite of steak, chewed it deliberately, then said, "Sure it is. If Canned-Ice believes you, you got no problem. If Canned-Ice believes her, you still got no problem. You just drag her wifely ass into the bedroom and tell her to shut her mouth. What you do outside the house is none of her business. Tell her she's got a nice deal going—lots of money, good clothes, nice furniture—and if she wants to hold on to it, she'll stay in line. She gets mouthy with you, take your belt to her. Either way, lay her down on the bed, do the job, be a man, Jack."

"That's what you'd do, huh?" Jack asked sarcastically.

Both men stopped to look at a comely brunette stroll by the table.

Joey said, "A man keeps his wife in line. He also keeps his mistress in line. That way, the wife doesn't suffer disrespect."

Jack Landis had heard about enough. He wasn't some poor little diner owner you bully into taking your vending machines. He was Jackson Hood Landis, he owned about half this town, and he could make one call to the Rangers and they'd beat the olive oil out of this cheap gangster. Except it would be inconvenient to explain his relationship to Joey Beans.

"Well, there's one problem, Joey," he said. "I'd be happy to take my wife into the bedroom and smack her around, except I don't know where she is!"

Joey Foglio stared at him.

"You keep losing women, Jack. You should burn a candle to Saint Anthony."

"My wife isn't some fat guinea with eight kids, a mustache, and signing privileges at Two Guys from Sicily Pizza Parlor," Jack said. "She's a smart businesswoman. If she gets mad and decides to divorce me, she can take about half that business with her, maybe more."

Wait a second. Now we're talking about *my* money, Joey thought.

"I think we need a new plan," Joey answered.

"Well, make it good this time," Jack snapped as he stood up to leave.

"Not to worry, Jack. Not to worry," Joey said. And that remark about my wife is going to cost you, by the way, you cracker bastard.

Landis huffed off.

"Harold, get on the horn and find out what's happening."

Joey looked up at the bridge, where another delectable piece of ass strolled in front of a little one-armed guy who was likewise ogling her.

Joey cut another bite of steak and debated whether to pursue the blonde or the brunette.

10

K aren sat down on the edge of the bed next to Neal.

"I'm sorry," she said. "I did my best."

"Don't apologize, you did great," Neal said. "I'm the one who screwed up. I thought I was taking Walter Withers for a ride, and he was taking me."

He played me like a piano, Neal thought.

"Anyway," Neal continued, "it looks like it might work itself out."

He gestured to the kitchen, where Polly and Candy sat at the table in earnest conversation.

"She's left her husband, you know," Karen said. "She had what's-his-name——"

"Charles?" Neal asked.

He wished Karen hadn't let Candy send old Charles and his little helper away. He would have liked to have asked Charles some questions——like how they got the mike in Hathaway's briefcase and what else they had heard in Kitteredge's office. It would be nice stuff to throw in Ed's face when he called to let him know the job was all but over.

"——Charles, call and tell him they'd found Polly, but not to say where."

"What's she going to do now?"

"She doesn't know," Karen answered. "I invited her to stay here."

That's nice. *What?*

"*Here?*"

"Until she figures things out," Karen said. "I mean, there's no point in running away now, is there? Candy doesn't want people to know where Polly is any more than we do. Besides, they have things to work out."

"So you're going to have a slumber party?" Neal asked. "Would you like me to go back out and get some popcorn, some stuff for hot-fudge sundaes, maybe an all-night supply of nail polish? I have to tell you, Karen, I thought they pretty much worked things out when Mrs. Landis called Polly a whore and Polly expressed the opinion that Candy was a, quote, 'frigid, ball-busting bitch.' "

"That was the female equivalent of a fistfight," Karen explained. "They're talking now."

"What's there to talk about?"

"Oh, I don't know, Neal," said Karen. "For starters, if it were me, I think I'd like to know if my husband of twenty-odd years was a rapist."

"Or a father," Neal said.

"Shit, I forgot."

"You forgot?" Neal asked. "How you could forget something like that!"

"Well, there was a little excitement around here, you know."

Candy Landis came to the doorway. She looked tired and somewhat chastened, not at all the superwife she was on television.

"If that invitation is still open, I'd like to take you up on it," she said shyly.

"If you can handle a foldout sofa," Karen answered.

Candy nodded and stood perfectly still in the doorway.

After a few moments, she said, "I think this has been the worst day of my life."

Karen held out her arms and Candy slid into them. Karen cuddled the sobbing Candy while Neal sat there paralyzed by this female display of emotion and feeling about as comfortable as a pork chop at a bar mitzvah.

The crying had settled into sniffles by the time Polly came in.

"Guess what, everybody?" she screeched. "I'm going to have a baby!"

Candy broke into sobs again.

"A baby!" Karen said, then she started to cry.

Neal left the three hugging, weeping women, went into the bathroom, and threw up. None of them even noticed when he slipped out to Brogan's.

Graham leaned his back against the painted brick wall and talked into the phone.

"I'm telling you, I'm staring at his ugly face right now," he said. He looked across the crowded floor of the Lone Star Cafe, where Joey Beans and his muscle sat at a table trying to chat up a leggy blond urban cowgirl and her redheaded friend.

"And you're sure it's him," Ed said.

"It's the same guy I saw get out of the limo," Graham said. "It sure as hell looks like Joey Beans."

"And you saw him talking with Jack Landis," Ed prompted.

"Are you going to repeat everything I tell you?" Graham asked. "Because this conversation is going to take a long time if we have to do it twice."

Maybe, Ed thought. He'd spent the whole damn night poring over the accountant's report, and it didn't look good.

"If I have to kick this up a level, I need to be sure," Ed answered.

"You want a positive ID?" Graham asked. He was getting irritated.

"I want a positive ID."

"I'll get you one," Graham said, and hung up the phone. He

worked his way across the room, sidling past cowboy boots and under cowboy hats, until he was at the bar. He ordered and got a glass of beer and leaned back to check out the scene.

This was no mob hangout. The crowd was young and affluent. The denim clothes were new and hadn't been faded by days of work in the sun. These were honky-tonking duds, from the matte finish of the well-blocked Stetsons to the shine of the boots.

The jukebox was hammering out a Texas two-step, so Graham had a hard time hearing anything, but it looked like Joey was making some progress with the young lady. At least she found him amusing—she was leaning forward listening to him and laughing, and Joey had a smug man-of-the-world look on his face as he made big gestures with his left hand and laid his right hand on her arm.

Graham found an empty chair and dragged it over to Foglio's table.

"You mind if I join you?"

Thr four of them looked a little surprised, but they were just drunk enough to give it a whirl.

Joey checked to make sure that the blonde was listening, then said, "I knew there was Sleepy, and Dopey, and Sneezy, but I didn't know there was a dwarf named Stumpy. Hey, I got friends in Vegas; maybe I can get you a job as a slot machine."

Harold and the blonde laughed. The redhead looked a little embarrassed. Foglio looked very pleased with himself.

"I want to tell you all a story," Graham said.

"Hey, we got our own court jester!" Foglio bellowed. "Stumpy the Clown! You ladies want to hear a story from Stumpy the Clown?"

Graham smiled at the young women and sat down. He leaned over the table and waited for quiet. The four partyers looked at each other, smiling and laughing, and then Foglio made a go-ahead gesture with his big hands.

"Once upon a time," Graham started as the women chuckled, "in a city far away, there was a young man named . . ." Graham looked up at Foglio. "Joey," he continued.

The party laughed again.

"How'd you know?" Foglio asked, looking enormously pleased.

Graham shook his head to dismiss the question, then went on. "Now Joey was a poor young man. He lived in a small apartment with his old mother and old father and life was very hard. But Joey was a determined young man with broad shoulders, a strong back, and big muscles, and he was resolved to make a better life."

Graham paused to take a sip of beer. He noticed that people at the next table had stopped their conversation and were listening in.

"So Joey went to see the king," Graham said.

"The city had a king?" the blonde asked.

"Every city has a king, darling," Graham continued, "and the name of this king was . . . King Alberto."

Graham noticed that Joey was smiling, but an edgy look had come into his eyes.

Graham raised his voice to include the people at the next tables and continued: "And Joey said to King Alberto, 'Your Majesty, I am a poor young man with a poor old mother and a poor old father, but I have broad shoulders, a strong back, and big muscles and am willing to work very hard for a better life. May I come and serve you?'

"And the king answered, 'Joey . . . I know your poor old mother and your poor old father and they are poor but honest. What can you do to serve me'? And Joey answered, 'I can walk all around your kingdom, Your Majesty, and collect your taxes,' because every shop in the city had to pay tribute to the king."

Graham smiled at Foglio, who didn't look so jovial now.

"Then what happened?" asked the redhead.

"So Joey went to work collecting taxes for the king," Graham said. "He went from shop to shop collecting taxes, and everything was going just fine until . . ."

"Until what?" Harold asked.

"Until one day Joey went to collect taxes from an old man who owned a vegetable stand."

Foglio's face turned deathly white.

"This better be a funny story, Stumpy the Clown," he said.

Graham held up his hand for silence. He had quite an audience now.

"When Joey asked the old man for money, the old man said no. Joey asked again, and again the old man said no. Joey was getting very angry, because he knew that his job with the king was on the line. So he demanded the money . . . and the old man said, 'I don't have to pay tribute to the king.'

"Joey lost his temper. He knew he had to teach this old man a lesson. So Joey, who had a strong back and broad shoulders and big muscles, tipped over the vegetable cart. Then he grabbed every crate and picked them up and threw the vegetables all over the street, called . . . Sullivan Street."

"Shut up, Stumpy," Foglio hissed.

"Hush!" the blonde said, and slapped Foglio's arm.

"By this time," Graham said, "a large crowd had gathered. They were shocked at what they saw, but Joey was very proud, and he shouted, 'This is what happens to anyone who refuses to pay tribute to the king!' And then . . . suddenly . . . standing there in Sullivan Street . . . was King Alberto himself, looking very angry indeed, and he asked, 'Did you do this, Joey?' And Joey was very proud and said, 'Yes, Your Majesty, I did!' "

"That's the end of the story," Foglio said through clenched jaws.

Graham shook his head.

"The king walked very slowly up to Joey and said, 'Joey, this old man is my uncle! My uncle does not pay tribute. Now, if you want to keep your job and the head on your broad shoulders, you will pick up all these vegetables you have thrown on the street and you will pay for any you have ruined out of your salary.''

"Awww," the blonde said.

"Serves him right," said the redhead.

"There's more," Graham added. "The crowd was laughing at Joey. His poor old mother and his poor old father were standing there ashamed. And then, just when Joey thought things couldn't get any worse, King Alberto said, 'And Joey, because it is a sin to waste food, you will eat any vegetables you destroyed in your foolishness.' And there in the gutter, in the mud and the muck and the mire, was a pile of green beans that Joey had smashed. And the crowd watched . . . and laughed . . . and hooted as Joey knelt down on that dirty street, picked up a handful of filthy muddy beans and started to eat them.''

"Icky," the blonde said.

"And from then on, everyone in the kingdom called him 'Joey Beans.' ''

The crowd burst into laughter.

"You son of a bitch!" Joey yelled as he lunged across the table.

Graham pushed his chair back and stood up. Joey's fingers grazed the front of his shirt.

"The end," Graham said.

Joey grabbed the bottom of the table and pushed it over. The women screamed and drinks crashed onto the floor.

"Careful, Joey," Graham warned as he stepped back, "or Albert Annunzio will make you lap those up.''

Joey went for him, but Harold grabbed his arms and held him back.

"You bastard!" Joey screamed. "I'll kill you, you little prick! I'll chop your other arm off!''

"And eat it?" Graham asked.

As Joey tried to tear himself from Harold's grasp, the young blond woman said, "Wait a second. Are *you* Joey Beans?"

The cruel sound of feminine laughter set Joey Beans off again. The whole bar watched as Harold had to wrestle him to the floor, where Joey kicked, roared, generally foamed at the mouth, and screamed, "I don't know who you are, you slimy little runt, but if I catch you, I'll take a week to kill you! I'll find you, you bastard! I'll bury you alive! You don't know who you're messing with. . . ."

Joe Graham smiled and backed out of the bar and onto the street. He could still hear Joey's muffled curses as he walked past the Alamo to the cab stand. He hopped a taxi back to his hotel, went up to his room, called Levine, and said, "I'm pretty sure it's him, Ed."

11

K aren answered the phone. "Hawley's Home for Wayward Women. Hawley speaking."

There was a long pause on the other end of the line.

Then Graham said, "Karen, have you been drinking?"

"Yep."

"Can I speak to Neal?"

"You could if he was here, but he's not here," Karen answered. "May I take a message?"

There was another silence while Graham considered what, if anything, to tell her. Just because Joey Beans was involved with Jack Landis didn't mean there was necessarily any danger, and he didn't want to alarm Karen.

"Yeah, why don't you have him call in, okay?" Graham said.

"No reason, I guess."

"How's everything going there?" Graham asked. "Okay?"

"Yeah . . ." Karen said as she debated what to tell Graham. She thought it would be better if Neal told him such little things as the fact that Candy Landis was sitting at her kitchen table eating frozen pizza with Polly Paget and discussing baby names. "Everything's fine."

"How's our friend?"

"Late."

"Huh?"

"I mean radiant," Karen said. "Our friend is radiant."

"Hey, Karen, take it easy on the sauce, okay?"

"You betcha."

"Have Neal call," Graham repeated. "Right away."

"Right away."

"Good night."

"Back at ya."

Karen hung up.

"Who was that?" Polly asked.

"Neal's dad," Karen answered. "And his mom, his grandfather, his best friend, teacher, and boss."

"We have one of those speaker phones," Candy said as she poured herself another glass of white zinfandel. This was her fifth glass, which matched her normal biannual intake of alcohol.

"You sounded a little tipsy on the phone," she warned Karen. "I think that Polly should answer the phone from now on, seeing as how she is not drinking. She can be the designated talker."

"Friends don't let friends talk drunk," Karen agreed.

Polly asked, "Is there any pizza left?"

Neal was halfway through his first beer at Brogan's when Walter Withers staggered in. Dust covered his rumpled suit and sweat stained his white shirt. The briefcase in his hand looked as if it weighed a good eighty pounds. And he was drunk.

But his tie is still knotted, Neal noticed with a mixture of admiration and disdain.

Withers's eyes narrowed like the gun slits on a tank as he shuffled toward Neal. When he was at least an inch from Neal's face, he spit out, "That was a low thing you did, Neal. I must have walked six miles before I got picked up."

Neal swiveled on his stool to face Withers.

"You walked!"

"Disappointed?"

"Didn't your buddy Charles come looking for you?" Neal asked.

"Who's Charles?"

"You can drop the act," Neal said. "You got the job done. Your client is sitting with Polly as we speak."

Withers hauled himself onto the bar stool, an action that his sore muscles might have made a lot more difficult save for a lifetime of practice.

"I don't think so," he answered. He couldn't imagine Ron Scarpelli even coming to this godforsaken wilderness, and besides, he hadn't told the lascivious voyeur where he was. Or had he?

"I'm telling you, Walter," Neal answered. "Candy Landis is bonding with Polly right now. Congratulations. You beat me, okay?"

As gratifying as that might be, my boy, although I do detect a trace of rancor in your inflection, Withers thought, the euphoniously named Candice Landis is not my client. However, if you do persist in believing that, there might be some small advantage to be found. . . .

"Experience, my boy, that's all," Walter said. "May I make it up to you by buying you a drink?"

"I have a drink," Neal answered. He swallowed some beer to demonstrate.

"Then may I make it up to you by buying myself a drink?" Withers asked. "A whiskey, please."

Brogan poured a shot, then set the glass and Withers's car keys on the bar. Walt picked up the glass.

"You can tell me where the 'Jehovah's Witness' went," Neal said.

Have I suffered that dreaded first blackout? Withers wondered. I seemed to have missed a Candy Landis and a Jehovah's Witness—at least.

"Perhaps into the Jehovah's Witness Protection Program," Withers suggested. "Does it matter?"

"I guess not," Neal said. "So what are you going to do now?"

"Well," Withers answered, "now that Chuck has seemingly abandoned me, I suppose I will try to find a room and then return to Reno in the morning. Unless, of course, you'd like to put me up."

I'd like to put you up on a sharp pole, Neal thought.

"Why don't you go to Reno tonight? The hotels are much better there."

"I'm a little tired, my boy," Withers answered. He drained his glass and added, "From all the exercise, I suppose."

"There's a motel across the street," Neal said.

"Yes, I think I'll just have a nightcap and hit the hay." He yawned dramatically.

Neal didn't believe him—not the nightcap, not the yawn, not one damn word he had to say. There was no reason on earth Walter Withers would hike even one mile if he thought he'd done his job, and he'd have been cocky, not angry, when he walked in. And most of all, he wouldn't be hanging around a bar with the opposition—he'd get his car keys and get the hell out of town.

"Open the briefcase," Neal ordered.

"I'm sure that you meant to say, 'Would you mind opening the briefcase, please?' " Withers said. "In either case, the answer is no."

"What I meant to say was, 'Open the briefcase,' " Neal repeated. "When I want a lesson in etiquette, I'll write to Miss Manners. Now open the briefcase and show me what's inside."

Withers ignored Neal and turned to Brogan. "May I have another drink, please, my good man?"

"I ain't your good man," Brogan rumbled. His voice

blended into the dog's low growl. "And I ain't selling you another drink. I ain't going to get my ass sued off when you drive that car into somebody, either."

He put his big hand over the car keys.

"I'm not accustomed to barmen getting cheeky with me," Withers said.

"Open the briefcase, Mr. Withers," Neal said.

Withers slid off his bar stool, picked up the briefcase, and pulled himself to his full height.

"Well, you can go to hell, my boy," he said as he weaved in front of them. "And you can go with him, my good man. I have never been treated so shabbily in my life. You can both rest assured that you will hear from my attorney, of the law firm of . . . of . . . Howard, Fine and Shep . . . an experience you will not enjoy . . . I assure you."

Neal got off his stool and caught him before he hit the floor.

"He's got a load on," Brogan said.

"I loaded him," said Neal.

He gently laid the unconscious Withers on the floor and took the briefcase out of his hand. Setting it on the bar, he said, "If you're squeamish about felonies, you might not want to watch this."

The nice thing about metal, Neal thought, is that it trains itself to the touch. After the owner dials the same combination a few hundred times, the dials simply respond to the touch and go right to the required numbers. Unless, of course, the owner changes the combination every month or so, which is what Walter Withers had apparently done, because the dials refused to cooperate.

"Impressive," Brogan muttered as he handed Neal a screwdriver.

"Thank you," Neal answered. There was nothing like having an unconscious victim, all the time in the world, and no need for secrecy. It was also nice not to have Joe Graham there to observe and make sarcastic comments. He ripped the lock open with the surgical delicacy of a stockyard butcher.

"Shit on toast," Brogan said.

"Yep," Neal agreed.

The briefcase was full of real cash. No outfit in the business would use this amount of real money as a prop. Neal figured that Withers's original story about *Top Drawer* magazine had been the truth, or as close to the truth as one ever came in a scam like this.

"I ain't gonna ask," Brogan said.

"Thanks," Neal answered. "If you can help me get him up, I think I can carry him across the street. Leave his keys on the bar; he can get them in the morning."

Brogan came around the bar and helped lift Withers into a fireman's carry over Neal's shoulder.

"What if he comes back tonight?" Brogan asked.

Neal answered, "I doubt he's going to come to soon, but if he comes back in, shoot him."

"Never shot a man wearing a tie before," Brogan observed as Neal staggered out of the bar.

Neal crossed the street and walked over to the motel. He knew that the door to the office—a double-wide trailer— would be unlocked. He went in, leaned Withers against the wall, and reached into the large Maxwell House can on a wooden shelf and pulled out a key. He took a twenty-dollar bill from his wallet and put it in the can. Hefting Withers over his shoulder, he crossed the gravel parking lot, let himself into room number four, and flopped the old detective down on the bed. He loosened Withers's tie and maneuvered his jacket off him.

Withers started to snore.

Neal took the opportunity to go through Withers's jacket. There were a few loose bills in his wallet, a driver's license, and an American Express card. Tucked under the bills were some slips of papers with names and phone numbers . . . Ron Scarpelli . . . Sammy Black . . . and someone named Gloria, whose phone number was the same as Neal and Karen's.

Neal put the wallet back and hung the jacket up.

He found a pad by the telephone and wrote, "Walter, a cheery good morning. I have your briefcase for safekeeping—both ours and yours. I guess you know where to call. You make any other calls and you can kiss the money good-bye."

He left the note on the pillow.

Overtime woke up and for a single second didn't know where he was. Then he recalled parking the car off a dirt road on the outskirts of town to get a little sleep. He needed the sleep to achieve sufficient clarity of thought.

Point one: Nobody at the target location had actually seen him, so his person was secure.

Point two: They might have seen the car, so the car was dangerous. He would have to acquire a new vehicle.

Point three: A question, a dangerous unknown. Who were the people who had come in behind him? Were they still in the house? Was the target still in the house?

The terrain has shifted, Overtime thought. The fog of battle has descended. The tactical situation was unclear.

So what to do? The cautious option would be to withdraw, to find a new staging area and contact the client. Advantage: Safety. Disadvantage: Acknowledgment of failure. Damage to reputation. Fresh contact with client.

It was one of his prime rules: Each contact with the client represents a danger of exposure—telephones tapped, tapes rolling, voiceprints tracking.

Reduce client contact to the minimum. Contact client only when absolutely necessary.

Question: Was it now necessary?

Analysis: You are in a small, remote town where individuals attract attention. The target may be at least aware that there is an exposure.

Question: Where is that idiotic private investigator, the oblivious screen?

Further analysis: The target may be deceived that the exposure has already occurred or been diverted. It is nighttime. The approach to the potential target area is simple and without risk. The escape from target area presents few problems—with a different vehicle.

Analysis: The situation is unclear but not without possibilities.

Decision: While disadvantages do exist, the overall gain, predicated on the acquisition of a new vehicle, suggests an attempt.

He got back in the car and headed for town.

12

*T*o the best of his recollection, Neal Carey had never taken LSD.

But he questioned this when he stepped back into the house, because the scene in front of him resembled everything he'd ever heard about an acid flashback.

The first weird and twisted hallucination that met his eyes was a distorted version of Candy Landis sitting on a chair in his kitchen. Her formerly sculpted blond hair was . . . *big* . . . *BIG* . . . teased into a high, wild golden forest of sprayed and moussed branches.

Neal looked more closely to see whether he could recognize Mrs. Landis's face beneath the mascara, rouge, pancake, and something wild and electric blue that sparkled on her eyelids.

Yeah . . . he thought tentatively, that was her in there. That was her mouth beneath the frosted hot-pink lipstick highlighted with brown pencil. Those were her fingers touching her mouth, her fingers with the scarlet stiletto fake nails.

Despite his best effort, Neal's eyes wandered downward, pulled by the sheer magnetic force of the black lace undergarment that peeked above one of Polly's red silk blouses. Gone was the prim white blouse with the bow tied at the chin. The top three buttons of the red silk were undone, showing the black bra that performed its structural function of producing—what was the term?—cleavage. Right, cleavage that revealed freckles on Mrs. Landis's chest. The freckles gave her a sort of vulnerable sweetness.

"Quit staring at her boobs and tell us what you think," Polly demanded.

Neal looked up and decided that he must be having a nervous breakdown, because there was another hallucination, this one more bizarre than the first. Polly Paget—at least he thought it was Polly—was standing behind Mrs. Landis with a comb in her hair, apparently trying to produce an even taller tower of hair. But this Polly . . . No, it couldn't be Polly, because this woman's hair had been washed, brushed to a shine, and cut so it hung thick and straight above her neck. Her hair was parted high on one side and then flipped over her forehead.

And this woman wore makeup so subtle that you could barely tell she had any on. Neal could actually see her eyes, which were even sexier without the accoutrement. And she was wearing one of her denim shirts over jeans. She looked like a tall, modern Joan of Arc with a sex drive.

"What?!" Polly demanded, blushing. She thought she looked good, but she just wasn't sure yet.

Her face flushed and Neal realized that he was staring.

He looked around the table to Karen, who was elbow-deep in a half-gallon carton of Häagen-Dazs chocolate-chocolate chip. She picked up a can of Reddi Wip, sprayed it onto the ice cream, and dug in her spoon.

"Want some?" she asked him.

He noticed the scissors on the table by her hand.

"What have you been doing?" he asked.

"Girl stuff," Karen answered.

"We decided," Polly explained, "that Candy's next husband is not going to take up with some sex kitten."

"He'll have the sex kitten at home," Candy said, then added, "Meow."

The woman is sloshed, Neal thought.

"And you're retiring from sex kittendom, I take it," Neal said.

"So whaddya tink?" Polly asked. Then she pushed up her chin and slowly repeated, "So . . . what do you think?"

"I'm speechless."

"Then we should do this more," Polly said.

Neal said, "I think you look great."

Polly curtsied.

"Let's do that thing for him," said Karen.

What thing? Neal wondered.

"What thing?" Polly asked.

But Neal noticed she said *thing,* not *ting.*

"That thing we practiced," Karen answered. She got up from her chair, stood next to Polly, and whispered in her ear.

After the requisite laughter, Polly pronounced, " 'The rain in Spain falls mainly in the plain.' "

" 'I think she's got it,' " Candy slurred.

" 'The rain in Spain falls mainly in the plain,' " Polly sang.

" 'By George she's got it,' " Candy hollered.

" 'Now, once again, where does it rain?' " Karen asked.

" 'On the plain! On the plain!' "

"And where's that nasty plain?' "

" 'In Spain! In Spain!' "

Neal left the three of them singing and dancing in the kitchen and retreated to the bedroom. He slid the briefcase under the bed, then went into the bathroom to brush his teeth. He dropped onto the mattress a few minutes later, determined to get some sleep. He wanted a clear head in the morning to work out a number of questions. Who was Gloria and why did she have their phone number? And what to do about Walter Withers?

Overtime spotted Withers's car parked outside Brogan's. No surprise there, Overtime thought. Hire a dipso detective and that's what you get. He made a mental note to tell the client that the next time he provided a screen, he wanted a sober one.

But it did give him an idea.

He parked his own car down the road and walked back to the saloon. Switching vehicles with a drunk like Withers should be a simple operation, and well worth the slight risk of exposing his identity in a dark bar. And the idea of sticking Withers with a murder charge was just too amusing to let slide.

He got out of the car and went into the saloon.

But Withers wasn't there. The place was empty save for a filthy man snoring away in a decrepit lounge chair and an enormous mongrel likewise snoring at his feet.

What I won't do for a client, Overtime thought, yearning for the clean sunshine of an immaculate Caribbean strand. He pushed the thought from his mind and spotted the set of car keys on the man's disgusting lap.

There are rewards for virtue, Overtime thought.

He leaned over the bar and saw the Hertz logo on the plastic tab.

Problem: I need a fresh vehicle.

Potential solution: Keys glistening before me.

Question: Can I get them without waking this loathsome specimen of the great unwashed? And his mutt?

Answer: I am a professional.

He paused to listen to the breathing rate of the endomorph in the suburban electric chair. The man's sound sleep was probably a result of alcohol ingestion. Overtime switched his attention to the dubious result of canine miscegenation. The dog was out. If it wasn't, it surely would have awoken when I came through the door.

Just then one of the beasts—was it the man or the dog?—released a gaseous effluence so noxious that it forced a decision. One had to leave; the question was whether it was with the keys or without.

Overtime stepped over to the man in the chair and reached to his right for the keys.

Now, Brezhnev had laid his nose in Brogan's crotch on thousands of occasions. The warm spot between his master's fat thighs represented a dizzying festival of smells, so the dog could understand the attraction. But he would be damned if he'd let a stranger grope around in there.

"*Son of a bitch!*" Overtime screamed with presumably unintentional irony as the big black dog sprang from the floor and clamped his jaws on his wrist.

At first, Brogan thought that the growls and screams were just part of a pleasant dream, but then he opened his eyes, to see Brezhnev drive an intruder to the floor and attempt to replace his clamp on the man's wrist with a more satisfying grip on his throat.

Overtime managed to pull his arm from the dog's jaws and lay it over his own throat. At least this temporarily saved his life, but it made it very awkward to pull his revolver from his shoulder holster.

"Do something!" he croaked.

Brogan reached for his shotgun but couldn't find an angle to shoot without a risk of hurting the dog.

Overtime got his wounded right leg up and under the dog's belly and kicked. Nothing happened.

Problem: Homicidal dog has sufficient mass and muscularity to retain its advantageous position.

Analysis: Continuing status quo will shortly result in my death.

Solution: Attack animal at weakest point.

He kicked the dog in the balls.

Brezhnev flew back several feet and landed on its haunches.

"That's enough, Brezhnev," Brogan said as the dog started forward again.

But by that time, Overtime had regained his feet, pulled his pistol, and pointed it at the dog.

Brogan swung the shotgun on the stranger.

"Don't," he said.

Temper, Overtime thought. Rein in your temper. You are not being paid to kill a revolting old man and his disgusting mongrel. Temper. But it would be so easy . . . and satisfying . . . and unprofessional.

Overtime lowered the pistol, then brought it up in an arc against the side of the man's head. The man and his shotgun dropped at Overtime's feet. The dog whimpered, crawled to his master's prone body, and started to lick the blood from his head.

"You recognize a gun, don't you, you bastard?" Overtime asked the cowering dog. He stepped over to the cash register and emptied the till. Then he picked up the keys and let himself into Withers's rented car.

The dog's fangs had shredded his right wrist but had missed the artery.

He was mad—at himself, at the dog, at this job. He'd come here to do a simple and clean removal. Instead, he'd tried to get too cute—a quality he despised about other so-called professionals in his business. They made things too complicated. The thing to do was spot the target, fix the target, and then walk in and shoot the target. And there was only one acceptable option now: Go to the target location and get it done.

Just in, just out.

Brezhnev licked and whimpered until Brogan opened his eyes and moaned. After his master pulled himself to his feet, Brezhnev wagged his tail and stopped whimpering. He sniffed the blood on the floor until he distinguished his master's from the intruder's, until the intruder's blood filled his senses. He would remember it.

He'd just been doing his job before. Now it was personal.

Karen slid under the covers and pressed against Neal. She slid her hand down and touched him until his eyes opened.

"You wanna do it?" she asked in a startlingly good imitation of Polly Paget.

"Do it?" Neal mumbled. "Do what?"

"It," Karen repeated, her motion demonstrating her meaning. She smiled and added, "Yeah, I think you want to do it."

"Are your guests asleep?"

"My shy boy," she said. "They're in the living room watching 'The Jack and Candy Family Hour.' We can be quiet. I can, anyway."

Afterward, she asked, "Do you think she's attractive?"

"Who?"

"Who," she mocked. "Polly!"

Neal recognized dangerous ground when he saw it.

"I think she's more attractive now than she was," he said.

Karen elbowed him in the ribs.

"You're such a diplomat," she said. "Would you like to do it with her?"

Would I? Neal thought.

"No."

"Good answer."

"Thank you."

But he still couldn't get to sleep.

Candy leaned across the sofa and studied Polly's face. Candy was in that phase of inebriation that is like the eye of a hurricane. For a little while, everything is still, calm, and clear. It is more sober than sobriety. It is the time when the terrible truths come.

"Did Jack really rape you?" she asked Polly.

Polly nodded.

Without all the makeup, Polly's eyes were remarkably

expressive. Candy knew right then that the woman was telling the truth.

"What happened?" she asked.

"You really want to know?"

"I don't. But I need to know."

"Jack comes to my apartment," Polly answered. "I tell him it's over, that I don't want to see him anymore because I feel so guilty, I can't ask Saint Anthony for even an earring and I'm too ashamed to go to confession. He says that's superstitious Catholic bullshit and that I don't have anything to feel guilty about because the two of you——"

Polly suddenly stopped.

"Didn't have sex anymore?" Candy asked. "That's a lie."

We just weren't having good sex anymore, Candy thought.

"Yeah . . . anyway, I tell him it doesn't make any difference, that I just don't want to see him anymore, and I try to close the door, and I guess that makes him mad, because he pushes it open and grabs me and starts trying to kiss me.

"I slap him, but I guess that just makes him madder, and he rips my nightgown open, which makes me pretty mad, because I'd just bought it and it was expensive, so I punch him and he pushes me on the floor, but I have hold of his jacket, so he falls on top of me, which isn't so smart on my part, I guess.

"He's strong, you know, and he pushes my legs open and says something like, 'You wanna play, huh?' And I'm telling him to stop, but he doesn't stop.

"After a while, he gets up and leaves. I call my friend Gloria and tell her and she doesn't think I should call the cops—you know, 'you play, you pay' attitude—but I did, and I guess you know the rest of it. And Candy . . . I'm really really sorry I did that to you. Even though I'd see you on TV, you were never a real person to me, but now you are, and I am so, so sorry."

Candy had seen a lot of young women cry, most of them ex-convicts who had stolen stuff. She had handed them tissues and recipes and monthly budget planners, but now she scooted across the couch and held this young woman and let her cry into her shoulder. She didn't think that's what a priest did in confession, but that's what she did. She watched the strange image of herself on television, a picture that now looked like some old documentary, held the young woman to whom she was strangely related, and wondered what would happen next.

13

Overtime was experiencing what von Clausewitz had called "the frictions of war."

His wrist was raw and radial pain throbbed into his hand. He had driven near the target house, couldn't find a decent angle from the front, so he had to work his way laboriously to the uphill slope behind the house before he found a workable shot.

But when he peered through the scope, the operational situation became confused. There were two women, not one, and neither looked like the picture he had of Polly Paget.

Problem: insufficient clarity of identification.

Analysis: Risk increases with proximity.

Solution: Nevertheless, there is nothing to do but move closer.

Charles Whiting heard a sound that was distinctly human. The long hours hiding in the drainage ditch were a testament to his bureau training and his own personal discipline. Hungry, cold, and tired, he had heard nothing but coyotes, an owl, and the occasional rabbit. But now he sensed movement, human movement, headed toward the house and Mrs. Landis. Charles started to bear-crawl toward the house.

It wasn't exactly a sound that woke up Neal; it was the feeling of a sound. He lay still for a few moments and identified the electric chatter from the television set and the nondistinct sound of the two women sitting in the living room. Karen slept beside him, breathing softly. But there was something else, something outside.

He slipped out of bed, put on a black sweatshirt, jeans, and tennis shoes, went into the bathroom, and lowered himself out the window.

That goddamn Walter, he thought as he moved quietly around the corner. Dead-drunk and he doesn't give up.

Overtime worked down the slope to get a better view through the window. He was almost in the backyard. He dropped into a sitting marksman's crouch, wrapped the sling around his aching arm, and looked through the scope.

Lesbians, he observed as he saw the women embracing. What a town: mad dogs and dykes.

There was nothing to do now but get in the house, identify the target, and dispatch her. And if someone got a look at his license plate, too bad for Walter Withers.

He started to edge down toward the house.

Then he saw the man crawling across the lawn. He raised his scope.

The force of the hit slammed Neal against the wall and drove the air from his lungs. A spectacular jolt shot up his spine and his legs collapsed under him. He would have fallen to the ground if the guy who'd rushed him hadn't grabbed him and held him against the wall.

"Who are you?" the guy hissed.

Neal didn't waste breath on an answer. He stalled with an unfeigned effort to catch his breath, then wrapped his ankles behind the tall man's knees, twisted his own body away from the wall, and pulled his heels back. The man's knees buckled and he started to fall forward. As Neal fell backward, he grabbed the man's shirt and pushed his upper arm so that they spun and he landed on top of his attacker. He brought his elbow forward and smashed it against the man's nose.

Neal heard a grunt, then his attacker came up with a knee, pivoted his hip, and threw Neal off. Lunging forward, he took Neal clean in the chest and knocked him backward. Neal rolled before the guy could grab him again, then kicked out and hit the side of the man's knee. The intruder crumpled to the ground.

Overtime watched the fight as he screwed the silencer onto his pistol and pulled the ski mask over his head. If he moved quickly enough, he could be out of this job tonight.

Just in, just out.

He ran for the house.

Karen reached the phone by the fourth ring. It was Brogan, and he sounded drunk. Karen couldn't make out what he was saying. She reached for Neal and was surprised that he wasn't there. He was probably in the kitchen getting his usual postcoital snack.

She found her sweatshirt and jeans on the floor, crawled into them, and hurried for the kitchen.

Neal put a headlock on his man and found himself flying through the air a second later.

He pulled himself to his knees and peered through the darkness at the tall man who likewise knelt in front of him sucking air.

"You wanna discuss a truce?" Neal asked.

Overtime raced up the steps to the deck, ducked under the kitchen window, and slid along the wall to the sliding glass door.

He found it unlocked, so he pushed it open and stepped into the living room. The two women on the couch looked up.

Which one? Overtime asked himself. Which one?

"Oh my Gawd," Polly said.

Then he knew which one was Polly.

A professional makes his own luck, Overtime decided.

He raised the pistol.

Neal heard the glass door slide open. He got up and sprinted toward the house.

Chuck Whiting raced after him.

They both heard the scream.

A lot of purists complain about the cheap *ping* an aluminum bat makes when it hits the ball. They miss the solid *thunk* of wood on leather. But Karen really leaned into her swing and her aluminum bat made a very traditional *crack* when it ripped into Overtime's lower back. There were some bonus sounds, too, because softballs don't generally scream after they've been hit or whimper after they drop to the ground.

Overtime held on to the pistol, though. He pointed it up at Karen even as pushed himself along the floor back toward the door. He was half-tempted to put one in her stomach as she stood there with the bat raised over her head, poised to bash his brains in.

Let's see how tough you are with your guts hanging out and your life pouring onto the floor, he thought.

Then he glanced outside to check his escape route and saw a pair of yellow eyes flashing in the night, and he popped the shot off at the eyes instead.

And missed.

That's what Overtime couldn't believe as the dog bit into the tendon above his collarbone. He had never missed a shot before and it was that bitch's fault.

He tried to squeeze another shot off but couldn't feel anything in his right hand.

He was remotely aware of the front door bursting open as he reached his left arm out the deck railing and pulled himself to the edge. Squeezing under the bottom rail, he levered the dog against the railing until the hell beast let go. Then he pushed himself under and dropped to the ground.

He remembered to roll, somehow got to his feet, and kept one thought in mind: Get to the car. *Get to the car.* The chaos in the house should let you get to the car.

As he ran, he could hear footsteps behind him.

And the panting of the dog.

"Are you all right?" Neal asked as Karen stood shaking in his arms.

She nodded her head in his shoulder and tried to stifle her crying. She looked up, embarrassed at her red eyes and tears, and said, "I'm sorry. I was terrified."

"You were great," Neal said. "I'm the one who's sorry."

Sorry I ever put you in this situation. Sorry I took this job so lightly, that I misunderstood Withers—not once, but twice— sorry I was out in the yard rolling around with the wrong guy while I left you to deal with a killer in our home. Sorry I got out there in time to see Withers's car roaring away. I'm one sorry son of a bitch.

"The dog's going to be all right," Candy said. She daubed Brezhnev's neck with antiseptic. The dog lay panting on the floor, with what looked like a satisfied smile on its face.

Karen bent over, stroked the dog's neck, and said, "You have a lifetime's supply of biscuits coming from me, kid."

I put her in a position where an old dog saved her life, Neal thought. *Just* saved her life.

"Are you sure you're all right?" he asked again.

"I'm okay. I'm shaken . . . I think we all are . . . but I'm okay."

Neal kissed the top of her head, then walked over to Polly,

who stood in the middle of the floor with that stupid expression on her face. It made him even angrier. He grabbed her by the wrist and pulled her toward the bedroom.

"What are you doing?" she asked.

But he noticed that she didn't resist.

"We're going to have a talk," he said.

He didn't wait for an answer or an argument, but hauled Polly into the bedroom and sat her down on the bed.

"I want the truth from you now," he said.

"Like what?"

"Like who is Gloria?" Neal snapped.

"She's my best friend," Polly said, "and my supervisor at work."

"Well, your best friend gave you up," Neal said.

"She wouldn't do that."

"How'd she know where you are?"

She chewed her lip.

I have to control my temper, Neal thought, because my temper isn't getting anywhere. She's perfectly capable of just dummying up if I keep getting angry.

He sat down next to her.

"You have to help me now, Polly," he said. "Someone wants to kill you, and someone came very close to killing Karen, so you have to help us."

"I called her."

Neal felt his face turn hot with anger. He fought to keep the bite out of his voice as he asked, "Why?"

"She's my best friend," Polly repeated. "We talk."

Not anymore, you don't.

"Does she have a man friend named Walter?"

"She has lots of man friends," Polly answered. "I don't know one named Walter."

"Do you know a guy named Walter Withers?"

"No."

The phone rang and Neal picked it up.

Polly took the chance to run out of the room.

"You were supposed to call me back," Graham said. "There may be some complications."

"Like a hit man coming to my house?" Neal asked.

"Hell no, nothing like that," Graham said. "Don't be paranoid."

"Okay, a button man just hit our place, but I'm sure it was nothing personal."

"What happened?" Graham asked.

"Someone just took a run at our honored guest."

"Is everyone all right?!"

"No thanks to me," Neal said. "Karen did a Mickey Mantle on his lumbar vertebrae. You told me this wasn't a mob thing, Dad. Can you still tell me that?"

Graham sounded ashamed. "No."

He briefed Neal on everything he'd learned. Neal, in turn, told him about Chuck Whiting, Mrs. Landis, Gloria, and Walt Withers.

"Walt Withers isn't a hit man," Graham said. "He's taken a fall, but not that far."

"Far enough to be a wheelman?" Neal asked. "The hitter got away in Walt's car."

Neal had his own doubts, though. He had left Withers just hours before, dead-drunk. It seemed barely possible that he could have driven a car, let alone made an assassination attempt.

"We'll get a team out there," Graham said. "Can you sit tight until morning?"

A team? Neal thought. So far, the old team had blown his location, let in at least three opposing players, and seemed to have given the other team copies of the playbook. He'd had about enough of the team. And there was a practical problem. With security so badly compromised, he couldn't be sure that any team that arrived didn't have one or more opposing players on it.

Neal answered, "I think I'll try a solo sport for a while."

"Don't do that."

"Well, I *am* doing that."

A long silence. Neal could almost see Graham rubbing his artificial fist into his real palm.

Then Graham said, "Son, every time something goes wrong, you go off on your own, and every time you do that, you fuck things up worse. You can't be doing that anymore. You have to stop running away like some sulking thirteen-year-old. You have to stay connected now, son. I know you're mad and you're scared, but it's time to grow up and stay connected."

"Fuck you, Graham."

But he's right, Neal thought. I can't handle this one on my own.

"What do you have in mind?" he asked.

Graham told him.

"Neal . . ." Karen stood in the doorway. She saw he was on the phone and so she sat down on the bed.

"Polly says you hate her and she wants to leave," she said.

"I'll drive her to the airport," Neal offered.

"Someone tried to kill her, Neal!"

"And almost killed you instead," Neal answered. "All because she had to get on the phone and blab to her buddy."

"She trusted her friend," Karen said. "Is that such a sin?"

"See?" Neal said. "Trust?"

"Neal . . ."

"As far as I'm concerned," Neal said, "she can take a hike. She's not worth it."

"I dunno," Karen said. "A deck *and* a hot tub?"

"We're going to have to run, you know," he said. He

reached for her and pulled her close. "I almost lost you. I couldn't take that."

"I wouldn't be so thrilled about it, either," she answered, stroking the back of his head. "How long will we have to run?"

"I don't know," Neal answered. "But we need to get going."

"I'm going with you," Candy Landis said, stepping into the room.

"Doesn't anybody in this house knock anymore?" Neal asked. "And no, you're not coming with us."

He was throwing things into a duffel bag when Chuck came back from Brogan's.

"He has a hell of a bruise and a possible fracture of the cheekbone," Chuck said. "That lady from the store is driving him to Fallon to check it out. They're going to stop by for the dog."

I owe Brogan, Neal thought—big-time. Not to mention the dog.

He could feel Chuck staring at him.

"Yeah?" Neal said. He didn't exactly have warm and fuzzy feelings toward old Chuck.

"I should remove Mrs. Landis from the area," Chuck said.

"Well, Chuckles, we're about to remove ourselves from the area," Neal said. "And Mrs. Landis is going with us."

"That's just not an option."

Neal turned from his packing and stared up at Whiting, who did not seem particularly intimidated.

"You want options, buy a Buick," Neal told him. "I don't think it's such a good idea, either, but the women insist, and I don't have the time to argue."

And between me and me, until I can figure out who is on whose side, I don't mind having a little leverage in the person of Mrs. Jackson Landis.

"Can you protect her?" Chuck asked.

Neal saw the little bones protrude at the base of Chuck's jaw and wondered if maybe this was a little more than business.

"I don't know," Neal answered. "Can you?"

"Of course."

Neal zipped up the duffel bag and said, "Yeah, you've done a pretty good job so far. She was, what, six feet from a gun barrel, would you say?"

The little bones looked as if they were going to pop right through his skin.

"The danger came precisely from her proximity to that . . . tramp," Chuck said.

"Agreed. You could have put that on the wreath," Neal said. "Look, I don't know what your feelings for Mrs. Landis are, but if you really want to help her, you'll let her work this out."

Chuck looked legitimately puzzled.

"Work what out?"

"See, that's the thing," Neal said. "You don't know and I don't know, so how can either of us help her? The best thing we can do is step away a little bit and let her do what she needs to do."

And besides all that good stuff, she's my trump card and I might need her handy.

"I don't think this is the time for feminist rhetoric," Chuck said.

"You're right," Neal said. "So try this: If Candice was a devious shit like me or you, she would have come here, found out what she needed to know, gone back to hubby, kept her mouth shut, and let him think everything was hunky-dory. And if you weren't so much in love with her, you wouldn't have made that call to Jack and blown what might have been a tremendous advantage. But she's not cold-blooded enough to be a mole in her own bedroom, and you're so jealous and so angry at Jack that you couldn't resist showing him the ace in the hole.

"Now Jack gets to calculate his next moves with the knowledge that Candy is no longer an ally, but an adversary—information that I'd have preferred he didn't have, but never mind—and we're left groping around in the fog as to his thoughts and intentions."

And I'm going to omit the happy news that Jack is apparently cheek-to-cheek with a known gangster who has caravans of empty trucks making deliveries to Candyland, because I don't know if you and Mrs. Landis already know that, and I don't want you to know that I know.

"I am not in love with Mrs. Landis," Chuck said.

"Whatever." Neal shrugged. "But I need your help and so does Mrs. Landis. Are you going to work with me on this, or what?"

Neal finished loading the jeep and walked back into the house. He'd hammered out a deal with Chuck, who left with the storekeeper—Evelyn, Brogan, and Brezhnev, so he was anxious to get moving.

He went back into the living room and said to Karen, "If the Sisterhood is ready to depart . . ."

"Funny," she answered. "Funny boy."

Polly asked, "Can't I just take my—"

"No," Neal answered for the fifteenth time. "There's not a lot of room and we have to travel light."

"Yeah, but I need—"

"We can buy things," Neal said.

We have lots of cash, he thought.

Karen drove because she was the better driver and so Neal could concentrate on what was outside. The first few minutes would be the worst. If someone was going to make a try at Polly in the jeep, he'd have to do it before or near the first possible turn, so Neal held his breath until they were headed west on Route 50 and out of town.

Karen turned down the dirt road that led to the Milkovsky place. Jackrabbits and the occasional coyote scampered from the headlights. The moonlight turned the sagebrush silver. Neal usually loved to drive through this country at night, but now the effect was eerie and frightening.

"Where you taking us, the moon?" Polly cracked, then with genuine alarm asked, "Hey, we're not going camping, are we?"

"Keep your head down like I told you to and shut up," Neal said. Polly seemed to have recovered her spirits, which was a mixed blessing.

Neal had Karen stop at the turnoff to the Milkovskys'. He felt a little edgy about making a stop there, since Withers knew about it and might figure they'd run there.

"How fast can you drive up to the house?" he asked Karen.

There was no point in sneaking in, and he wanted to give anyone inside as little time as possible to get ready.

"Please," she said. She stood on the gas pedal and the little jeep hurtled, bounced, and leapt toward the house. She hit the brake and the jeep fishtailed to a stop in the gravel driveway.

"Are we there yet?" Polly asked.

"We're just looking for a place to park," Karen answered.

"Shut up!" Neal hissed.

"I've got to pee," Polly whined. "Those bumps . . ."

Neal glared down at her and then listened.

He didn't hear a sound, which didn't mean much, but he got out of the jeep anyway and stepped up on the porch of the house. He walked around to the kitchen door and let himself in. The house was dark and quiet.

Neal felt the tingling sensation he always got in his arms when he was going into a dark and potentially hostile room. He wondered whether he was ever going to get over that. Joe

Graham's opinion was that if he ever got over it, he should get out of the business.

I should get out of the business, anyway, Neal thought. If something's going to happen, it's going to happen now.

He reached over and flipped the light switch.

Nothing.

Neal opened a drawer under the countertop and found two sets of keys. He used one to open Steve's gun cabinet. Steve wasn't big on pistols, but Neal found a .44 revolver that was bigger than he wanted but would have to do. The pistol in his hand, he walked through the rest of the house and found it empty. He went back out on the porch and hollered, "If you want to use the bathroom, now's the time to do it!"

While the women were thus engaged, Neal went back to the gun cabinet and selected a lever-action Winchester .30-30, a twelve-gauge pump, and found the matching ammunition.

"You think you have enough firepower there?" Karen asked.

"I hope so. Give me a hand with this, will you?"

They loaded the rifle and shotgun, carried them out to the open shed that served as a garage, and arranged them under the front seats of Steve's new Laredo. Neal backed it out of the shed, they transferred the bags, and Karen pulled her jeep into the shed.

"Think we'll be back before Steve and Peggy?" she asked.

"I hope so."

Neal took the wheel this time. He turned south toward a fifty-mile stretch of rugged dirt road that was the loneliest part of the High Lonely. It would take him straight down the Reese River Valley, then west over the Shoshone Mountains, then down into the low desert. He had driven it many times in daylight and never seen a single other car, and he sure didn't want to see one tonight.

"Where are we going?" Polly asked.

"God knows," Neal answered.

Polly thought a few seconds before she asked, "Is that in California?"

No, Neal thought.

Las Vegas.

Part Two

Candyland

14

Marc Merolla opened the door before the bell stopped chiming.

Ed liked the door, black exterior enamel with a brass knob at waist height. The refurbished mock-Federal door epitomized the recent Yuppie homesteading in the old neighborhood on Providence's east side. Once shabby and bohemian, it was becoming the place to be for young doctors, lawyers, and business types who could buy an old house cheaply and put the money they saved into renovations. The general rule seemed to be that the new owners would freshen up the exteriors, leaving the Colonial flavor intact, and gut the insides. Behind the tranquil quaint facades, contractors knocked down walls, exposed beams, sank tubs, and installed kitchen islands over which to hand stylish copper pots and pans that were much too expensive to mess up with food.

"Ed, hello," Marc said. "Come in."

Marc was a small man, compact and trim. His thick dark brown hair was short and he wore a neat mustache. His eyes, almond-shaped and deep brown, were soft and expressive, betraying the basic component of Marc's personality——kindness.

Marc Merolla was unfailingly kind. Soft-spoken and polite, he was a successful stock trader and investor who wanted to do well by doing good and had pulled it off so far. Even his clothes seemed calculated not to threaten. Today he was wearing a plum polo shirt with the collar turned up over a cream-colored sweater. His dull brown corduroy trousers were baggy and fell over suede shoes.

"Sorry to disturb your Saturday morning," Ed said.

Ed had taken the 3:00 A.M. train from New York, gone to the offices in the bank to shower and change clothes, then taken a cab to Merolla's.

"You're never a disturbance, Ed," Marc said as he ushered him in. "Let me tell Theresa you're here."

He took Ed's jacket and hung it on an antique coat rack in the hallway. He motioned for Ed to wait, then returned a few moments later with his wife and two young children.

Small and dark, Theresa was a perfect match for Marc. Her black hair framed sharp, pretty features and her brown eyes seemed to engage without challenging. She and Marc had dated since high school, all the way through college, and then married.

Theresa had an arm around each child's shoulder as she whispered to them and pushed them forward to shake their guest's hand.

Ed squatted to greet them. He made small talk with Theresa for a few minutes before she excused herself and the children to return to the kitchen, where they were busy baking a cake.

"Do you want to come in the library?" Marc asked. "And can I make you a cappuccino? It's my Saturday-morning indulgence."

"Sounds great. Thanks."

Marc opened the library door, just off the hallway, and gestured to a Danish-modern chair.

"I'll be right back."

Ed took a walk around the large room. Floor-to-ceiling bookcases held collections of the classics and an assortment of reference books. Several music stands, their surfaces laid flat, held oversized, open photography books, most of them of Italian country scenes. The walls were decorated with opera posters, mementos, and framed photographs of Marc and Theresa, their family, and their friends.

As Ed surveyed the pictures, music came piping softly from speakers in the bookcases. Opera, Ed thought with a smile. A typical Marc Merolla gesture, because Marc and Ed had first met at the opera. It was a charity event that Kitteredge had been desperate to dodge, so he'd sent Ed instead. To his own great surprise, Ed had enjoyed the music and also the Merollas.

Marc came in juggling two large cups of cappuccino. He set them both on his desk, handed one to Ed, then sat down. Ed sat down across from him.

Marc said, "You look awful."

It wasn't an insult, but an opening.

"I wouldn't bother you with this, Marc," Ed said. "But it's a real crisis."

"We're Friends of the Family, right?"

Marc had several large accounts at the bank.

"It's nice of you to think of it that way."

"What do you need?"

Ed sighed and then spit it out.

"I need to talk with your grandfather."

"Don't look so embarrassed," Marc said. "I talk with him all the time. I just don't work with him."

Ed heard the slight stress on the word *work*.

"This is business," Ed said.

"I don't know anything about his business," Marc said. "Every three or four years, I seem to have to convince the FBI of that, but I didn't think I'd have to convince you."

"You don't," Ed asserted. He knew that Marc Merolla had never been involved in the family business. He also knew how hard it was for Italian-Americans to shake the mob label, especially in a wholly owned Mafia subsidiary like Rhode Island. "I know who you are, Marc."

"Then why are you asking me this?"

"One of my people is in trouble. I need help. I was hoping maybe your grandfather could open a door for me."

Marc chuckled softly. "He's in prison, Ed. If he could open doors . . ."

It was no secret that Dominic Merolla ran New England from a suite at the Adult Correctional Institution.

"If I could just talk with him," Ed said.

Marc was quiet while he seemed to be listening to the aria and sipping cappuccino. He was thinking it through.

After a long while, he said, "We go to see him every other week, Theresa and the boys and I. The boys ask me if Poppy is a bad man and I tell them that he's not a bad man but that he has old ways that get him into trouble.

"He's seventy-eight years old and he's sick. Do you know why the state prosecuted?"

"No."

"To beat the feds to the punch so he could be near his family instead of at Leavenworth," Marc answered. "He's my grandfather, Ed, and I love him, but I don't get involved with his business. Sorry."

Ed drank some coffee to be polite. He didn't really want any. His stomach was raw from the battery acid he'd consumed on Amtrak.

"This really isn't anything to do with his business," Ed said. "I guess what I really need is an introduction."

"To . . ."

"You don't want to know, do you?"

"But someone of his standing."

"Yeah." Ed set his cup and saucer back on the desk. He bent forward so far, his head was almost touching his knees. He felt very tired. "Marc, I'm afraid. I'm afraid one of my people is going to get killed. I need to reach out, but my arms aren't long enough."

"Shit."

"I know."

Ed looked up and saw Marc's smile.

"I'll make a couple of calls," Marc said. "No promises. He hates you Waspy types."

"I'm Jewish."

"I meant the bank."

"I know," Ed answered. "Thanks, Marc."

"Would you like to stay for lunch?"

Lunch was three hours away. Even third-generation Yuppie Italians will always press you to stay for the next meal, Ed thought. They still cook in big pots.

"I have to get back to the office," Ed said as he stood up. "Rain check?"

"You'll be in town?"

"Right by the phone."

"I'll call. Come say good-bye to Theresa and the boys, or I'll be in trouble all day."

Ed went into the kitchen, where Johnny and Peter were wearing the ingredients of a big chocolate cake, and said his good-byes. He licked some frosting off the beater, kissed Theresa on the cheek, and made his way out without eating anything else. Marc shook his hand and gave him a little hug at the door.

Ed decided to walk down the hill to the office. As he walked, he thought it might be nice to get into another line of work, something that didn't make you so paranoid. Something that didn't set off internal alarm bells just because you saw a fraternity photograph of Marc Merolla arm in arm with Peter Hathaway.

* * *

Walter Withers woke up rough.

A Saharan thirst parched his throat, his head was full of cotton wadding, and he was shaking. Also, he didn't know where he was. He rolled out of bed, shuffled to the bathroom, and threw up. He poured three glasses of water down his throat and threw up again.

I have to cut back on the sauce, he thought.

He went back into the bedroom and edged a corner of the drape open. Even the pale morning sunlight hurt his eyes as he looked out onto a deserted Route 50 and remembered where he was.

Austin, Nevada.

His mouth tasted like a mop that had just cleaned a subway rest room—or what he imagined that must taste like—and he desperately wanted to brush his teeth. The problem was that he couldn't seem to locate his bag.

Deciding that he must have left it in his car, he opened the motel-room door, didn't see any cars at all, and tried to remember the last time he had seen his.

Outside that grubby saloon.

He looked out the window again and didn't see his car.

He found his shoes under the bed, pried his feet into them, went outside, looked up and down, and didn't see the red Sunbird.

This has the potential of making things very awkward at the return counter, he thought.

Then he remembered a dispute over car keys, which led to a recollection of Neal Carey's disgraceful behavior and the alcoholic marathon back from the far reaches of the tundra. The door to the saloon was unlocked, so he went in.

Deserted. Neither the smelly old man nor the smelly old dog were to be seen. Withers vaguely recalled an episode of an old television show—back when people actually bothered to write them——where a man woke up in an uninhabited world and found out that he was in hell.

Withers walked behind the bar, poured himself a bourbon, and considered the possibility that he was dead. Or asleep, dreaming that he was dead . . . or dreaming that he was awake, sitting at a bar considering the possibility that he was dead or asleep, or . . .

This was getting him nowhere.

Get thee behind me, Satan, Withers thought as he pushed the bottle away. There is work to be done——Neal Careys to be dealt with, automobiles to be recovered, young ladies to be located and bribed——

The briefcase.

Oh Lord, the briefcase.

Surely it was in the room and he had overlooked it.

He rushed out of the bar, across the street, and into the room. It wasn't on the chair or the bed; it wasn't on the floor under the luggage rack; it wasn't under the bed. He considered the awful possibility that the briefcase was with the automobile——gone——and went back into the bathroom for another bout of expurgation.

Then he saw the note on the bed.

There was no phone in the room, so he had to go to the booth on the street. His hand shook as he dialed the number. He let it ring about twenty times before he concluded that no one was going to answer, then he leaned against the glass, feeling sick for five minutes before he dialed again.

Never send to ask for whom the bell tolls, Withers thought. It tolls for thee.

After thirty-five rings, he decided that this earthly existence was a dark endless cycle of meaningless despair.

In something like eighteen hours, he thought, I have misplaced the subject, a car, $20,000——give or take——and my toothbrush. Whoever said that God takes care of fools and drunks was wrong on both counts.

He checked his wallet and saw that God had taken care of him to the tune of a couple of hundred bucks.

A two-dime stake, Walter thought. There was only one place in the world where he could build that back up. Now if only the Deity will make a bus run from here to Las Vegas.

Overtime had overslept.

The sun was up well before he was and that made him mad at himself. He'd wanted a few more hours of darkness to drive in but had been too exhausted.

Last night was too close, he thought. He'd barely reached the car ahead of the snapping dog and then had switched vehicles again in such a hurry that he hadn't had time to change clothes until he'd pulled the car off a dirt road east of town.

The car was clean; that was not the problem. The problem was his distinctive wounds. If he was stopped for any reason, the dog bites would clearly mark him as the attempted killer. Attempted murder, Overtime thought. Hardly a charge for a professional. He'd be laughed at.

The thought hurt almost as much as his wounds, and he couldn't decide which of those hurt most. His back felt as if someone had laced it with a baseball bat. The bitch. The Amazonian bull dyke bitch. As he arched his back to try to stretch the muscles, he regretted not killing her.

He unwrapped the gauze bandage he'd hastily applied last night. The dried blood stuck to the bandage and he could still feel the stinging pain as he'd poured hydrogen peroxide onto the raw flesh and into the puncture wounds. It always surprised him how many professionals didn't carry a basic first-aid kit as a standard part of their equipment. It was a serious oversight, because once you went to a doctor or an ER you were entered into the information network, and that could be extremely disadvantageous.

He opened his kit and removed a small pair of scissors. It was difficult with his left hand, but he carefully snipped away the shreds of loose flesh and neatened the wounds. Then he daubed them with a cotton swab soaked in peroxide and applied a topical antibacterial ointment. He threaded surgical filament into a needle and slowly stitched the cuts that needed closure. The pain made sweat pop out on his forehead, but he controlled his breathing, relaxed, and concentrated on the task.

Pain is ephemeral, he told himself. Infection can be permanent.

When he was done, he wrapped the wrist in fresh gauze, tore the edge in half with his teeth, and tied it off.

He treated the puncture wounds on his shoulder as best he could, but by using the rearview mirror, he could see that one was especially deep and would need attention soon.

He popped a couple of codeine tablets and pulled out on the road. He didn't dare take a pass back through town. The risk didn't justify the gain.

No, he thought, the bird saw the dog, the bird flew, and the dog got me.

Now he would have to contact the client, inform him that the target had escaped before he'd had a good chance to execute, and start again. Bad for the reputation.

A reputation is like glass, he thought. Once it's chipped, it shatters easily.

If the real story ever gets out, I'm finished. No one paid Overtime's kind of fee for anything less than success. The legendary Overtime, "Sudden Death" himself, trashed by a dog and a woman.

Problem: damaged reputation reduces marketability.

Analysis: Revenge, although a personal indulgence, will restore said reputation. As will a spectacular two-for-one execution.

Solution: Locate targets and dispatch both. Polly Paget *and* the woman with the baseball bat.

But now he needed to reorganize. Find a good crooked doctor and a safe place to sleep. He pulled the car onto Highway 376 and headed south for the one place that could provide what he needed: Vegas.

15

*B*reakfast didn't taste good to Jack Landis, even though it was the breakfast that Candice would never let him eat. He had taken advantage of her absence to order Pedro to fix him his "Early Retirement Heart Attack Special"—three fried eggs, bacon and sausage, rye toast dripping with real butter, a pot of strong coffee, a cinnamon roll, and a big old cigar.

Pedro balked at first, whining something about "Mrs. Landis wouldn't want me to," but Jack reminded him that Mrs. Landis wasn't there to rescue his wetback ass if Jack started feeling vengeful about the Alamo, so he'd better shut his mouth and fix breakfast or he'd be frying tortillas in Nuevo Laredo by lunchtime.

That seemed to do it. Jack got his artery clogger, but somehow he couldn't enjoy it. He ate it all right, but it didn't taste as good as it usually did. Pedro said that maybe he was tense.

Well shit, Jack thought, I don't know what I have to be tense about. My former girlfriend is accusing me of rape, that prick Hathaway is about to take my network from me, I'm neck-deep into an amusement park more labor-intensive than the Great Wall of China, a lunatic mobster is hitting me up for money, I got about three days of canned shows left before 50 million members of the viewing public start wondering where my loving wife is, and that same lady is about to cut off my balls, stuff them in my mouth, and parade me bare-assed down Broadway as an object lesson to any other husband who might be thinking about unleashing his hound outside the sacred confines of the old home place. Tense? Why, I'm as tranquil as one of them crazy monks when they pour gas all over themselves and strike a match.

Jack lighted the cigar and walked all over the big mansion, puffing as much smoke as he could into every room. He paid particular attention to Candy's personal bathroom, on the odd chance that if the ice sculpture did come home, it would really piss her off. She'd probably get the house anyway, the cars, half the restaurants, and half of what was left of the TV stations after Hathaway was finished sucking the meat off the bones.

The worst thing, the absolutely worst thing, was that the old ball and chain was gone and yet Jack couldn't do the one thing he really wanted to do. The breakfast was okay, so were the whiskey and cigars and boxing matches on cable, the ones where two skinny Mexicans you couldn't tell apart beat the guacamole out of each other. All just fine. But, thanks to the recent publicity, he couldn't do the one thing he really wanted to do.

Jack Landis couldn't get laid.

Nope, Jack thought. Here I am with more money than brains, my hound dog straining at the leash, and I absolutely, positively cannot let it hunt.

For the first time in a lifetime spent in the relenting pursuit of the dollar, Jack Landis asked himself what all that money was worth, anyway. He was rich, but he was a lot less free than he was back in the days when he went door-to-door selling vacuum cleaners and giving away hoses.

He had a shitload of money stowed away in the Cayman Islands, anyway . . . oh, peanuts compared to his aboveboard net worth in the old U.S. of A., but more than enough to live out a long retirement in the Caribbean. He didn't know if they made chicken-fried steak down there, but given enough long green, they could probably learn. And he could probably learn to like rum, and the women . . . well, he had heard that the women down there hadn't even heard of Gloria Germaine Greer Steinem or whatever the hell that uppity broad's name was.

"Pedro!" he yelled.

Jorge's name wasn't Pedro, but it was easier just to answer. "Yes, Mr. Landis?"

"This was a better country before the women started getting hyphens in their names like those inbred British chromosome cases!"

Jorge didn't think it was worth making the point that neither Mrs. Landis nor Polly Paget had hyphens in their names, so he said, "Yes, Mr. Landis!"

Jack thought he heard a little cheek in his voice anyway, so he hollered, "Pedro! You ever hear of the Goliad massacre?"

"No, Mr. Landis!" Jorge answered, wondering why the boss's husband was bringing up an unfortunate incident 150 years ago in which Santa Anna's troops had executed some Texas rebels.

"Well, I'm still mad about it!"

"Yes, Mr. Landis!"

"So watch yourself!"

"Yes, Mr. Landis!" Jorge agreed. Then he decided he had to do a little something to preserve his self-respect. "Mr. Landis, when is Mrs. Landis coming home?"

Jack pretended not to hear and stormed out the front door.

Actually, that's a good question, he thought. He went to find Joey Foglio and ask him how things were going up in Nevada.

Driving gave Neal some time to think, an activity he hadn't exactly been overdoing up to that point.

He knew that even if he'd cut himself off from Friends of the Family, Friends hadn't cut him off from them. Graham would be doggedly finding out whether this Joey Beans had put a contract out on Polly Paget and Levine would be working the paper trail. Kitteredge would be politely blowing a gasket because he didn't like to get mixed up with mob business.

Neither did Neal, of course, but he knew that he had to let go of his irritation at Friends and concentrate on keeping the three women in the car safe. What he had to do now was focus on what he had in front of him. The first step in that process was to look back.

So start with what you know, he thought. Three sets of intruders located Polly at the house. The first was Walter Withers, the second was Candy Landis and her boy Chuckles, and the third was a would-be hit man.

Withers apparently got the location from Polly telling Gloria and was dumb enough to keep it in writing. He was probably more afraid of forgetting phone numbers than he was of compromising his source.

Landis and Whiting claim they got the location by bugging Peter Hathaway's office and half of Austin. They have no apparent reason to lie at this point.

The would-be button man got the location . . . how?

From Candy Landis and Chuckles? Not unless they're the best actors in the history of deception, and they aren't. Which still leaves the possibility that they leaked it unintentionally.

From Withers? The hitter drove away in Withers's car, but only after beating up Brogan to get the car keys, although that might have been an accident touched off by the dog. And Withers had the blood-alcohol level of a Saturday night in Moscow, unless he was faking it for an alibi, and I don't think anyone could fake it that well.

Withers did have a pile of cash on him, which matched his *Top Drawer* story, but he gave up that tale in a heartbeat when I thought he was working with Whiting. And the cash could have been front-end money on the hit, but then why would Withers carry it around?

Whatever the case, Walt Withers is at the center of this thing, whether he knows it or not. The answers to Withers's involvement rest in two places: *Top Drawer* magazine and Polly's best friend, Gloria.

Neal pulled the car over at a gas station in Luning, a back-route crossroads in the mineral-rich desert of southwest Nevada. The left fork led to the Sierra Madres and California; a right turn took you down through the desert to Las Vegas. Karen, next to him, in the front seat, woke up when he stopped. Polly remained sound asleep, her head on Candy's shoulder.

"Be back in a sec," Neal said.

He went into the phone booth, dialed information, and got the offices of *Top Drawer* magazine. An annoyed answering service operator told him that no one, especially Mr. Scarpelli, was in the office on a Saturday.

"Do you like your job?" Neal asked.

The operator answered that except for a few stupid calls, she liked it a lot.

"Then I suggest you find a way to get in touch with Ron Scarpelli right away and tell him that Walter Withers is at two-oh-five five-five-five three-four-four-six and that he has thirty minutes to call."

The operator asked if he was nuts.

Neal replied that he probably was but that if she wanted to take the chance he wasn't, that was up to her. He hung up as Karen got out of the Jeep and walked over.

"You want something from inside?" she asked.

"Coffee would be great," he answered. "And maybe you should buy some food for the road. The Haynes sisters are going to be hungry if they ever decide to wake up."

White Christmas was one of Karen's favorite movies. Karen would watch *White Christmas* on an August afternoon when the temp was 102.

She brought him a plain doughnut and black coffee and he was surprised at how good they both tasted as he stood waiting in the phone booth. Twenty minutes later, the phone rang.

"Walter?" Ron Scarpelli asked. "Where the hell are you? Did you find Polly?"

Neal hung up.

Either Walter Withers had an extremely elaborate cover or the hit man had used him as a bird dog.

Neal had heard of a button man who liked to do that, a guy who preferred to stay in the background, let other people shake things loose, and then step in. But he'd always thought he was just a legend, one of those apocryphal underworld superkillers that turn out to be just a legend. In the whispers he'd heard, the guy even had a jive name, like boxers often gave themselves. What was it?

Neal got back in the car and turned left.

"Neal, you're heading for Las Vegas," Karen said.

"I know."

"Half the mobsters in the country live in Vegas and the other half vacation there! Why the hell——"

"It's neutral ground, a money machine as long as the tourists feel safe. The wise guys don't do hits in Las Vegas."

He'd driven about five minutes when he remembered the legend's name. Overtime——because it means sudden death.

Sudden death, my butt. We'll play for the tie.

Jack Landis stood on the terrace and gazed out across the Great Family Plaza that formed the center of Candyland. The Candy Club Condos, or the shells of them anyway, rose unsteadily from the ground on the far side.

"I have a vision," he said.

"Who's that dicking around on the water slide?" Joey asked him. The gigantic structure loomed to his immediate left.

Jack turned and looked up about one hundred feet in the air where a small man stood on the starting platform.

"That's just old Musashi," he said.

"Who's Musashi?" Joey asked. He didn't like people who didn't work for him messing around on the construction site, in case a ladder rung snapped or a piece of wall gave way or something.

"He's the engineer who designed the damn thing," Jack said. "Candice heard the Japs were the best for moving water. Something about Zen, I think."

"Oh."

"He used to be a kamikaze pilot," Jack added. "Don't you want to hear about my vision?"

Joey didn't want to hear about Jack Landis's vision. Joey figured the lights were about to go out on Jack Landis's vision, anyway. Unless Polly was smart enough to keep her mouth shut, which wasn't likely, the afternoon papers would be screaming about the attempted hit.

Jack would be the prime suspect—which was okay with Joey, except he'd better arrange to suck as much cash out of Jack while it was still there to suck.

"What's your vision?" Joey asked, rolling his eyes at Harold.

Jack's eyes got dreamy.

"I see that big empty plaza filled with thousands of happy people," Jack said, "each one of them carrying a Jack and Candy souvenir. Over yonder, I see the condos all built, a hundred percent occupancy and a waiting list. I see people in line for rides, people in line for food . . . shit, people in line just to get in."

I see people in line to get a chunk of your ass, Joey thought, unless we can get to Polly.

"I have a vision, too," Joey said.

"We ain't naming the water slide after your hooter," Landis said.

"No," Joey continued. "I have a vision of a terrible fire at night, the water slide crumbling to the ground, the condominiums as burnt-out shells. I see Candyland as a big black wasteland."

Jack turned and looked up at him.

"Your plan didn't work, did it?" Jack asked.

"Construction insurance, Jack," Joey said. "This is a beautiful country."

"Arson?!"

"Let's just call it nonspontaneous combustion."

"This is the biggest theme park in the world!" Jack yelled. "You'd need a goddamn tankerful of gas to burn this down!"

"Or a couple of guys from Louisiana," Joey said.

"We used the finest fire-resistant materials——"

Joey shook his head.

"No, we didn't."

"We didn't?"

"We *billed* for the finest fire-resistant materials," Joey explained. "We *used* the cheapest shit we could find."

"And half of that we hijacked," Harold added.

"You got a big discount, Jack," said Joey.

"I thought you were just padding the labor." Jack groaned.

"Nah," Joey answered.

Jack turned around and gazed across the plaza. His dream was looking more like a nightmare.

"None of this stuff can pass a safety inspection, can it?" he asked.

Joey and Harold cracked up.

"Shit," Jack muttered.

Joey put a big paw around his shoulder.

"Don't worry," Joey said. "We'll get a big insurance check, and then we can build it all over again."

All over again? Jack thought.

It'd be nice to be able to do it all over again.

16

*L*as Vegas, Neal thought, is a town designed to make people feel like winners, using money paid by losers.

He crossed the viaduct over the electric lava flow, wound his way around the tiled hot springs, eased past a trio of chariot drivers, and found his way to the registration desk. The lobby of The Last Days of Pompeii Resort and Casino Hotel was crowded with tourists, conventioneers, and gamblers.

"May I help you?" the clerk asked in a voice hinting that this was a doubtful proposition. The young man wore a simple white toga with a cloth belt, indicating that he was a "household slave."

"Mr. Heskins," Neal said. "I have a reservation for two adjoining rooms."

The household slave punched some buttons on his computer.

"I don't see you," he said.

"Thomas Heskins," Neal said. "I made these reservations months ago."

The slave punched some more buttons.

"You're not in here," he said with the barely concealed delight of a teenager wielding power, "and I'm afraid we're completely booked. The convention, you know."

"I do know. I'm with the convention."

Neal, Polly, and Candy had waited in a tiny motel north of Vegas while Karen went in to check things out. She came back with the information that the Association of Adult Film Makers was holding its annual bash at The Last Days of Pompeii.

Neal figured that was as good a cover as any for a man traveling with three women. The cover wouldn't last long, not in this town, but he wanted to buy every minute he could.

"You must have something for me," Neal continued. "Tommy Heskins? Moonlight Productions?"

The slave shook his head and frowned.

"*The Swap Meet?*" Neal asked. "*Swap Around the Clock? Swap Around the Clock, Down Under?* I did the Swapper series."

"You made *Swap Around the Clock!*" the slave said with admiration.

"Did you see it?" Neal asked.

"Yeah," the clerk said.

You did? I thought I made it up.

"I'll get you stills," Neal promised. He looked at the clerk's name tag: ATTICUS.

"My name's really Bobby."

A tall woman clad in a way-off-the-shoulder toga stuck a tray of drinks under Neal's nose.

"Complimentary ambrosia of the gods?" she asked.

Neal took a Bloody Mary, thanked her, and turned back to the desk clerk. "Bobby, can you help me out here?"

"We do have emergency set-asides for VIPs . . ." Bobby said doubtfully.

"One room's for my wife and myself. Two of my top stars will share the other room," Neal said with a wink.

"Were they in *Swap?*" Bobby asked.

"Remember the scene on the rubber raft?"

Bobby went back to the computer.

"And how would you like to pay for this, sir?"

Neal opened Withers's briefcase on the counter.

"With cash," Bobby said as he typed into the computer. "I'll need names for the other room, sir."

I should have known you would, Neal thought. I wish I had a couple.

"Amber Flame and . . . Desire," he said, because it was the best he could come up with.

"Just Desire?" Bobby gulped.

"Sometimes just desire is enough," Neal answered with what he hoped was a knowing wink.

Bobby finished the paperwork and handed Neal four plastic key cards.

Now all I have to do is sneak Amber and Desire up to the room, Neal thought.

Bobby greeted the next guest, "May I help you, sir?"

"Ron Scarpelli, *Top Drawer* magazine," the guest said as Neal's ears spun 180 degrees and stood up. "I get the convention rate, right?"

Or I could just leap into the lava, Neal thought.

Walter Withers was out of luck.

He bombed at twenty-one—or "XXI," as it was known in the Vesuvius Room—got burned by old VII at the dice table in the Molten Lava Pit, and was out-and-out killed by a steely-eyed gladiator holding three kings over VIII's in The Coliseum Poker Arena.

He did not make back Ron Scarpelli's fifty thousand. Instead, he'd tapped his cash, maxed out both Visa and MasterCard, and been laughed at by the woman on the AmEx 800 line. She told him that not only could he not get another cash advance; he couldn't even get a room unless she had a cashier's check by noon.

He was on his last day in Pompeii.

He found a phone booth with a stool and perused the late games. Then he dialed Sammy Black's number. Sammy would take his bet on account and maybe he could get well on San Diego with the points.

A recorded voice came on to tell him that the number had been disconnected.

That's strange, he thought. I hope Sammy hasn't been arrested.

He called the Blarney Stone and was relieved to hear Arthur's live, familiar voice.

"Walter! How are you doing?"

It was refreshing to hear a little warm bonhomie again.

"All right, Arthur, all right. Listen, I tried to call Sammy just now, but his number has been disconnected."

There was an uncharacteristic silence from Arthur.

"Uh, Walt, I thought you knew that," Arthur said.

"How would I know that?"

Because you did the disconnecting, Arthur thought. But he said, "Walter, Sammy is dead, remember?"

"Dead! Good God, man, what happened?"

Arthur got it then, and he was offended. Withers was calling to make sure his alibi was intact.

"A guy walked into the bar and shot him," Arthur said. "*And* Chick.*"

Walter Withers was shocked. New York had achieved a promiscuity of violence that was simply unacceptable.

"Who would want to do a thing like that?" Withers asked.

"I don't know," Arthur said pointedly. "I was in the can."

"How traumatic for you, Arthur."

Arthur hung up thinking that Walter Withers was one cold-blooded cookie.

Walter hung up and tried Gloria again. Perhaps she had heard from Polly. If he could just get a lead on Polly, he could probably persuade Scarpelli to give him another advance on the expense money.

"Hi!" Gloria's voice said brightly.

"Hello," Withers said.

"I'm sorry I can't come to the phone right now," Gloria's

voice continued, "but I would love to get a message from y-o-u. So leave one at the sound of the beep."

"Gloria, it's Walter again. I'm wondering if you heard from your friend. Please ring me. Please."

He hung up and wandered into the lobby to score another free drink.

He approached one of the fabulous showgirls in the revealing togas and tried not to stare at her breasts as he requested a drink.

She looked down at him suspiciously and asked, "Are you really with the convention?"

"Certainly."

"There's supposed to be a three ambrosia per guest maximum," she said. Then she saw his face crumple in disappointment and added, "I can give you a virgin ambrosia; it's just tomato juice. A lot of the Triple-X people are in the program; maybe you should try it."

Withers looked dolefully at the vegetable concoction.

"What am I supposed to do with it?" he asked. "Sacrifice it to the volcano?"

"Huh?"

"Never mind." He sighed. "And no thank you."

"I'm a friend of Bill's," she confided.

He looked unabashedly down her toga and said, "Bill must be a happy soul."

She looked around quickly and handed him a real drink.

"You're a kind person, Calpurnia," Withers said.

"There's a meeting in the Sandals Sandals room tonight," she whispered. "You should check it out."

"Are you and Bill going?"

"You're a funny guy," she said as she padded off to inflict hospitality on other guests.

"You're a stitch," Ron Scarpelli agreed. "Where's my money?"

"Ron!" Withers exclaimed.

"Call me Mr. Scarpelli," Ron growled. He was dressed for business: a three-piece white suit, black silk shirt open at the neck, gold chain, and white loafers, with no socks.

Ms. Haber, in a white tube top and white pantaloons, stood over his shoulder like an erotic backdrop.

"What are you doing here?" Withers asked.

"What am *I* doing here?" Ron shouted. "What are *you* doing here! You're supposed to be out getting me Polly Paget!"

A few heads in the lobby turned at the name. Ms. Haber steered the two men to a banquette behind an enormous palm tree.

This gave Withers a few seconds to think. There was only one thing to do: Lie.

"That is precisely what I am doing," he said quietly. He leaned closer to Scarpelli. "She's here."

"In Vegas?"

And keep lying.

"Right here in this hotel."

"Is that why you called?"

Is that why I called? . . . Is that why I called? . . . Did I call?

"Yes," Withers said.

Scarpelli leaned closer. The smell of Brut was overpowering.

"Why'd you hang up on me?" he asked.

"I was about to lose her," Withers said. "Had to go. I've been on the trail ever since, so I couldn't call back. That's why I look so . . ."

"Shitty?"

"Exactly."

"You're making this up," Scarpelli accused.

"Certainly not," Withers answered.

"Ron," Ms. Haber said, "if she's in this hotel, is it possible she's signing with the film people?"

Scarpelli looked genuinely alarmed.

"Hard-core?" he asked. "That'd be a terrible mistake. We'd pay her more for one spread than she'd make in a dozen movies!"

"All the major magazines are here, too," Ms. Haber warned.

"Shit," Scarpelli said. "Walt, we gotta make our move. Where is she?"

Where is she? . . . Where is she? . . . Let me think now. . . . Where is she?

Polly Paget knelt in the front seat of the Laredo and applied the last touches of makeup to Candy Landis.

She inspected her handiwork and said, "Your own mother wouldn't recognize you."

Candy looked into the rearview mirror.

"If she did, she'd have a heart attack," Candy said. "I look like a whore."

"Better," Polly said.

Polly, on the other hand, looked like a young gym teacher with her newly shorn hair and unadorned face, over a University of Nevada/Reno sweatshirt, sweatpants, and tennis shoes.

Neal knocked on the window and Karen opened the door.

"Okay," Neal said. "You and I are married."

"Neal, we're going to check into a hotel pretending we're married? How cute."

"Who am I supposed to be?" Candy asked.

Neal looked at the cohost of "The Jack and Candy Family Hour" for several moments before he found the nerve to answer, "Desire."

"I beg your pardon?"

"A pornographic film actress," Neal said. "You, too, Polly."

"Thanks a lot."

"A pornographic film actress!" Candy repeated, her eyes wide. "Neal, I don't know if I can . . ."

"It's just for the paperwork," he assured her.

"But aren't I a little old?"

"Ah, you're only as old as you feel," Polly said. "What's my name?"

"Amber Flame."

"Amber Flame?"

"Shut up."

Neal started to haul baggage out of the back of the Laredo.

"Polly," he said, "lose the sunglasses. People take a second look at someone wearing sunglasses indoors, and we don't want second looks. We're just going to walk in, get in an elevator, and walk to our rooms. Don't try to be sneaky; don't try to be inconspicuous. Questions?"

Polly asked, "Why can't I be Desire and she can be Amber Flame?"

"Is her hair red?"

"It can be," Polly said.

"It's not going to be," said Candy. "They're naked in these shows, aren't they?"

"No, they keep their shoes on," Polly said.

"You've seen them!" Candy shrieked.

"Sure, haven't you?"

"No!"

"Someone want to take a bag?" Neal asked. "Mrs. Heskins? Amber? Desire?"

"Where have you seen these movies?" Candy asked as she walked toward the elevator.

"If you really want to know, Jack used to have me rent the videos. He wouldn't go himself because he was afraid he'd be recognized," Polly answered.

"Weren't you embarrassed?"

"Watching or renting?" Polly asked.

"Renting."

"No."

"Watching?" Candy asked.

"Uhhhh . . . no."

Candy reverted to her talk-show voice, "Did you find them stimulating?"

Polly thought about it for a while.

"I liked the clothes," she said.

This is wonderful, Neal thought. I've got a desk clerk who's a big fan of movies that don't exist, a skin-magazine mogul whose cash I'm using to hide the woman he's paying to find, and the woman herself, who watches porn films for fashion tips.

"Desire and Amber Flame," Karen said, enjoying herself immensely. "How can a simple mountain woman like me ever understand what goes on in the mind of the man who shares my bed?"

"I had to think of something on the spot," Neal said.

"So they came from your unconscious. Interesting."

"Shut up."

"Do you have an actual plan or are you pretty much making this up as you go along?"

"I have a plan," Neal answered.

Which I'm pretty much making up as I go along, he added to himself.

"She's in a room under an assumed name," Withers said.

"What room? What name?" Ron Scarpelli asked quickly. He sounded like an overcaffeinated chipmunk.

Withers watched three muscle-bound gladiators pass by. He waited for them to get way out of earshot. He would have waited for them to leave town if he could have gotten away with it, but Scarpelli was actually chewing on his gold chain.

"I have a call set up with my snitch," he said. "She'll have the room and the name."

"Who's the snitch?" asked Ron.

Withers looked at the charm dangling from the chain in Scarpelli's mouth. It looked like a little spoon.

Withers answered, "I can't reveal a source."

"You can if you're paying this source with my money."

"What if you were captured?" Withers asked. "Then what?"

"Captured! What are you, drunk or something?"

"This is a virgin ambrosia," he told him. "I'm undercover, you know."

Ms. Haber rescued him by gliding onto the banquette and whispering urgently, "The buzz in the lobby is that Tommy Heskins is here with some kind of big deal. Everyone's talking about it."

"Who the fuck is Tommy Heskins?" Ron asked.

"The Swapper series, Ron?" Ms. Haber prompted. She hadn't heard of the Swapper series until three minutes ago, but everyone was talking about it, and it was her job to keep current.

"Shit," Ron answered. He'd never heard of Heskins or his Swapper movies, but he didn't want to appear unhip in front of her. "He has juice."

This confused Withers, who thought it was Bill who had the juice.

"Megajuice," Ms. Haber agreed.

"And tomato juice," Withers added, wanting to contribute.

"Walt, get on the phone to your snitch," Ron ordered, remembering even in this moment of crisis to speak with authority. "We need the name and room now! And Haber, find out where Heskins is staying so we can keep an eye on him!"

Ms. Haber rushed off to charm a desk clerk.

Withers sat on the banquette to finish his drink.

"What are you waiting for?" Ron asked.

I'm not really sure, Withers thought, but I'm probably waiting for Gloria to stagger back into her apartment for a Saturday matinee in the company of some man she picked up in a bar.

The room had lava lamps, of course—big ones—and thick shiny red curtains and a red cover on a big round bed. The carpet was stone gray flecked with red and the wallpaper was black with red and gray splotches on it.

The bathroom was black, with a black sink, black sunken bathtub-Jacuzzi and black shower stall. The plumbing fixtures were fake gold.

"I think the theme suggests that impending death by molten lava is an aphrodisiac," Karen said. "Does it do anything for you?"

"No," Neal answered.

"Me, neither."

There was a knock on the adjoining wall.

"Come in!" Karen yelled.

"Our room is beautiful!" Polly warbled. "It's just like yours!"

Candy made a face behind her back.

"Okay," Neal said, "here are the rules. Basically, you are prisoners here, ladies. You don't answer the phone; you don't answer the door. You don't make any phone calls."

He looked pointedly at Polly, who looked innocently back at him.

Neal continued: "All meals will be through room service. Karen or I will call them in and have them delivered to this room. When the maids clean your room, you will be in our room. When the maids clean our room, we will be with you. Any unexpected knocks on the door, you will repair to the bathroom. Any questions?"

"When do we get to gamble?" Polly asked.

"I don't think I'm making myself clear," Neal said. "You can't leave these rooms."

"For how long?" Polly asked.

"Forever," Neal said. "You will be here until the day you die."

Or until we're caught, whichever comes first. In a town where they know who draws to eighteen down, in which hotel security is tighter than on an Israeli airliner, and where both the mob and the feds have permanent staffs watching the airport, someone is going to make us. But hopefully not before we can cut a deal.

"During the duration of this ordeal," Neal pronounced, "we will continue in the education of Polly Paget. I say *we* because I am hoping that both of you other ladies will add your considerable talents to this monumental effort."

"You're taking a shot at me, right?" Polly asked.

"Better me than someone in a ski mask," Neal answered.

"I have a question," Candy said. She had washed off the makeup, done her face, and looked like her tightly wrapped self again. "What, if anything, are you planning to do about my husband? I mean, it seems like this hit man thing has put us on the defensive. I don't know about you all, but I would like to go on the attack. When do we do that?"

Neal checked his watch.

"I think right about now," he said. "Polly, I want you to make one more phone call."

"What would you like to drink, sweetie?" Gloria asked. She leaned forward to let her guest see the coming attractions.

"A scotch, please," Joe Graham said. He looked at the top of her breasts while wondering if her glasses were clean. The woman looked a little sloppy. Of course, most women who picked you up in the Blarney Stone at 1:30 on a Saturday afternoon were not going to look like Loretta Young coming downstairs.

Then again, he probably didn't look so hot himself, having spent half the night on an airplane.

The place is a mess, Joe thought as Gloria fixed the drinks in the kitchen. The carpet needs shampooing, the coffee table needs dusting, and the faded picture of Bobby Kennedy needs a good Windexing. Plus, it's overheated and smells of stale cigarette smoke.

Graham looked at his watch. He'd cut this a little too close. Then again, it had been a long time since he'd picked up a woman in a saloon.

"Hey, Gloria, forget the drink, huh?"

"What's the matter, Joe? Are you in a hurry, or are you afraid it'll wilt your asparagus?"

My asparagus? I have to get out of here.

"I was wondering if you'd heard from Walter Withers lately."

Her hand stopped above the glass for a half second, then she relaxed, poured the drink, and smiled.

"You know Walter?" she asked.

"From the insurance business," Joe answered. "You know, sometimes when you get a claim you think isn't kosher, you call a guy like Walter. I know he hangs around that bar."

She came in from the kitchen, sat down, and crossed her legs to show the maximum amount of thigh. Graham thought it looked pretty silly for a woman her age.

"I don't think Walter's been getting so many calls these days," she said. "He hangs around the bar too much."

"Yeah, well."

"When you get to the point where you can't handle your booze . . ." Gloria added, letting the point trail off.

Graham picked it up.

"So, have you heard from him?"

She opened a mock leather cigarette case, took out a filtered Winston, and waited for him to light it. When he didn't, she shrugged and reached for a lighter in her purse. Joe saw that she sensed something was wrong, but she was trying to keep it light.

"I had a drink with him about a week ago, I guess," Gloria said. "Are we going to talk about me and Walter or me and you?"

"When you saw Walt about a week ago," Joe said, "did you talk about your friend Polly?"

"Who are you?"

"Did you?"

"Maybe."

The phone rang. She lighted her cigarette and made no move to answer it.

Joe walked over to the window, opened it a foot, and stood in the fresh air. It was something he had always taught Neal— when you take over, take over. Make the space your own— little things lead to bigger things. It was the same with interrogations. Usually, your goal was to make people swallow a big ugly, so you're better off feeding it to them in small bites.

"It's okay with me if you don't want to answer your own phone," Graham said. "Anyway, your machine is on, so we can both listen."

She leaned over to turn it off. Graham grabbed her hand and forced it to the receiver.

"Hello," she said.

"Hi, it's me," Polly said.

"Kid, how are you?"

"I'm fine, but I'm scared. Someone tried to kill me."

"Oh my God!"

She looks surprised, Graham thought.

"Gloria, look, I want you to know where I am in case something happens. I'm at the Bluebird Motel in Sparks, Nevada. Room one-oh-three."

"Got it, kid. Listen, maybe you should call the cops."

"No!"

"All right, kid. Stay in touch, huh?"

Gloria hung up and looked at Graham.

"I brought you up here thinking we could have a few laughs," she said. "It isn't too late. . . ."

She looked pathetic.

"You're a very attractive woman and I'm attracted," Graham lied, "Unfortunately, we have a problem we need to work out. . . ."

"What problem?" Gloria asked.

Now she looked scared. He sat down next to her on the couch.

"What do you owe Joey Beans?" he asked.

Yeah, that's it, Graham thought. It's right there in your eyes.

Gloria said, "I didn't know he was going to kill her."

"No, you thought he was going to have roses delivered," Graham said. "Did Walt know about the hit?"

She laughed. "Walt! Walt thought he was getting her to pose for dirty pictures."

"He was a decoy."

"Who are you?"

"I'm a friend of the family," Graham answered. "Now, are you going to do the right thing, Gloria?"

She took a short hit on the cigarette before she answered, "If I knew what the right thing was."

Graham handed her the phone. "Make the call."

"You're kidding."

"Yeah, I'm a real comedian," Graham said. "Make the call. And remember, Joey Beans can't protect you up here."

She took the phone and dialed.

"Hello, Harold?" she said. "Take this down."

After she finished giving Harold Polly's new whereabouts, Graham said, "I'm curious. How much did you owe Joey Beans? What's a friend's life go for these days?"

The phone rang.

"Saved by the bell," Gloria said as she reached for the phone.

Graham shook his head.

After the beep, they listened to Walter Withers's plaintive voice ask Gloria to call him.

"You aren't home when he calls," Graham told her. "Leave him out of this now."

"Sure."

"I mean it."

"Okay, okay."

She leaned back on the couch and studied him.

"If you call Joey back, I'll know about it," Graham lied.

"You can trust me," she said.

Not while your heart's beating, Graham thought. He got up and walked out without looking back.

17

M y informant doesn't know which room yet," Withers told Scarpelli. "But soon."

"If butts were gold, baboons would be billionaires," Ron answered.

Withers figured that Scarpelli has doubtless heard that tasteful analogy at one of those motivational seminars. He also figured that he was about at the end of his rope with the publisher of *Top Drawer,* and if he didn't produce something soon, Scarpelli was going to start asking nasty questions about his fifty thousand dollars.

The lovely, efficient Ms. Haber rode to his rescue once again when she returned, predictably, with results.

"Heskins is in twelve-thirty-eight and twelve-thirty-nine," she said in that cold tone that Withers found inexplicably erotic. "We owe a kid at the desk named Bobby a lifetime subscription."

"Two rooms? What is he, fat?" Ron asked.

"He has his wife and two actresses with him," Ms. Haber reported. "A Ms. Flame and a Ms. Desire."

Withers saw a chance to buy a little time.

"Code names," he said in his most professional voice.

Ron shook his head and said, "Nom de porno. A lot of the girls use them."

Withers hung in there.

"Code names," he repeated. "At least it's worth checking out."

"You got any bright ideas on how to do that?" Ron asked.

"Yes, actually I do," Withers said.

And he actually did.

Two minutes later, Ms. Haber approached Bobby at the desk and asked him how he'd like to have a date with Miss July.

Karen sat on the edge of the bed and tapped her foot impatiently. The room-service manager finally came on the line.

"Yes," Karen said, trying to keep her voice soft and even. "We ordered four Vesuvius burgers with everything an hour and a half ago. We were told then it would be forty minutes. The next time I called back, I was told it would be up in twenty minutes. Now your guy tells me it'll be another half an hour. What do you have to do to get some food around here?"

The exasperated manager sighed and said, "You want the truth?"

"I can take it," Karen said.

"It's that adult-film convention," he said, sounding close to tears. "The waiters go up to a room and they don't come back."

"You're joking."

"Wish I was. I've already fired two kids, but what can I do, fire them all?"

Karen's stomach was growling and Polly had already worked her way through the snack food in the courtesy bar.

"Don't you have any waitresses?" Karen asked.

"I used to," he answered. "Half of them are signing contracts as we speak. Look, I'll tell you what. I'll have the cook burn your burgers again and I'll bring them up, okay? To tell you the truth, I could use the break."

"Well, that's nice of you."

"Not at all," he said. Then he spotted a waiter coming

through the door. "Oops, hold on. I've got one of the horny bastards right here. He'll be right up."

Karen called into the next room, "They're coming now!"

"Yeah, right!" Neal answered. He turned back to Polly. "Once again: The long thing in the middle of your face is your nose. It's for breathing and things to do with mucus we don't need to discuss right now. The oval-shaped thing beneath it, the one crammed with chocolate at the moment, is your mouth. It's for speaking, and, as you already know, eating. The idea is to inhale through your nose and exhale through your mouth in the form of speech. Swallow first."

Polly swallowed a mouthful of $4.50-a-bar Toblerone, inhaled deeply, and said, "I first met Jack Landis when I was a typist in his New Yawk office."

"Not bad. But there's an r in York. Try it again."

"I first met Jack Landis when I was a typist in his New York office."

"Good. Breathe deeply, because that gives you the nice soft tone. When you don't breathe, you sound tinny."

"Cheap," Candy suggested.

"Thank you, Mrs. Landis," Neal said. "Go on."

"I tought—"

"Thought," Neal corrected.

"—thought he was handsome, and I guess he thought I was cute, and it wasn't long befaw—"

"Before."

"—before one thing led to another."

"You got that r. Great."

There was a knock on the door in the other room. Neal put his fingers to his lips, switched places with Karen, and shut the adjoining door. He put the pistol in his belt, at the small of his back, and slipped on his jacket.

"Room service!"

Neal opened the door and saw Walter Withers, in a white tunic and sandals, standing beside the cart.

They stared at each other for a half second, then Neal grabbed him by the front of the tunic, kicked the door shut with his foot, and shoved him down the hallway and into the alcove with the ice machine in it. Turning so he could keep an eye on the hallway, he pushed Withers against the wall and stuck the gun barrel in his face.

"You dirty lying alkie son of a bitch," Neal said. "I should shoot you right here."

"You stole my money," Withers accused.

"I am going to shoot you," Neal said. He would have cocked the hammer for effect, but he was nervous around guns, his hands had the adrenaline shakes, and he only wanted to blow Withers's head off in fantasy. "Is that the money you took for setting Polly up?"

"It's the front money," Walter explained. "Neal, they're downstairs waiting."

"What, and you came up to warn me? How did you find us?"

"It was an accident, I swear."

Neal pushed the barrel into Withers's cheek.

"I know. I don't believe it myself," Withers said. "But I got lucky."

"How?" Neal asked.

"You made quite a splash as a pornographer, my boy," he answered. "I'm afraid you overplayed your cover."

First I underplay. Now I overplay. I should have it bracketed now.

"Who are you working for?" Neal asked.

"*Top Drawer*—Ron Scarpelli. It's his money you took. Neal, I'm in big trouble."

"You've got that right."

But I'm not in much better shape, Neal thought, and Withers knows it. He can blow the whistle and we'll have the media around our ears in about twelve seconds. And we're not ready for that yet.

Buy some time.

"I'll give you ten thousand of it now to keep your mouth shut," Neal said. "The rest goes to you in New York in two days if everything stays nice and quiet."

"That just puts me even, Neal. I need something for my trouble."

"You unbearable little shit . . ."

"My boy, I need something," Withers said, his eyes twinkling with the joy of combat, "or I'll have no choice but to sell this information to the media."

You'd do it, too, Neal thought. In a heartbeat, if you had one.

"Okay, another ten for your so-called trouble," Neal said, "In one week's time, not before."

"Twenty in three days."

"Fifteen in five."

"Done," Withers said. "A pleasure doing business with you."

Neal slipped the gun back under his belt and released his grip on Walt.

"I'll go get your damn money," he said.

"That's wonderful, my boy, wonderful," Withers said, straightening his tunic. "But do you suppose you might advance me, say, a thousand? I find myself fiscally embarrassed."

"I'm giving you ten large!" Neal protested.

"Unfortunately, I have to remit that to my soon-to-be-former employer, Mr. Scarpelli. Thank you for releasing me from the clutches of that tawdry flesh peddler, my boy."

"Wait here," Neal said. "And quit calling me that."

Neal went into the room, took $11,000 from the briefcase, went back out into the hall, and handed it to Withers.

"If I see you poking around here—no, if I see anyone poking around here, I will shoot you, Walter," Neal said.

"You're a gentleman and a scholar," Walt said.

And a dope, Neal thought.

He pushed the room-service cart into the room, checked it for electronic bugs, and called the ladies to dinner.

Withers strolled into Scarpelli's suite, walked to the bar, and made himself a martini. Then he sat down on the couch and put his feet on the coffee table, which was shaped like a lyre.

"I saw her," he announced to the startled Scarpelli and Haber. "She's in the room with Heskins."

"That's terrible!" Scarpelli said. "Or great . . . Which?"

"It's great, Ron," Ms. Haber said, "if we can get access to her."

"Access," Scarpelli repeated. He was pretty sure he'd been to a seminar on access. He couldn't recall what was said about access, but he did remember it was an important thing. "We need access."

"We could access Heskins," Ms. Haber suggested.

"We could . . ." Ron said thoughtfully.

"Why would we want to do that?" asked Withers.

"Tell him, Haber."

"To make a deal," she explained. "We can buy and sell Heskins. We'll make him an offer he can't refuse."

Still flush with success from his deal with Neal, Withers asked, "Why pay twice? Why not go right to the source?"

"How do we access her?" she asked.

"Actually, *access* is not a verb, my dear," Withers said. "And why don't you leave that little problem to professionals such as myself? I think you'd have to agree that I've done pretty well for you so far. And Ron, would you mind horribly if we settled up on my expenses? I hate to let these things go too far.''

Because, Withers thought, when Lady Luck is kind enough to land in your hand, work the faithless strumpet to death.

18

*O*vertime drove past the Bluebird Motel three times before he eased into the parking lot, turned off the motor and the lights, and watched. There was a car parked in front of 103 and lights shone through the cheap drapes. He could even see the flicker of the television.

Overtime didn't want a long wait. His right arm throbbed from the shoulder on down and his back was stiff. But he'd bungled the last operation by rushing in, and he wasn't going to make that mistake again.

Someone would come out the door. Someone always did. It was proof of the lack of discipline that infected Western society. Even people in great danger would eventually get bored or careless and throw their lives away going to the soda machine, or for something they forgot in their car, or just for a breath of fresh air.

Most people didn't have the patience for hiding, not in the long run—especially not women. Besides, these people would think they had dodged the bullet. They wouldn't expect another attack this soon.

He had angled the car to place the driver's side window toward room 103. Now he opened his Haliburton briefcase and screwed an aluminum tube into the back of the sniper rifle. He considered using the nightscope but decided that the lights of the motel soffit were sufficient.

Overtime popped two amphetamines, rolled down the driver's window, then lowered himself down against the passenger door and waited.

Chuck Whiting watched from room 120. He had to admit that Carey had picked the rooms well—the hit man had parked on the opposite side of the lot from 103, which put him close to 120. Chuck had seen the man was alone and now could clearly see the top of the man's head in the passenger window.

Chuck hadn't been on a stakeout for years. He'd forgotten how tedious and nerve-racking it was. As a good Mormon, he didn't drink coffee or smoke, so all he could do to pass the time was think about Mrs. Landis. The hours spent waiting to see whether a hit man would arrive had been soul-torturing. In the long hours of forced introspection, Charles Whiting had to admit to himself that Neal Carey had been right: He did have feelings—strong feelings—for her.

It's true, he thought, I'm in love with Candice Landis.

In the *old* Mormon Church . . . Never mind.

He forced his thoughts back to the alleged perpetrator in the vehicle. Carey had said just to watch, but Chuck didn't feel obliged to put himself under Carey's authority, even if he did have some mysterious influence over Mrs. Landis. Carey viewed this as strictly an intelligence-gathering operation, but now Chuck had the chance to capture the perpetrator. All he had to do was sneak out the door and come up behind him.

The door would be the difficult part.

Charles Whiting crouched in the darkness and thought about it.

Overtime felt eyes on him.

Paranoia, he thought as images of frothing dogs and baseball bats skidded across his brain.

Control yourself. Breathe. Focus on the target.

Goddamn it, there are eyes on me. I can feel them in the back of my head.

For one awful moment, he imagined the crosshairs lining up on the back of his head. His breath caught in his throat. He wanted to slip lower into the seat but was afraid that would trigger the shot.

Trigger . . . so to speak.

That's good. You've retained a sense of humor.

Professional. Analyze your situation.

Hypothesis: They set you up.

Supposition: They're behind you.

Potential solution: Turn and shoot.

Analysis: One, you won't have the time to turn, roll over, find the target, and shoot. Two, there'll be cross fire coming from 103. Three, they'll shoot the tires out and then take their time.

He paused to suppress the rising terror.

Breathe.

Dismiss image of bullet smashing into your brainpan.

Return to analysis. And hurry up.

Potential solution: Escape.

Analysis: One, you're facing the ignition and steering wheel. Two, you can push yourself forward and offer a minimal target. Three, you'll be out of good fire angles quickly.

He thought it was the best solution. If he could only get himself to move. An unfamiliar emotion suffused his being: humiliation. He recognized that he had the contemptible deer-in-the-headlights syndrome, and he was—for the first time in his life—deeply humiliated.

Overtime resolved there and then that if he ever got out of there, he was going to kill someone for this.

* * *

Charles Whiting couldn't make up his mind.

He recognized the problem. He was inexperienced in solo ops—the bureau just didn't do them. If this was a bureau operation, there'd be a dozen well-armed agents in several rooms, on the roof, and on the street. They'd give one warning on the bullhorn and then open fire.

And he was too old for this. His legs already hurt from crouching and he wasn't sure he had the agility or speed to make the requisite moves.

And I'm scared, he thought.

That revelation hurt almost as much as the realization that he loved Mrs. Landis. Life had become an uncertain experience after he'd left the bureau.

Now or never, he thought. He pulled his .38 from its shoulder holster and duckwalked to the door.

Overtime sensed the motion and threw himself forward. His head smashed into the steering wheel and the gun butt slammed into his upper ribs. Lying on the seat, he turned the ignition, put his foot on the gas, reached up to the steering wheel, then cranked it hard to the right.

The car careened in a wavering arc out into the road. Overtime's foot found the brake and got just enough of it to stop the car. He straightened the wheels and hit the gas again. When the car was ten yards down the road, he sat up.

His vision was blurred from the blood dripping into his left eye and he felt like someone had lighted a match and stuck it into his ribs.

I hate these people, he thought.

Whiting picked himself up. He'd tripped on the threshold and gone sprawling across the landing. Relieved and embarrassed—and embarrassed that he was relieved—he watched the car speed away.

It was almost time for Carey's call. This time, at least there'd be something to tell him.

And he was looking forward to getting back to San Antonio, even if it did mean blaspheming his religion.

"It doesn't make sense," Neal said to Graham. "Why would Foglio put a hit on Polly Paget?"

"To shut her up," Graham answered. He was having a hard time holding the receiver with his chin while trying to pack with one hand. "I'm telling you, I sat there and watched her make the call. Then you tell me a hit man shows up at the Bluebird Motel. You don't need motive if you've got evidence."

Neal sat back on the bed. Karen dozed beside him.

Neal pressed the point. "Why shut her up? What is she going to say that she hasn't already said?"

"Son, we traced the leak: Polly to Gloria, Gloria to Harold, Harold to Foglio, Foglio to the hit man. What more do you want?"

Neal said, "Certainty."

"Not in this life, kid," Graham said. "Sit tight. We're reaching out."

Sit tight, Neal thought. What else am I going to do?

He knocked on the adjoining door and went in to tell the ladies the happy news.

"Gloria wouldn't do that," Polly said when Neal told her about the dye test that ended at the Bluebird Motel.

She was sitting up in her bed. Candy sat on the other twin. An old black-and-white movie flickered in the background.

"But she did," Neal answered. "Joe Graham watched her do it."

"Are you sure Chuck is all right?" asked Candy. When Neal nodded, she asked, "Why would this Joey Beans person want to kill Polly?"

That was the question Neal thought Polly might have asked, but he guessed she was too focused on Gloria's betrayal.

"You're not going to like this," he warned Candy.

The woman was just getting used to the fact that her husband was an adulterer and a rapist. Now she was going to get to hear that he was a crook.

"Joey Foglio has been skimming off your construction project," Neal explained. "Polly's rape allegation is busting his rice bowl. If he can shut Polly up, money will start flowing through Candyland and into his hands again."

He watched Candy absorb this new information.

Then she said, "It's hard to imagine this could happen without Jack knowing about it."

"It is."

"Or participating in it," Candy continued. "Do you think he's involved in the murder attempt?"

Neal shrugged. "I would say that's a possibility."

"Dear Lord," Candy said. "What can I do to start making this right?"

"Nothing right now," Neal said.

All we can do right now is wait for my boss to go see an old man in prison.

19

*E*than Kitteredge stood in the waiting room of the visitors' center of the Adult Correctional Institution clutching a brown paper bag of expensive yellow peppers.

Kitteredge was not happy. He had never gone to visit any of the several bank customers who had passed time in white-collar federal facilities with tennis courts, manicured lawns, and well-appointed lounges, so he was especially displeased to find himself in this impossibly squalid human storage bin.

Why Dominic Merolla preferred this hovel to, say, Danbury was a mystery to Kitteredge. But Merolla had told the prosecutor and the judge that if he had to do time, he wanted to do it in Providence, prompting one wag on the local paper to observe that living in Providence at all was like being in prison, so going to prison in Providence was an irrational redundancy. But Merolla owned the prosecutor and the judge, who checked their law texts, bank books, and life-insurance policies and agreed that justice demanded Dominic Merolla be confined to the state prison for twenty years or the rest of his life, whichever came first.

Kitteredge felt horribly out of place in the waiting room, among the sweating mob composed mostly of overweight young women dressed in stained frocks that resembled used tents. Each woman seemed to have the same tired, blank expression, and oddly, they all seemed to have at their hips carbon copies of the same three filthy children, who in turn each seemed to have an identical health condition, the most apparent symptom of which were layers of dried mustard yellow mucus caked between their nostrils and upper lips.

Kitteredge had intended to spend this weekend cruising the blue water south of Newport on his boat *Haridan*. He had acquired several bottles of excellent wine and ordered some very good smoked salmon from his grocer. It was going to be a lovely weekend. Instead, he was standing in the visitors' waiting room, feeling sartorially inappropriate in his brown three-piece corduroy suit, white button-down shirt, and knit tie, all because Dominic Merolla would talk only to "the boss."

After a Dantesque eternity, a guard shouted, "Kitteredge!"

Kitteredge made his way through the crowd to the double-chambered doorway. The guard looked at his clothes suspiciously.

"You a lawyer?" the guard asked.

"No."

Ethan Kitteredge did not realize the significance of the question, unaware that prison guards loathed attorneys and tended to subject them to strip searches and all manner of hassles.

"ACLU?" the guard asked.

"Certainly not," answered Kitteredge, who believed that the term *civil liberties* was possibly oxymoronic and, in any case, a bad idea.

"What's in the bag?"

"Peppers."

"Peppers?"

"Peppers."

"You don't look like a *paisan,*" the guard observed as he pawed through the vegetables.

"Nor do I feel like one," Kitteredge said.

A senior guard behind a glass booth leaned out, tapped his

associate on the shoulder, pointed at a clipboard in his other hand, and said, "He's here to see Don Merolla."

The younger guard flushed, hurriedly put the peppers back in the bag, and escorted Kitteredge down a hallway, saying, "Sorry about that. Uh, I have a brother-in-law who's Italian."

They walked down a long narrow corridor to a metal door. The guard knocked and a heavyset guy with silver hair opened the door, looked Kitteredge over, and handed the guard a twenty-dollar bill. The guard left.

"You this banker?" the guy asked.

"I'm Ethan Kitteredge."

"Yeah, that's right. Come on in."

If Ethan Kitteredge had ever seen an Italian social club, he would have known that this large room in the middle of a maximum-security prison was indistinguishable from one.

The converted recreation room had a fully equipped kitchen in the northeast corner. Two large pots bubbled on the stove and a stooped old man gently stirred the contents of a saucepan. Kitteredge noticed to his horror that a complete cutlery set went along with the several cutting boards and the chopping block, at which a tall young man was wielding a cleaver on what looked to be a large piece of veal.

A long table with metal folding chairs occupied the center of the room.

In the southern half of the room, a dozen or so men were playing gin at three folding card tables, while another three or four were sitting in easy chairs or on a big sofa and watching two large-screen color televisions.

The silver-haired convict noticed Kitteredge's odd stare and explained, "The 'General Hospital' guys were fighting with the 'Guiding Light' guys. On Sundays, it's the Giants and the Patriots. It was easier to have two TVs. Wait right here."

Kitteredge watched him walk over to the old man stirring the sauce and whisper in his ear. The old man set his spoon down on the stove and shuffled over to Kitteredge.

Kitteredge was shocked at how frail Dominic Merolla appeared. He was thin and stooped, and what little hair he had left was cotton white. Liver spots marked his olive skin and his blue eyes were rheumy. He wore a plaid wool shirt, baggy khaki trousers, and old slippers.

"Did you bring the peppers?" he asked.

Kitteredge held up the paper bag. Merolla's hand shook as he reached out. He opened the bag, took a pepper, gently squeezed it, sniffed it, and handed it to the silver-haired man. He seemed satisfied.

"You know my grandson?" he asked.

Kitteredge nodded. "Very well."

"He's a good kid," Merolla said.

Merolla faltered as he made his way over to the long table and sat down. The silver-haired man gestured for Kitteredge to sit down.

Merolla said, "It's Sunday. We cook a big meal. I wanted you here and gone before the families arrive."

"This shouldn't take long."

"I hate you pricks," Merolla said. The silver-haired man set a glass of heavy red wine next to Merolla, who swallowed some wine and continued. "Do you know what I'm here for? Two guys steal my money; I have them killed. The police shoot thieves, they get medals. Dominic Merolla gets twenty to life. You old-money Yankees think you're safer because Dominic Merolla is in prison. Now there's no gambling, no loan-sharking, no vice in New England, huh?"

Kitteredge vaguely remembered that two brothers had been gunned down while eating pasta in a Federal Hill restaurant. As he recalled, the newspaper photos were rather bloody.

"I'm seventy-eight years old," Merolla said. "What do they think I could do on the outside I can't do on the inside? Chase broads? If I could still do that, I could get a broad in here, no problem. I eat, I sleep, I watch TV, I cook. I take care of business.''

"I came—"

Merolla interrupted. "I hate you pricks because you're hypocrites. I buy you all, then you go on television and call me a danger to society. Accuse me of bribery. Okay, I'm the briber. I'm here. Look around the room. Do you see the bribees? No. Do you know where you'll see them? At your cocktail parties and charity galas. On your boat. Yeah, I know all about you, you prick.''

Kitteredge understood why Merolla had insisted he come personally—to stand in for the old WASP establishment and take a beating. Kitteredge leaned back in his chair.

Merolla went on. "I knew your father before you and his father before him. All pricks. Your grandfather and my father did business. I can remember walking downtown with my father and seeing your grandfather walking with his family . . . and your grandfather walked past my father like he wasn't there.

. "Your grandfather hid money all over New England. He hid bootlegging money, gambling money, smuggling money. Then he wouldn't even look down his nose at my father. So I'm glad you came today to ask for your favor, so I could say no to your face. I have to check my sauce.''

Merolla tottered to the kitchen. The young man at the chopping block had cut up the yellow peppers. Merolla inspected the peppers and stirred them into the sauce.

Kitteredge got up and stood next to him at the stove.

"I'm not asking for a favor so much as—"

"Doing business," Merolla said. "You're the same prick your father was.''

Merolla dipped the spoon in the pan and tasted the sauce.

"When I started, we had the numbers," he said, "and it was

illegal. Now you have the lottery. We had booze. Now you can buy booze at the drugstore. We had the bookies. That's still illegal, but the same newspaper that calls me a criminal prints the point spreads. We made dirty movies. Now you can go to Loew's, see dirty movies. Dope? Now Hollywood actors joke about cocaine on the television and everybody laughs. But Dominic Merolla is locked up, so everything must be okay. You—''

Kitteredge said, "I've heard enough of your self-serving, self-pitying diatribe, Mr. Merolla. You cannot create corruption and then curse it. You are a murderer, a usurer, an extortionist, and a whoremaster. While it may be true that you simply take advantage of human frailties, it's also true that you and your ilk prey upon this society like carrion birds, except that you don't even have the decency to wait for your vice-wounded victims to die.

"A sterner society would stand you all up against a wall and shoot you, and were I asked to serve on such a firing squad, I would do so cheerfully and then take myself out for a very good lunch and eat it in good appetite.

"As for the relationship between our families, it is a sad reality that earthly exigencies sometimes force one to handle excrement, but one is expected to wash one's hands afterward. I'm glad my grandfather snubbed you, Mr. Merolla. I only regret such standards have lapsed and that we seem to be living in a society that embraces filth. Personally, I am sick to my stomach that I have to do business with you.

"You may not have comprehended this unfortunately long-winded soliloquy of mine, Mr. Merolla, so let me put it in words you might understand: Fuck you.''

During the seemingly interminable silence that followed, Kitteredge listened to the desultory sounds of the televisions droning what he assumed to be a football match. He wondered whether he had just botched the negotiation. It would have been better to have sent Ed Levine, who was much better at this sort of thing.

Merolla resumed stirring the sauce and said, "You're a prick, like your whole family. What do you want?"

"An introduction to Carmine Bascaglia."

Merolla's laugh sounded like a dry cough.

"That's funny! The banker wants to meet The Banker!" he crowed. "Why come to me? Carmine has his business in New Orleans; I have mine in New England."

"Because he would never see me without an introduction."

"That's right."

Merolla set down the spoon and wandered along the counter to check a tray of antipasto. He swiped a sliver of salami from the tray and popped it in his mouth.

"You have a problem in New Orleans, prick?" he asked.

"Possibly."

"Possibly. You didn't lower yourself to come here for 'possibly.'"

Merolla shuffled back to the long table and sat down, forcing Kitteredge to follow him around like a lovesick suitor.

"We believe that it is in Mr. Bascaglia's interests to talk with us," Kitteredge said.

"Carmine will let you know what's in his interests," Merolla said. "I can do this for you. It's a phone call."

Kitteredge felt the cool breath of relief.

"But why should I?" Merolla asked. "Why should I do anything for you?"

"Perhaps you can tell me."

"Tell you what?"

"What it is that you want in exchange," Kitteredge said. "You wouldn't have asked to see me if you didn't think that there was something I could do for you."

Merolla bent over and gestured with his fingers for Kitteredge to do the same. Kitteredge found himself inches away from the old man's face. The old man's breath smelled of fresh garlic and stale cigars.

"This thing of ours, it's over," Merolla said. His rheumy eyes looked teary now. "The Chinese, the South Americans, even the niggers are running us out. I can't fart without the Justice Department telling me what I had for lunch, and every time I turn on the TV, I see another associate singing songs to congressmen.

"I have grandkids, great-grandkids. You understand?"

"I think so."

Merolla grabbed Kitteredge's hands.

"I'll put you with Bascaglia," he said. "I don't want anything from you, prick. But maybe my grandkids, my great-grandkids will need a favor sometime. . . ."

Merolla's hands felt like old musty paper.

Kitteredge slid his own hands away, swallowed hard, and said, "I'd be pleased to assist them in any way."

Merolla wiped his hand on his trousers.

"Favor for favor," he said. "Like the movie."

"Sorry?"

"That movie. With Brando," Merolla explained. *"The God-father."*

"Yes, of course," Kitteredge answered, making a mental note to ask Levine to watch this film and brief him. Kitteredge had gone to a movie theater once and hadn't liked it. He could scarcely hear the hopelessly banal dialogue over the incessant bovine sound of popcorn chomping, an overly involved viewer spoke back to the actors during the entire ordeal, and his shoes got stuck on spilled soda as he tried to leave. He recalled it as a thoroughly miserable fifteen minutes.

Merolla shakily rose to his feet, signaling that the meeting was over.

"You'll be hearing from Jimmy," Merolla said, pointing his

chin at the silver-haired man. "Get out of here before the families come in."

He turned and shuffled back to the kitchen counter.

Jimmy walked Kitteredge to the door.

"I'm afraid I'm unacquainted with prison etiquette," Kitteredge said at the doorway. "Do I tip the guard on the way out?"

Jimmy answered, "We got it covered, chief."

Kitteredge had the driver take him to the bank. He stopped in the rest room to scrub his hands, then went into the office. Ed Levine was poring over books at the conference table.

"How did it go?" asked Ed, concerned that Kitteredge looked so tired.

"He will make the introduction," Kitteredge said. He sat down behind his desk and began to stroke the thread lines on the model of his boat, the *Haridan*.

"What's it going to cost?" Ed asked.

"Have you seen a film called *The Godfather?*"

"Sure."

"So has Dominic Merolla," Kitteredge said. "He wants a return favor for his grandchildren or great-grandchildren. In exchange for a telephone call, the Merolla crime family has our marker for potentially the next century."

The news didn't surprise Ed, but it did add heat to the heartburn he'd been feeling for the last hour or so, ever since he'd figured out what had been bothering him about Marc Merolla's fraternity picture.

"I've been doing some research," Ed started. "Guess who was Peter Hathaway's college roommate."

Kitteredge had a headache. He didn't want to guess. "Who?"

"Marc Merolla."

Kitteredge gazed at the sleek lines of his boat. He longed to be skimming through the clean blue water of the open ocean.

After a while he smiled and said, "We've been had, Edward."

"We don't know that yet, sir," Ed answered. "It might be a coincidence. I have people working on it now."

Kitteredge nodded, but his instincts told him the truth: Dominic Merolla had just committed him to the Mafia takeover of the Landis television empire.

"It brings rather a new meaning to the Family Cable Network, doesn't it?" he asked.

"There's something else."

"Oh, good."

"Just an oddity, really," Ed added quickly. "He had another roommate at Brown."

"Martin Bormann?"

"Kenny Lafreniere."

Kitteredge stared at him blankly.

"Dr. Kenneth Lafreniere," Ed prompted. "Seven years ago, he sliced up his wife and took a header off the Newport Bridge. It was in all the papers."

Ethan Kitteredge realized that he had never managed to make Ed understand that the only newspaper articles he ever saw were the ones that Ed clipped out and made him read.

"Small world," Kitteredge said. "Providence."

Perhaps it's time to retire, he thought, attend board meetings, social functions and the like, and let Ed run Friends. The board would have to be persuaded to allow someone outside of the family in that post, but perhaps they could be persuaded that times had changed.

Kitteredge sighed. "Does it seem to you that the world becomes more vulgar every day?"

"I live in New York," Ed answered.

Kitteredge stood up.

"I'll be at home," he said. "Check out Marc's involvement; let me know the second our mob associates call."

"Yes, sir."

"And Ed, visit with a realtor, would you?" Kitteredge said from the doorway. "I might want you to relocate to Providence. I'm thinking of taking a long trip when this is over."

"Where to, sir?"

To the clean open ocean, Kitteredge thought, away from all . . . this.

"I was thinking of the nineteenth century," Kitteredge said as he walked out the door.

20

*T*he light came on over the confessional booth and Joey politely waved an old lady in front of him. She smiled and tottered over to confess her sins.

Joey smiled back. He didn't give a shit about the old lady, but he was trying to maneuver the situation so that he could get the priest in the other booth. Joey liked to confess to Mexican priests who didn't understand a single word he was saying. This Catholic thing was the best deal in the world if you worked it right.

The other booth opened up and Joey hustled over. He knelt down, the window slid open, and he fought the urge to order a double cheeseburger, fries, and a large diet soda. Instead, he mumbled, "Bless me, father, for I have sinned. It has been one day since my last confession."

He went on to relate the usual litany of fraud, larceny, extortion, blackmail, and fornication, got sentenced to three Hail Marys and a Sincere Act of Contrition, went out and did them, then met Harold at the back of the church.

"If I died right now, Harold," he boasted, "I'd go straight to heaven."

Joey was always trying to get Harold to go to confession but insisted that he do it in another jurisdiction, like Guatemala or someplace like that. He didn't fully trust Harold to confess his own sins and keep him out of it, and the nuns had never been really clear—despite Joey's constant questions—on what happened if someone dropped a dime on you instead of you doing it yourself.

"God send you a long life, boss," Harold said.

Joey wasn't entirely happy that his bodyguard seemed to be leaving this matter to God, but he had other things on his mind. "Have you located that one-armed midget yet?"

"Get this, Joey. Yesterday, it's like he drops off the face of the earth. This morning, he's sitting out on the River Walk eating breakfast like he doesn't have a care in the world."

"I'll give him a care," Joey said as he got into the car.

This worried Harold.

"Joey," he said, sliding into the driver's seat, "you remember Carmine said you were supposed to keep a low profile here. I don't think he'd like you trashing some guy on the River Walk on a Sunday morning."

"I'm just gonna talk to him."

This didn't do much to soothe Harold. He'd been present at one of Joey's conversations, when his boss smacked the listener in the face with a tire iron and then peed into the guy's shattered mouth. True, that conversation had been in the back of a warehouse, but Harold had also tried to restrain Joey the night he'd made the late Sammy Black take his clothes off, stroll through a shocked crowd of theatergoers on Times Square, and recite, "I will never hold back on Joey Foglio. I will never hold back on Joey Foglio." Both those evenings had started off by Joey saying that he just wanted to talk.

Harold thought he owed it to Joey to try again, because Carmine "The Banker" Bascaglia wasn't going to put up with this kind of shit. The reason Don Carmine was called "The Banker" instead of "The Butcher," even though the latter sounded better, was because he was all business. He had warned Joey in no uncertain terms that he was there to make money, not headlines.

So Harold said, "Joey, you know this is going to end in an ass kicking. I'm just saying, let me do it. I'll get the guy under a bridge, then give him a couple of shots. You can stand on the bridge and watch."

Joey thought this over. In normal times, he'd make the smart-mouth son of a bitch beg to die, but these weren't normal times. Despite going to confession, Joey had an anxiety. Some smart bastard had sandbagged Overtime last night—which meant they were on to Gloria—and the assassin was highly pissed off. It had taken an hour to settle him down, and even then it meant causing some trouble in New York. Too bad about Gloria, but she had it coming.

He needed something to make him feel better.

"How about it, huh, Joey?" Harold was saying.

"Okay," Joey said, "but you have to throw him in the river."

"Aw, Joey!"

"If you won't, I will," Joey warned.

"Come on, Joey."

"In the river."

Rip off his fake arm, throw him in the river, and don't give him back the arm until he repeats "Mr. Foglio, Mr. Foglio" a hundred times.

Harold saw that Joey's imagination was slipping into high gear, so he said, "Okay. I'll throw him in the river."

Satisfied, Joey Beans went back to worrying what the hell was going on in Nevada.

Joe Graham was wondering the same thing as he finished his breakfast at an outdoor table on the River Walk.

The whole Polly Paget operation had been undertaken in haste and executed in ignorance. Friends should never have taken Polly over until they had thoroughly scouted the opposition. And Eddie and Kitteredge blowing a safe house was beyond explanation. And it wasn't even our safe house—it was Neal's. The kid finally finds a home and we blow it up on him.

We're getting sloppy, Graham thought. We have some success and start to think we're better than we are.

He leaned back and let the morning sun hit his face. He glanced over to his right at a footbridge to see whether the goon was still there. He was. Graham wondered what the hell was keeping Joey Beans.

The room-service guy must have fingered me, Graham thought, because Joey's goon picked me up at the hotel and followed me down here. Maybe the waiter was getting back at me for taking silverware. And I've been sitting here like a signpost for an hour and a half. If Joey Beans wants me, he's taking his sweet time. Maybe he's too smart. I hope not.

Graham opened his newspaper to the sports section and was disappointed to find that there was very little interest in the New York Giants in San Antonio. This was to be expected, however, from a city where the food squirts at you.

Foglio's head goon, Harold, walked onto the bridge.

Don't go away, Graham thought. It's time to play. He set his newspaper down, signed the credit-card slip, got up, and walked south toward the bridge. He looked up, pretended to see them for the first time, then tentatively kept walking.

Let's see what you want me to do, Graham thought. If you want me to walk south, you'll let me pass the base of the bridge and fall in behind me. If you want me to head north, you'll block my path and let me turn around. If you want my ugly Irish butt now, you'll meet me at the base of the bridge.

Graham watched as Harold slipped down to the base of the bridge and let himself be seen in the middle of the sidewalk. So he "spotted" Harold, turned around, and started to walk north.

This means that Joey Beans is in front of me somewhere, thought Graham. If they just wanted to give me a beating, both of them would be coming. But they're taking this seriously, and Harold is herding me toward his boss, because mob guys never do anything alone, so it's going to be Harold and Joey. And it's going to be a beating, not a killing, because even Joey Beans isn't crazy enough to do a hit in downtown San Antonio on a Sunday morning. So this is good.

Joe Graham had assigned himself the task of cooling out Joey Beans.

He'd made a point of scouting the River Walk a few dozen times, so he was getting to know it pretty well. About three blocks north, the river made a big bend under the Convent Street Bridge. So the north side of Convent would be the place to do it. Graham figured he had nothing to worry about until Convent Street.

Graham looked back over his shoulder at Harold, then picked up his pace to let the bodyguard think he was doing the chasing. Harold matched his pace, which made Graham think he was right about Joey being up ahead somewhere, because Harold wasn't trying to shorten the gap, just stay even.

Graham tested the theory by stopping suddenly. Harold hit the brakes.

Graham started out again and wondered when Harold would start to close in. It would have to be pretty soon if the shit was going to hit the fan at Convent, because Harold shouldn't leave him too much room to maneuver after he'd spotted Joey.

Sure enough, Harold picked up his pace and lengthened his stride. Graham made a token effort to walk a little faster just to keep up the show.

It's refreshing to work against a professional, Graham thought. That made him remember Walter Withers in his heyday——the smoothest street man on the slickest streets. He pushed the memory from his mind because it was too painful and because he spotted Joey Beans, grinning and waving at him from the top of the Convent Street Bridge.

"Hello, Stumpy the Clown!" Joey yelled.

This is where Harold moves in and I make the frantic effort to escape, Graham thought as he felt Harold's hand on his shoulder. He tried to go under the arm, but predictably, Harold spun him and pushed him up against the arc of the bridge.

They picked a good spot, Joe thought. The bridge was a wide concrete job, and the curve of the river put the underside out of view.

"Do yourself a favor and hop in the water," Harold muttered. "I'm supposed to hit you a few shots, but I don't feel right about hitting a guy with one arm."

"Then hit me with both arms," answered Graham, who didn't know the word *syntax* but recognized a straight line when he heard one.

"What's your story?" Harold asked, then moaned as he saw Joey come down the staircase.

"Yeah, what's your story?" Joey asked.

"Get back on the bridge," said Harold.

"You giving the orders now?" Joey said. "Turn the monkey around where I can get a look at his ugly face."

"Speaking of ugly," Graham said as he was spun around, "you look like it's Roy Rogers night at a wise guy costume party, with your snakeskin boots, Stetson hat, and big fat gut hanging over your longhorn belt buckle. You guys should stick to the open shirt, gold chain, black ankle boot thing. It still looks stupid, but not this stupid."

"You're still in a funny mood," Joey said.

"Something about you brings the chuckles out in me. I don't know," Graham said. "Maybe it's the image of Don Annunzio making you eat all that garbage. That's funny stuff."

Graham didn't wait for the punch he knew was coming. Harold had him by the shoulders—too high—so it gave him plenty of room to swing his heavy artificial arm down in an arc, which had an effect similar to a croquet mallet whacking a ball.

Graham's fist whacked *both* Harold's balls, though, driving them up somewhere near his chin.

This inspired Harold to release him immediately and bend deeply at the waist. Foglio went right for Graham's throat but stopped suddenly when the serrated edge of the steak knife pressed against his scrotum.

"Did you ever want to sing in the Vienna Boys' Choir?" Graham asked as he pressed the knife and stepped forward, forcing Joey to take baby steps back toward the edge of the water. "Or wait on the nice ladies in a Turkish harem? Or change your name to Joey No Balls? If the answer to any of these questions is yes, or if you never want your compass to point north again, just get stupid now, Joey Beans."

"What do you want?" Joey croaked.

"You know about *famiglia,* right, Joey?"

"I know about family."

"Well, you've been fucking around in Nevada," Graham said, "And you almost hurt one of my *famiglia. Capisce?*"

"I don't know what—"

A little pressure of the blade stopped him.

"Don't bother," Graham hissed. "Just listen. There's been a misunderstanding of some kind. We're going to get it straightened out. That might take a few days. In the meantime, you call off your dogs. You got that?"

"You don't know what you're messing with."

"Right now, I'm messing with you, Joey," Graham said. He saw Harold start to straighten up and noticed that Joey saw it, too. "You want me to mess you up permanently, Joey, you have Harold make a move."

Joey looked at Harold and shook his head.

Graham continued: "You're right, though. I don't know what I'm messing with, but I'm going to get it all straightened out. And nothing better happen to any of my family."

Graham pressed the knife just enough to close the deal.

"Okay," Foglio said. "You through now?"

Graham heard a tourist barge heading toward them from upstream.

"Not quite," he said. "There's still that 'Stumpy' business."

He brought his rubber forearm up and smacked Foglio in the chest. Foglio waved his arms to try to keep balance, then crashed into the muddy water. It was shallow, only chest-high, and Foglio was on his feet quickly, but the tourists on the barge were amused.

Graham saw Harold reach inside his jacket and said, "Yeah, dummy, shoot. Unless you don't think there are enough witnesses."

He pushed past Harold and trotted up to the Convent Street Bridge. He paused only long enough to enjoy the sight of Harold fishing the soaked, muddy Joey Beans out of the river and the sound of laughter. Then he picked up his bag at the hotel and caught a taxi to the airport.

21

Ed Levine took a cab up College Hill. He could have walked, but he wanted to get this over with as soon as possible.

Marc must have been waiting at the door, because he opened it before Ed could ring the bell. He took one look at Ed's serious face and said, "You know, don't you?"

"Yeah," Ed answered. "But I don't know why."

"Come on in."

Marc led him into the den this time and sat next to him on the sofa. He turned the volume off on a late game from the West Coast but left the television on.

"Theresa and the boys are at her mother's," he said.

"Sorry I missed them."

"Being Peter Hathaway's partner isn't a crime, Ed."

"Then why keep it a secret?" Ed asked.

Marc's smile was bitter.

"Because I'm Dominic Merolla's grandson and Salvatore Merolla's son."

"What does that mean?" Ed asked, annoyed. He had come for answers from a friend.

"It means, among other things, that the FCC would never grant me a license," Marc said. "It means that I have to be a silent partner. It means I need a front man like Peter if I want to pursue certain opportunities."

"You're a successful businessman, Marc!" Ed yelled. "A lot more successful than I realized. You own almost half of the Family Cable Network."

"Peter has quite a piece," Marc said quietly.

"Is it mob money?" Ed asked. "Do you do your grandfather's laundry?"

Marc shrugged.

"You're asking two questions," he said. "I have a trust fund, various monies from my grandfather and father, which I've invested. Most of the money I put in the network comes from good investments I've made. So, is Dominic's money in FCN? To the extent that he gave it to me, yes. Do I launder his business profits? Of course not, and I'm offended by the question."

"Are you telling me Dominic's not involved?" Ed asked.

"See, that's what I mean," Marc said. "I have to answer that question. Every Italian businessman in this country has to live with the assumption, at least the suspicion, that his success is due to his underworld contacts—myself more than most.

"You say I'm richer than you thought. I'm richer than you know. We live modestly. If I built a big mansion, everybody would say, there's Don Merolla's grandson, living on mob money. If I owned racehorses, boats, fancy cars, same thing. If I tried to buy a television network, I'd have the FCC, FBI, IRS, the whole alphabet on my neck. Not that they don't come around, anyway. I can't have a birthday party for one of my boys without the DEA trying to bug the ice cream cake.

"I'll tell you this one time, Ed, because we're friends: I'm not involved with the wise guys. I'm a businessman. I'm clean."

Ed looked at the anger in Marc's eyes and knew they weren't going to be friends anymore.

"You took his money," Ed said.

"He's my grandfather."

Their eyes were drawn by a burst of activity on the television screen. A home-team player caught a bomb and tossed the ball to the crowd.

"He did us a favor," Ed said.

"You do business with him; I don't."

"Why did he give you our marker?"

"This is the first I've heard of it. Ask him."

"Marc . . ."

"He's my grandfather," Marc said. "He wants to look out for me."

"And that's it."

Marc stood up.

"I'm through being interrogated by you," he said. "You want to blow us up with the FCC, do it. And keep your damn marker; I don't need you."

Ed stayed seated. The television replayed the touchdown while an invisible hand drew squiggly white lines all over the screen.

"That's the funny thing," he said. "I think you do."

"What do you mean?"

"You've heard of Carmine Bascaglia?"

"I read the papers."

"One of his captains has a hook into Jack Landis. He's bleeding you dry."

On the screen, two buxom women mocked orgasm over a light beer.

Marc said, "I'm calling the cops."

"Don't."

"Why not?"

A truck bounced up a muddy road to the summit of a mountain. A man and a woman got out and embraced as they shared the stunning panorama below.

Ed answered, "People will get hurt and you'll lose your money."

There was a long silence. The afternoon sun was falling and the den was getting dark. Marc turned on a lamp, sat down, and raised the volume on the football game.

San Diego was down by three points to Pittsburgh.

They watched the game for a few minutes, then Marc said, "You're going to make a deal, aren't you?"

"We're going to try."

"And it'll leave Bascaglia's people with a piece of the business," Marc said. "Otherwise, you couldn't make the deal."

"That's right."

"That stinks."

"I agree."

Ed watched the game for a few minutes, then he got up and left. Marc didn't see him to the door.

"What do you want to drink, sweetie?" Gloria asked.

"I don't drink," her guest said.

She leaned forward to give him a preview of coming attractions and asked, "Do you have any vices, I hope?"

And what is it with hands this weekend? First she brings home a guy with one hand; now she picks up a stray with a bandaged paw.

"Well," the guy answered, 'just last night I got fucked at the Bluebird Motel."

He had the pistol on her before she could scream.

"Now go ahead and have your drink," he said.

Will they ever come out of there? Walter Withers wondered as he lay on the floor next to the door of his hotel room. He had been listening for over twenty-four hours, which far exceeded the timetable in his plan.

It was such a good plan, too. The indomitable Ms. Haber had bribed the ever-tumescent young Bobby—who now had dates with several months' worth of young ladies with strong exhibitionist tendencies—to arrange a room directly across the hall from that young snake Neal and the valuable Polly Paget.

Then Withers had been spirited up the room in the bottom of a delivery cart—an uncomfortable journey; however, not without a certain whimsical quality—where the plan had called for him to listen vigilantly for the opening of doors and watch the hallway through the peephole until opportunity arose—opportunity for access to Ms. Paget.

A fine plan, Withers thought as he lay on the floor by the door, save for the target's unreasonable stubbornness in holding to their fortress and the treacherous presence of a cabinet stuffed to bursting with spirits.

The courtesy bar was calling to Withers.

It's the damn boredom, he thought, the bane of surveillance. The brain-killing, spirit-stifling, buttocks-numbing tedium of interminable waiting. A condition that could be ameliorated by the contents of the courtesy bar. Yes, its contents could soften the suffering, take the edge off boredom's sharp blade, surround one in the comfort of an old friend's embrace.

Think of the money, he told himself. You are no longer a young sprite, and it is high time to think of building a retirement fund, a fund that could be well started on the photographic reproduction of Ms. Paget's nubile body, which lies just across the hall as the object of your vigilance.

Spurn the sweet, soft song of the liquor cabinet for the cold, hard logic of cash.

Still, there must be a better way.

If only Gloria would return his calls, perhaps she could persuade Polly to come across the hall.

If I can just make the pitch, he thought.

He dialed Gloria's number again. Again, the damnably cheerful message warbled through the phone.

"Gloria, it's me again, Walter," he said. "I really do wish you would return my call. I have located Polly—small thanks to you, I might add—and am, in fact, just across the hallway from her. Please call. I am in room twelve-forty, The Last Days of Pompeii Resort and Casino Hotel, oh two-five five five-four six six three.''

I have such a headache, Withers thought. Perhaps one little drink.

He found the key and opened the courtesy bar.

Gloria never heard the phone.

She was lying in a tubful of hot water and her own blood.

She had told him everything, of course, while he was forcing her to gulp the scotch down. She told him about the one-armed man and the phone call long before he told her to swallow the pills.

Overtime heard Withers's message, though. He had just finished wiping the knife handle and pressing her fingerprints onto the handle.

Poor drunken slut, he thought. Prey to the sad but banal combination of booze, drugs, and guilt.

He erased the message tape and left for the airport.

22

*A*t about the time Gloria died, a black limousine pulled up to an iron-gated courtyard off St. Claude Street in New Orleans's French Quarter. The driver's window rolled down; the uniformed guard checked out the driver and the three passengers and waved the limousine in.

The driver parked at the top of an oval driveway next to a three-story Spanish neoclassical building, replete with terra-cotta-tiled roof, wrought-iron balconies, and creeping ivy. Two bodyguards walked Joe Graham up the stone steps and into the building.

The floors were highly polished octagonal black-and-white tiles. The walls were painted chalk white and held large gilt-framed oil paintings of New Orleans street scenes. A marble staircase, flanked by a wrought-iron railing, curved up to the right, and the bodyguards led Graham up these stairs. Video cameras were recessed on swivels in the plaster ceiling.

A guard sat at an antique table at the top of the stairs, the bulge of a pistol prominent under his jacket. He nodded to the two guards, pressed the button on the intercom, and said that Mr. Bascaglia's two o'clock appointment had arrived. A feminine voice replied that he should be sent right in.

They walked past the table, down the hall to a large mahogany door. The first bodyguard knocked. There was an electric buzz, the lock sprang open, and they were in a narrow waiting room decorated in a blue Napoleonic theme.

An attractive older woman in a blue business suit sat at another antique table. She smiled at them, knocked on a door behind her, stuck her head in, and announced them.

"You can go right in," she said.

Carmine Bascaglia sat behind a large table. Behind him, a floor-to-ceiling window of thick bulletproof glass allowed a splendid view of old New Orleans, from the private courtyard garden directly below to the shabbily genteel old buildings of the French Quarter down the street.

Bascaglia's desk was spare except for two stacks of paper— one on the left, one on the right—a gold fountain pen, a pitcher of water, and a single glass.

One wooden chair, smaller and plainer than the Queen Anne Bascaglia sat on, had been set directly in front of the desk. The walls of the office were covered with thick gold-and-blue wallpaper. Portraits of Spanish ladies, also gilt-framed, hung on the walls.

Bascaglia looked tall even sitting down. He wore an elegantly tailored slate gray suit with subtle white striping, an off-white Italian shirt with cuff links, and a blood red tie. His gray hair, starting to thin, was brushed straight back and he wore gold-rimmed glasses on his Roman nose.

The bodyguards led Graham to the chair in front of the desk and then took their places in the corners.

"I have fifteen minutes for you, Mr. Graham," he said without introduction. "I will begin. One: You think you are a funny son of a bitch, but you are not a funny son of a bitch."

He paused to let Graham agree.

Graham nodded.

"Two: When we want comedians, we hire them and they perform in nightclubs. They tell humorous jokes and we laugh. They do not tell allegorical anecdotes in restaurants or shove people into rivers."

He paused again and stared at Graham.

Graham nodded.

"Three: I have no sense of humor. I don't have the time for one. Neither do you. Are we in agreement?"

"Yes, we are, Mr. Bascaglia," Graham said.

"Good," Bascaglia said. "The only reason I gave you an appointment is that Dominic Merolla requested it. I required that you represent your organization because I wanted to tell you personally that the antics in San Antonio are to stop forthwith."

"There won't be any more, Mr. Bascaglia."

"Now, what seems to be the problem, Mr. Graham?"

Graham felt butterflies in his stomach the way he used to when he was sent to the Mother Superior's office as a kid, except worse. The nun might hit you with a ruler; Carmine Bascaglia might make you a concrete lawn ornament at the bottom of the Mississippi.

Graham said, "One of your subordinates in Texas, a Mr. Foglio, is engaged in business practices that are proving harmful to interests we represent."

"Mr. Foglio's business is to make money," Bascaglia answered. "I assume you're referring to that amusement park?"

"Candyland, yeah."

"Joe Foglio is a contractor on the project," Bascaglia said. "It's all aboveboard."

Graham coughed and said, "As a matter of fact, sir, there's quite a bit that's uh, below-board."

"Let's not play games," Bascaglia said. "In recent years, we have made a successful effort to move our monies into legitimate businesses such as construction, trucking, entertainment, and various investments. If Joe Foglio traded on certain names to acquire business . . ."

Bascaglia held his palms up.

"Our client is happy for Mr. Foglio's various companies to

have the work," Graham continued. "They'd be happier, though, if he'd stop robbing them blind."

"I don't make it my habit to pry into the details of my associates' businesses, and Mr. Foglio's profit margins are a detail best left to him."

Graham started to rub his artificial fist into his real palm. He thought for a minute and then said, "Years ago, I worked for a guy who owned a chain of movie theaters. He hired me to see how much the staff was stealing. And he told me, 'Joe, if they're just stealing supper, let 'em. I don't want to know.' It turned out that they were stealing dinner money. They were happy; he was happy. But Joey Foglio is stealing supper, lunch, breakfast, midday snacks, the table, the chairs, the cabinets, and the kitchen linoleum.

"Sir, when the old men threw Joey out of New York, you took him on because you thought he could make money, I know that. But now he's got his hands around the throat of the golden goose. If that's not enough for you, he's also ordered a hit on a young woman who isn't involved in your business, and he's aligned himself—and you, I guess—against the direct interests of the Merolla family."

Graham saw a scary, cold look come across Bascaglia's eyes. "What's the Merolla family got to do with this?" he asked.

"The grandkid is Jack Landis's partner."

"The grandson isn't in the family business," Bascaglia said. "His grandfather loves him, anyway."

Bascaglia took his sweet time thinking this over while Graham pictured chunks of himself floating into the Gulf of Mexico.

"I've always believed," Bascaglia finally said, "that violence is the first recourse of the foolish man and the last resort of the wise man."

Graham was relieved to hear that.

"I don't want a war with the Merolla family," Bascaglia concluded.

"No one's talking war here, sir."

Bascaglia seemed to be thinking out loud when he said, "But I can't take Joe Foglio's business away from him."

Graham was thinking that a man rumored to have arranged the assassination of a United States President could probably blow off a bum like Joey Beans, but he didn't voice the opinion.

"We believe that there's a lot of room for negotiation here," Graham said. "Funny, but it all kind of hinges on this woman who says Landis raped her."

"Paula somebody."

"Polly Paget, yeah."

"How is she central to this dispute?"

"She's got FCN by the short hairs, and if she takes the company down, everybody loses," Graham explained. "See, Joey's trying to whack her; we're trying to protect her; Merolla and Hathaway are trying to use her. . . ."

"Can you deliver her?" Bascaglia asked.

I hope so, Joe thought.

"We have influence," he said. "With the right deal—"

"Yes or no, Mr. Graham."

This in a voice telling me that I deliver her to a deal or you deliver her to a morgue, and somehow I don't see Neal standing by waving olé to a hit on this woman.

"Yes," Graham said. "But—"

"No *buts.*"

"But I need an absolute guarantee of a truce while we negotiate," Graham insisted. "You have to put Joey Beans on a short leash . . . sir."

"I think you made that point to him already," Bascaglia said. "You'll be our guest in New Orleans during the negotiations. My secretary will make hotel reservations for you and you'll have an office in this building during the day. I'll have her contact your Mr. Kitteredge to get started."

"Mr. Bascaglia, with all due respect, I think we better get started right now," Graham said. "This is one of those things that gets hotter the longer it goes."

"Oh?"

"Mr. Kitteredge is standing by on his phone," Graham said.

Bascaglia actually smiled.

"You're an extraordinary man, Mr. Graham," he said.

"You're the extraordinary man. I'm a working stiff."

"If you ever want to work for me, I'll have a job for you," Bascaglia said. He took a piece of paper from the left pile, glanced at it, initialed it, and set it on the right pile. Then he picked up the phone.

Nothing, Graham thought, better go wrong with this deal.

23

"N̲o," Polly said.

"What do you mean, no?" Neal asked.

"You know——no. N-O," Polly insisted. She sat on the bed in Neal's room, looking defensive and hostile. Neal sat on the bed beside her, Candy watched from a chair, and Karen stood beside the television set, on which Jack and Candy were hawking time-shares at Candyland. "No means no."

"Isn't that where this whole thing started?" Karen asked.

"Right?" Polly asked.

Candy nodded vigorously.

"If the NOW meeting is over . . ." Neal said.

"What's NOW?" asked Polly.

"The National Organization of Women," Karen explained.

Polly said, "That's a good idea."

"You ain't kidding."

The exchange stopped at the sound of Neal's head rhythmically smacking into his hands.

"Polly," Neal said. "Two million dollars. Two . . . million . . . dollars."

All in all, Neal thought, it's a good settlement, hammered out over a long night. Polly would get the $2 million in exchange for dropping the suit. Neither she nor Jack would discuss the affair, the paternity, or the alleged rape with the press.

On the business level, Jack would sell enough shares at fair market price to give Peter Hathaway majority ownership, but Jack and Candy would own their show and sell it to FCN at top dollar.

As for Candyland, Hathaway would agree to let the project continue. Foglio would retain his contracts but perform real work at reasonable costs. He would also acquire certain maintenance contracts on the same terms. Kitteredge and Bascaglia would appoint a mutually agreeable comptroller to monitor costs.

It was a good settlement and Neal could see Kitteredge's careful fingerprints all over it.

"All you talk about is money," Polly said.

"You launched a civil suit," Neal reminded her.

"Because he should pay for what he did," Polly argued.

"Two million freaking dollars!" Neal said. "And he loses control of his company! That's paying!"

Polly chewed on her bottom lip and thought.

Please take it, Neal thought. So I can go back to my life. So Carmine Bascaglia doesn't kill us all.

His eyes caught Candy's.

He wondered what she could be thinking, having okayed a deal that would send her back to her scummy husband for two years. She was apparently willing to trade two years of misery to save her life's work. Such are life's bargains.

He didn't have to wonder what Karen was thinking. She reminded him at every private moment. She was pissed off. She thought the whole thing stank. She was a cowgirl who thought they should just shoot it out, in the courtroom or wherever, and take their chances. He loved her madly, but she just didn't realize that they didn't have a chance against Bascaglia.

Polly seemed to be wavering.

"I'll try to get two-five," Neal said, hoping to push her over the edge.

Karen grunted in disgust.

"I'll take it," Polly said.

Thank you, God.

"If he says he raped me."

Thanks, God. Thanks a lot.

Karen applauded.

"Good for you," she said.

"Polly," Neal started again, "if he admits he raped you, 'The Jack and Candy Family Hour' will fall off the charts. The network will lose millions of dollars and Candyland will never be built. There won't be enough money to finance the deal. Jack might as well take his chances in front of a jury."

And we can take our chances in front of a firing squad.

"That's fine with me," Polly said. "That's what I wanted in the first place. That's what you were supposed to be helping me with, wasn't it?"

"We didn't know the mob was involved," Neal said.

"So the mob is involved, that makes it okay to rape me?"

"And keep raping her?" Karen asked.

That's a damn good point, Neal thought.

"This is not the time for tired feminist cant," he said. "The point is—"

"Oh, goodie," Karen said. "Neal's going to tell us what the point is."

"The point is that we can talk right and wrong, fair and unfair until the sun goes down, but at the end of the day we have to look at what is possible," Neal said. "This is about the best deal we're going to get."

"What do you think?" Polly asked Candy.

Swell, Neal thought. First she's boffing her husband, now she thinks the woman is her big sister.

"I'm not the one who was raped," Candy said.

"I don't know about that," said Karen.

"Will you stop?" Neal asked her.

Karen shrugged.

"I don't know," said Candy. She watched herself whip up a low-fat noncholesterol 'His First Night Home from the Hospital Dinner' while Jack made funny faces to the camera. "I'm kind of tired of cooking for the son of a bitch."

"Will you talk to them?" Neal asked Karen. "Tell them it's a great deal."

Karen talked to them.

"This deal sucks," Neal said into the telephone a few minutes later.

"It doesn't suck," Ed answered tightly as he watched Kitteredge look quizzical and Hathaway turn pale. "It's a terrific deal."

"It sucks!" Neal repeated. "Two million lousy dollars! He forks over some chump change and walks away from raping her? It's a terrific deal all right—for Jack! How am I supposed to sell this to her?"

Please tell me, Ed. Nothing I've tried so far has worked.

"I'm putting you on speaker phone, Neal," Ed answered. That would help settle Neal down, if he knew he was talking directly to Kitteredge. "Could you summarize her objections to this proposal for Mr. Kitteredge and Mr. Hathaway?"

"Yeah, it sucks!" Neal bellowed. He repeated the rationale.

"Neal, Ethan Kitteredge here!" Kitteredge shouted. Kitteredge thought the speaker phone was yet another symptom of societal decline. "How are you?"

Oh, I'm trapped in a hotel room in the wise guy capital of the world with three women who want to take on both the Merolla and Bascaglia crime families, the entire Family Cable Network, and you. One of the women is pregnant, another is discovering herself, and the third one is just nuts.

"Fine, sir. And yourself?"

"I'm a bit puzzled. Perhaps you can enlighten me," Kitteredge said, "as to why Ms. Paget feels this arrangement—how did she phrase it . . . ?"

"Sucks, sir."

"Yes . . . sucks."

"It eats shit!" Polly yelled.

"Was that Ms. Paget?" Kitteredge asked.

"Yes it was."

"Your tutorials aren't going especially well, are they?" Kitteredge asked.

Neal filled him in on Polly's demand that Jack confess to raping her.

Kitteredge listened and said, "I'm afraid that's just not possible, Neal. Perhaps she would consider another million as an alternative."

You're afraid? You're not sitting next to the human bull's-eye here. And you've been lowballing us?!

"Three million, no confession," he said to Polly.

"Eat shit," Polly answered.

"She declined the offer, sir."

"I heard her, Neal."

"Because she pronounced her *t*'s," Neal said. Let's not be defaming my tutorials. "A week ago, she would have said, 'Eeh shih.' "

"Ask this jerk who he thinks he is," Hathaway demanded.

"He can hear you," Ed said.

"Who do you think you are?" Hathaway asked.

"There is some confusion on that score," Neal admitted.

"I mean, are you her agent now?" Hathaway asked. Now that Polly had served her purpose, he wanted this matter settled quietly. The scandal that was such an asset was becoming a liability. "Are you getting a piece of her settlement?"

"No, Mr. Hathaway," Neal answered. "The only person who is gaining financially from Ms. Paget's rape is you. And by the way——"

Ed flicked off the speaker.

"——eat shit," Neal concluded. "Hi, Ed."

"Hi, Neal," Ed said pleasantly. "Neal, a number of highly placed people have worked very hard to put this package together. Just in case you've forgotten, we don't represent Polly Paget; we represent Mr. Hathaway. Mr. Hathaway is satisfied with this arrangement. If Ms. Paget persists in being stubborn, we will just have to walk away from her. She can hire her own lawyer, her own speech coach, and her own security. You can go back to doing whatever the hell it is that you do. Got it?"

"Got it," Neal said.

Of course Kitteredge would have a backup plan.

"Three million," Ed said, "no confession. Final offer."

Neal cradled the receiver in his neck, turned to Polly, and said, "Take it or leave it. If you don't take it, you're on your own. We leave."

Karen's head snapped up and her face flushed in anger.

"Neal," she said, "we can't—"

"So leave," Polly said.

Neal told Ed it was no deal.

"Pack your things and get out," Ed answered. "While the truce is still on."

Neal set the phone down.

Karen glared at him and said, "I'm not leaving. And—"

"I'm trying to think," Neal said, cutting her off.

And you, of all people, should know how hard that is for me. What the hell are we going to do?

"They want me to do what?!" Jack yelled. His voice bounced off the Alamo's old stone walls.

Joey Foglio calmly repeated what they wanted him to do.

He thought the Alamo would be a good place to have this meeting. The plaza was usually empty on a Monday morning. The only people here were some Mexican workers who were cleaning the place, and if any of them spoke enough English to understand anything, they probably wouldn't give a shit, anyway. Still and all, there was no use taking chances with Jack turning red and screaming.

"Why don't I just go out there," Jack yelled, "stick a knife in my guts, and disembowel myself! Would they like that, too?"

Joey thought the Japanese tourists would probably get a charge out of it, as a matter of fact.

Jack continued: "No, no, no . . . I've got a better one. Why don't I just smile at the camera, take a meat cleaver, and whack my johnson off! Then Candy could mix it up with a little sautéed onion, some red peppers maybe, a little hot sauce, and serve it to me on the show! There's an idea!"

Harold belched.

"Excuse me," he said.

Jack stalked over toward the chapel.

Joey followed him and said, "Your girlfriend won't take the deal. We gotta do something."

Actually, Joey was pleased that Polly was shooting down this deal. It would give him more room to maneuver. Jack didn't seem to be listening, just staring up at the old Alamo.

"You know who stood there?" Jack asked, his eyes glistening.

"Okay, who?" Joey sighed. He was already late getting to confession. If he got hit by a bus or something . . .

"John Wayne," Jack said. "John Wayne stood there. And fought to the death."

"John Wayne died here?" Harold asked.

"For freedom," Jack said reverentially. "John Wayne stood here and fought to the death for my freedom."

Joey had serious doubts that the Duke laid down his life so Jack Landis could nail some skank, but Jack was a local, so he must know the history.

"That's nice he did that," Joey said. "What's it got to do with—"

"And you want me," Jack said, his voice quivering with emotion, "to go before the people of this great country and . . . surrender? You want me, in the shadow of the Alamo, to spit on the memory of John Wayne?"

He's lost it, Joey thought. He's got one foot planted firmly in the enchanted forest.

"You can't ask him to do that, boss," Harold said. He looked as if he was going to cry. "You just can't. I mean . . . John Wayne."

They're both nuts, Joey thought. I'm the only sane guy here.

"I knew John Wayne," he said, wrapping a big arm around Jack's shoulder, "back on . . . Iwo Jima. We was in a foxhole together, surrounded by the enemy. I'm telling you, Jack, Mexicans everywhere. And the Duke said to me, 'Big Joe, sometimes a man just has to stand up and be a man and do the right thing. Like a man.' Do you understand, Jack? Do you hear what I'm trying to say to you?"

Jack ducked out from under Foglio's arm and said, "You want me to eat a shit sandwich and smile."

"That's it," Joey said, relieved he could now get to church. He was very careful crossing the street.

Kneeling in the pew, Charles Whiting felt as if he was in another country. Most of the worshipers were Hispanic women with their heads covered in black veils, and the painted statues of saints in various stages of martyred agony, their sad eyes shedding tears and blood dripping from their hands, gave the church a foreign atmosphere.

Whiting thought that he would probably be consigned to an eternity in hell just for being in this church, never mind for the horrible sin he hoped to commit soon.

And the entire idea of confession made him uncomfortable, not only for the obvious blasphemy but also because—were he indeed a Catholic—he had so much he would have to confess.

His feelings for Mrs. Landis weighed heavily on his soul. He thought about the betrayal of his wife and nine children and then about the wisdom of the old Mormon elders, who knew that monogamy was not natural for men.

He thought about his admiration for Candy Landis, her commitment to family values, the way she spoke of morality and ethics, the way her golden hair touched the soft skin on her neck, how it would look falling back on a satin pillow as she opened her arms, and he wished that Foglio would hurry up and get into the damn church. He wanted to get this over with.

An old woman came out of the confessional booth he was watching. He crossed himself in imitation of the veiled ladies, slid down the pew, parted the curtain of the confessional, and knelt.

"Bless me, father, for I have sinned," he recited, knowing that his Mormon ancestors were spinning in their graves. Reaching into his pocket, he found the tiny microphone with the little suction cup.

"It has been . . . uh . . . ten years . . . since my last confession," Chuck said, promising himself that he would never, ever do another undercover job as long as he lived. Why didn't the priest say something? "Uh . . . it's been so long because . . . I've been in a coma."

The priest mumbled something incomprehensible.

Chuck attached the suction cup to the underside of a piece of molding, then pressed it to make sure it stuck.

He thought he heard the priest say something about sin.

"I . . . I'm in love . . . with a woman who's not my wife," Chuck confessed, because he felt he had to say something.

Then it all came tumbling out, how he had come to work for the woman and her husband, how the husband cheated on her, how he had come to see a softer side of her, how . . .

The priest kept trying to interrupt with some mumbo jumbo, but Charles kept spewing guilt about how he had constant carnal images of the woman that he couldn't suppress and how he wished that her husband would die and his own wife would run off with a Gentile and then he could persuade the woman to convert and stuff, until he ran out of breath and the priest said something that sounded like "Hentile?"

Charles felt better as he went to the old truck parked around the corner.

"Does it work?" he asked Culver.

Culver took off his headset and asked, "You've got a boner for Candy Landis?"

Evidently it works, Chuck thought.

Joey Foglio went back to the car with a shiny new soul and a fresh resolve to take more advantage of Jack Landis's crumbling empire. He had ridden Jack about as far as he could. It was time to change horses.

"Did you arrange a clean phone?" he asked Harold.

"Joey, don't you think—" Harold started.

"No, I don't think," Joey said without a trace of irony. "Carmine's been acting like a banker so long, he thinks he is one. That's the crucial difference between him and me. I know who I am. I'm a criminal. I commit crimes."

The crucial difference, Harold thought, is that Carmine has several hundred soldiers to do his bidding and you have several.

"Carmine isn't going to like you messing around in the middle of a deal," Harold said.

"He's the one who's messing," Joey said.

"You'll still make money."

"I don't want to *make* money," Joey answered. "If I wanted to *make* money, I'd sell insurance. I want to *take* money. That's who I am. It's the me of me."

Harold took him to a phone booth on Flores Street and handed him the phone number in Rhode Island.

"What is this phone?" Joey asked.

"Another phone booth."

"Clean?"

"Guy promises it is," Harold assured him, aware of Joey's paranoia about wiretaps.

The guy answered on the third ring.

"Hello?" Joey said.

"Hello," Hathaway answered. "Why am I talking to you?"

"Because you like to make money," Joey answered. "Because you're tired of working like a donkey and giving the money to Marc Merolla."

He outlined his proposal to Hathaway.

Hathaway was definitely interested when he heard the profit margins. Joey let him drool over the potential riches for a minute before he said, "There's a problem, though."

"What's that?"

"That broad that says she was raped?" Joey said. "I was paying her to shag Jack."

There was a long silence, so long that Joey was afraid he had blown the deal.

"Jesus," Hathaway said. "You, too?"

24

*A*re you really afraid of these people?" Karen demanded as Neal packed.

"Do you mean *really* in the sense of *actually*, or *really* in the sense of *very?*" Neal asked.

Karen looked annoyed.

"First one, then the other," she said.

"Okay. I am actually very afraid of these people," he answered. "Really."

She sat down on the bed.

"I thought they only killed their own," she said.

"Did you tell that to the guy in the ski mask?" he asked.

"No," she answered. "I hit him with a bat."

He turned from his packing.

"You're saying we should—"

Polly came into the room.

"You guys should see this," she said.

"What?" Neal asked.

"Jack!"

They followed her back into her room, where Candy sat transfixed, watching Jack standing all by himself, center stage on their set.

"What's up?" Neal asked.

Candy shook her head.

* * *

Jack Landis stood stock-still, looked at the hushed audience, then said, "You're probably wondering where Candy is."

The audience assented.

"So am I," Jack said.

There was some nervous laughter in the crowd.

"Earlier today," Jack continued, "I stood in the shadow of the Alamo and thought about those brave men who stood up for what they believed—and died for it.

"Well, I'd rather die than tell you what I have to tell you, but that would be the coward's way out, and I guess I wouldn't want to go out a coward. The ghosts of Travis, Bowie, and Crockett would haunt me."

"What's he doing?" Karen asked.

"They're playing the card," Neal said.

"What?"

"Watch."

Jack looked directly into the camera. "What I have to stand up and say is that I did have an affair with Polly Paget."

The audience gasped.

"Holy shit," Karen said.

"Miss Paget seduced me in my office in New York . . ."

"Lying sack of crud," Polly said.

". . . and I regret to say that I fell to temptation. The affair was short-lived, but it happened, and I am deeply, deeply sorry."

"He's good," Neal said.

"He sold used cars in Beaumont," Candy said.

The camera zoomed in for a tighter close-up as Jack's eyes brimmed with tears. His voice broke as he blurted, "I have betrayed you. I have betrayed you. I have betrayed my family . . . my audience . . . and my God. . . ."

He broke down, dropped his head into his hands, and sobbed. His shoulders heaved up and down as members of the audience wept and cried, "No!" A woman in the front row fainted and had to be carried out.

The camera eased back to a head-and-shoulders shot as Jack struggled to compose himself, then continued. "I have decided to take a leave of absence from my duties at FCN."

More shouts of "No!"

Jack continued, "I want to use that time to seek spiritual counseling and take a long hard look to find out just who is this man named Jackson Hood Landis."

He bowed his head.

When he lifted it, he tightened his jaw, aimed his focus an inch higher, and said, "One thing I know about Jack Landis, though. . . .

" 'He's not a rapist,' " Neal murmured.

"He's not a rapist," Jack said. "That charge is utterly, completely, and absolutely false. I'm sorry to say that Miss Paget is a far sicker individual than I ever thought, and when I told her that I was going to end our relationship, she made up this horrible story for revenge. She told me that's what she was going to do, and that's what she did."

"In your dreams," Polly growled.

The camera tightened in on Jack's tear-streaked face.

"One word more," he said, "to my beloved wife, Candice."

The tears poured down his face and little snot bubbles came out of his nose as he stared into the camera and choked out, "Candy darling, I know I've hurt you . . . but I love you . . . and if . . . you could ever find it in your heart . . . to forgive me . . ."

He broke into sobs, shook his head, and walked off the stage.

A stentorian voice announced, "And now, on FCN, 'Flipper'!"

* * *

Jack Landis came off the stage.

A weeping apprentice handed him a towel and said, "That was beautiful, Mr. Landis. Deeply moving."

"Fuck you," Jack said.

He wiped the sweat off his face and walked out of the studio.

"Wow," Karen said over strains of "*They call him Flipper, Flipper, faster than lightning.*"

"We're hosed," Neal said. Jack's virtuoso performance had just taken Polly's cards out of her hands.

"Why did he do that?" Polly asked.

"They'll get instant polls," Neal said, "and see how it went over. If the public bought it, they can rebuild FCN without dealing with you."

You, who basically told Carmine Bascaglia to stick it up his ass.

"So?"

Neal didn't want to tell her the whole truth. It wouldn't do her any good. He knew that it might not happen right away, but it would happen. Sometime after Polly faded from the headlines, sometime after she tried to rebuild a life, someone would come and snuff it out.

"*And you know Flipper, Flipper lives in a world full of wonder . . .*"

He picked up the ringing phone.

"He was great, wasn't he?" Ed gloated.

"He was terrific," Neal admitted.

Ed said, "Listen, the client decided to enter an agreement with Mr. Landis, and he doesn't think he can go forward with Ms. Paget in good faith."

"Good faith, Ed?" Neal scoffed. "Are you reading from a card or something?"

"If Ms. Paget decides to pursue her litigation, of course that is her right," Ed continued. "But it would be a conflict of interest for our attorneys to represent her."

Now it's a conflict of interest?

"So Friends' role is finished," Ed said. "Mr. Kitteredge asked me to thank you for your good work, apologize for any inconveniences, and instruct you to stand down."

"That's an oxymoron," Neal observed. "Stand down."

"You're not hearing me, Neal. The job is over. Go home."

"Let me make sure I have this straight," Neal said. "We pick Polly up because we think she's useful, then when she's served our purposes, we throw her to the sharks. Is that it?"

"She shouldn't have gotten greedy," Ed answered.

"Yeah, wanting the truth."

"Do you think we could protect her if we wanted to?" Ed asked. "When are you going to grow up?"

"I've grown up," Neal said. "I'm packing. We're out of here. The job's over, like you said."

He hung up and looked back at the three women who were staring at him.

"Hey." He shrugged. "You gotta do what you gotta do."

So we might as well do it right now.

By the evening news, Jack had become a figure of sympathy, and Polly got the wrong end of the media's magic wand as she slid from sexy victim on the run to love-crazed psycho female in a single afternoon.

The radio talk shows led it off. Calls started at about four to three for Jack and then jumped to two to one in his favor when the men got to their car phones at rush hour.

The afternoon papers rushed WHERE IS CANDY? sidebars onto the JACK CONFESSES headline stories, and the evening news commentators opened with, " 'I have betrayed you,' said restaurant and media magnate Jack Landis today as he admitted an affair with a vengeful Polly Paget. Landis firmly denied,

237

however, allegations of rape" before cutting to footage of Jack's tearful television address.

By nighttime, "Jack's Confession" parties had broken out on college campuses all over the country. Students who habitually set their VCRs for "The Jack and Candy Family Hour" invited friends, made popcorn, consumed massive quantities of beer, and howled uncontrollably as they reran the "I have betrayed you" segment, until hysterical exhaustion forced an end to the festivities.

By the late news, polls came in that were strongly in Jack's favor on the alleged rape, feature reporters dug up men who had been "exactly in Jack Landis's shoes" at one time, and "woman in the street" interviews gave the strong impression that America's women thought Candy should give Jack another chance.

On one late-night talk show, the host delivered a deliberately lame joke in his monologue, paused, and blubbered, "I have betrayed you," to thunderous applause, while on another network, a serious news show offered psychologists' views on "recovering from adultery," two friends of Candy who thought that she and Jack—with time and prayer—would rebuild their marriage, and a gentleman from the Men's Liberation Front who warned about vengeful women and rape charges.

On a late-late talk show, two actresses dressed as Polly and Candy identified themselves in the studio audience, then slugged it out in the aisle, and each subsequent guest desperately tried to give his or her new movie or book a "Jack hook."

By the time this show aired on the West Coast, Polly was firmly entrenched as the other woman, the vengeful other woman, whose mendacity was proven by the very fact that she would not—as Jack had done—come out and tell the truth. She was, in the public opinion, afraid to show her face. "At least," said one woman caller on a late-night radio show, "she has some sense of shame."

By that time, Joey Foglio's "Jack's Confession" party was winding down in a hotel bedroom with three young ladies.

By that time, Candy had reached Jack at home, telling him she loved him and forgave him and that's she'd be coming home tomorrow to start working out their problems.

By that time, Walter Withers was unconscious and therefore missed the camera crew that came as quietly as it could to the room across the hall.

25

The television woke Withers up.

His eyes popped open when he heard, "exclusive interview with Polly Paget." He sat bolt upright on the floor and remembered within minutes exactly where he was.

A dozen or so miniature booze bottles lying empty on the floor provided the first clue. By the time he vomited the contents of those bottles into the john, he had it all pieced together.

Oh dear, Withers thought, I have succumbed.

But at least I have my toothbrush, he thought brightly, proceeding to scrub the previous evening from his cottony mouth until he remembered "exclusive interview with Polly Paget" and rushed to the television.

A sincere-looking young woman with a vaguely famous face was speaking softly but urgently to the camera. "Last night, I flew in great secrecy to a location I promised not to disclose for the purpose of interviewing Polly Paget. When 'Morning' returns, you will see that interview in its entirety."

Withers watched a commercial extolling the benefits of fiber while he tried to work this out.

Who had called the media?

Didn't I threaten to call the media?

Good God, did I?

He looked under the bed. The money was still there, so he decided that it couldn't have been him.

The phone jangled.

"Are you watching this?" Scarpelli asked. Withers thought he detected a nasty edge to his voice.

"Ms. Paget is being interviewed on television," Withers said.

"No kidding," Scarpelli said. "I thought you were supposed to be watching their door."

"I just didn't think it was the time to make a move," he answered. Because I was unconscious.

"Well, it better be time to make a move now," Scarpelli said. "I want Polly Paget—right now—or my goddamn money back, or you're in more trouble than you know about. You understand?"

"Yes, I think I do."

"I don't like being scammed."

"No, of course you don't."

"I got friends in this town, you know what I mean?"

Withers had difficulty imagining Scarpelli having friends anywhere, never mind gangster friends in Vegas, but he kept it to himself.

"I'll get you Polly Paget," he said.

You don't have to threaten me.

Jack Landis had Pedro bring him his breakfast in the den so he could eat and admire his performance as it was rerun on the morning news. He had pulled the thick drapes to ignore the mob of reporters out by the gate. Security wanted to chase them off, but Jack wanted them to get nice shots of Candy as she returned home—lots of footage of them hugging and shit. He already had the writers working on the big reunion show.

Things are going to change, he thought as he snipped the end of his cigar. I'll eat crow for a little bit, then explain to Canned-Ice that this whole thing was her fault. Shit, she has lots of money, nice clothes, nice furniture . . . maybe I will take a belt to her just to drive the point home.

Teach any of these bitches to go up against Jackson Hood Landis. . . .

He speared a strip of bacon, scooped a forkful of *huevos rancheros* under it, and turned on the television.

"I first met Jack Landis when I was a secretary in his New York office," Polly was saying. "I thought he was handsome . . . and I guess he thought I was cute, and one thing led to another and——"

Oh shit, Jack thought.

"She looks great," Ed Levine admitted as he watched the rented TV they had brought into Kitteredge's office earlier for Jack's performance.

"She seems to be a nice young lady, really," Kitteredge agreed. "Fire Neal the next time you talk to him, would you, Ed? Sever all connections."

"Yes, sir," Ed answered, even though he knew it was easier said than done. No way was Joe Graham going to sever his connection with Neal.

But if this interview kept going the way it was going, Jack Landis would be toast by afternoon. "The Jack and Candy Family Hour" would be history, Candyland the world's most expensive vacant lot, and there would be a whole lot of angry people in Providence, San Antonio, and New Orleans.

Ed's stomach turned progressively more sour as he watched the whole carefully crafted deal go down the toilet.

Because Polly was killing them. In contrast to Jack's bathetic posturing, Polly was coming across as soft, sincere, and . . . goddamn it . . . truthful. Connie Kelly, one of America's real sweethearts, sure believed Polly. She nodded as Polly answered, and lowered her voice, and there were tears in her eyes as she whispered, "Could you . . . if you can . . . tell us about the rape?"

The rape, Ed thought. Not the alleged rape, but the rape.

"Jack came over that night," Polly began, "And I told him that I was ending our relationship."

"So *you* told *him,* is that right?" Connie asked.

"Yes, and Jack got very angry and grabbed me. . . ."

Polly's description of the assault was devastating.

"We might as well turn this off," Kitteredge said.

"There'll be more," Ed said. "Neal won't stop at tit for tat. He'll go one up."

"But what does he have?" Kitteredge asked.

A piece of rye toast flew out of Jack's mouth when Candy came on the screen, sat down next to Polly, and put her arm around her.

Standing over Jack's shoulder, Jorge announced, "Look! It's Mrs. Landis!"

"I know who it is," Jack snapped. "Shit, I'm married to her, ain't I?"

Not for long, thought Jorge.

"Connie," Candy said, "I think it's so important that the viewers out there understand that rape is not always committed by strangers in a dark alley. Sometimes it's someone you know. . . ."

Jorge handed Jack the phone.

"What!" Jack yelled.

"Are you watching this?" Joey screamed. "That's your wife!"

"I recognized her."

"What's she doing on there!"

"Sawing my balls off," Jack said. The world was starting to

close in——black, hot and stuffy as an East Texas summer night. You want to get out, get away from the suffocating heat, and there's no place to go but to more of the same.

"The bitch lied to me. . . ." Jack mumbled, more to himself than to Joey. "She said she forgave me . . . coming home . . ."

"I find it incredible that the two of you have become such close friends," Connie said. "How in the world did that happen?"

"Well, of course we had something in common," Candy said.

As Connie giggled and shook her head, Jack handed Jorge the phone.

"Tell that son of a bitch I'm going to the Grand Caymans," he muttered. "He can have fucking Candyland."

The world was spinning.

"You're a son of a bitch and Mr. Landis is going to the Grand Canyon," Jorge said. "You can fuck having Candyland."

Visions of a Caribbean beach, women with skin like cocoa butter, and a cool grass shack sparkled in Jack's eyes as his arm went numb, his heartburn returned, and he felt as if someone was wrapping barbed wire around his chest.

"And then when someone tried to kill her . . ." Candy drawled.

Joey was trying to figure out why Jack was going to the Grand Canyon when he heard the bit about someone trying to kill Polly.

"Wait a second. That's me!" Joey yelled indignantly. "Why the hell does she have to drag me into it? What the hell did I ever do to her?"

"You stole a boatload of money from her," Harold suggested.

"Yeah, but she doesn't know that!" Joey whined. "That's not fair!"

"Why would someone want to kill you?" asked Connie breathlessly.

Please, please, please, please, please, Harold prayed. Don't say it.

Please, please, please, please, please, Joey prayed. Don't say it. Carmine will have me melted into a wax candle and burn an inch or two of me every day.

"I don't know," Polly answered. "There are a lot of crazies out there."

Thank God, thought Harold.

Thank God, thought Joey.

"She's a stand-up broad," Harold said when he got his breath again.

"Yeah, she's okay," Joey said when he realized that it still wasn't too late to knock her off.

If that numbnuts Overtime can get it right for once.

Overtime limped down the hallway and rapped softly on Withers's door.

"Who is it?" Withers asked.

"Open the door before someone sees me," Overtime hissed.

Walter cracked the door, Overtime pushed it open, shut it behind him, and grabbed Withers by the lapels.

"Listen, you drunken buffoon," Overtime said. "You're going to deliver the target the way you're supposed to so I can get the job done."

"Who are you?" Withers asked. "Do you work for Scarpelli?"

"Yeah, okay," Overtime answered.

One more float, he thought, in this endless parade of idiots.

* * *

Why would they want to kill her? Neal asked himself as he watched the interview. *What could she say that she hasn't said already?*

"It's going great, isn't it?" Karen said.

"Yeah," Neal said.

"What?" Karen asked, picking up on his mood. Neal was such a damn perfectionist. Polly had probably dropped a *t* or an *r* or put a diphthong where there wasn't supposed to be one or something.

What could she say that she hasn't said already?

She talked about the affair; she talked about the rape—what else was there to Pollygate? Joey Foglio, obviously, but she didn't even know about that until we found out that her good buddy Gloria was giving her up. . . .

From the Book of Joseph Graham, book one, chapter one, verse one: Don't look so hard at what's there that you forget what's missing.

So when you told Polly that Gloria ratted on her, she never asked, "Who's Joey Foglio? How does Gloria know him? What does Gloria have to do with a mobster?" Nothing, just that same stupid, resentful acceptance that all men are shits, so it was no surprise Joey turned on her.

"What did Gloria owe Joey Beans?" Neal asked.

Polly kept her eyes on the television and said, "I didn't know Gloria even knew Joey Beans."

Joey Beans, just like that. Not "Joey who?" Not "That's a funny name." Nothing. Which is strange, because I never called him Joey Beans before. Neal watched her beautiful, honest image on the screen—the one he'd worked so well to bring out—and got an awful sinking feeling.

"I thought they only killed their own," Karen had said.

I'm afraid you were right.

What could she say she hadn't already said? That she worked

for Joey Beans. She was Joey's hook into Landis. That she pulled out too soon and Joey Beans was pissed off and scared—so pissed off and scared, he put a hit on her.

"Awwwww," Neal groaned.

"What?" Karen said.

"How much was he paying you?" Neal asked.

"Who?" Polly said.

"Who?" Neal mocked. "You mean there was more than one!"

She got that defensive look in her eye, the one he hadn't seen since . . . the moments after the attempted murder.

"I don't know what you're talking about," she said.

"I don't either," Karen said. "What *are* you talking about?"

"Aw, man," Neal groaned again. "She's a player."

"What do you mean?" asked Karen.

"Because I slept with Jack Landis?" Polly asked.

"Because you took money from Joey Beans to sleep with Jack Landis," Neal said.

"I did not!" Polly yelled as she stood up.

Yeah, you did, Neal thought. It's in your eyes; it's in your voice.

"How'd it happen?" he asked.

"It happened just the way I told Connie——"

"Look, I've told more stories than the frigging Brothers Grimm," Neal said. "Don't bother."

"I——"

"No, seriously," Neal said. "I was stupid enough to believe you; it's my fault. You and Joey ran a scam on Jack. Hathaway made you a better offer. You took a shot. . . . I hope it works out for you. Now just shut up."

Because I need to think how to get the hell out of this.

"He raped me!"

"Yeah," Neal said. "Listen, you should have taken the three mil. What did you think, that the TV performance was going to up the ante? Now they'll get on the phone and offer you five? What Joey Beans is going to offer you is a mouthful of concrete somewhere. But I'm not going with you, Polly, and neither is Karen.''

"He raped me!" Polly screamed.

"And that wasn't part of the deal, was it?"

"No!"

Neal sat down on the bed.

"Bummer, huh?" he said to Karen.

Karen said, "Polly, how could you let us put ourselves on the line like that and not—"

Polly pushed past and ran out of the room.

"Let her go," Neal said.

"We can't just—"

They heard the door slam behind her.

Walter Withers saw Polly come out the door.

Nothing ventured, nothing gained, he thought. Walter, this is your big moment. One moment to do it all right and redeem yourself, a fresh start.

He tightened the knot on his tie, opened the door, and stepped into the hallway.

Miss Paget was weeping.

Perhaps the gallant approach.

"Excuse me, my dear," Withers said. "I could not help but notice that you seem to be in some distress. May I be of assistance?"

"I don't have no one," Polly wept.

"Ah, loneliness, perhaps my greatest area of expertise," Withers said. That treacherous young weasel Carey will be out here any second. Must move with dispatch. "Didn't I just see you on television?"

"No."

"Yes, you're Polly Paget, aren't you?" he asked. "No wonder you're weeping. You've been through a great ordeal. Please allow me to help.''

''How can you help?''

Here it is, Withers thought. My make-or-break moment.

''I can offer you half a million dollars.''

Polly wiped her eyes and looked at him. She'd need money to hide from Joey Beans now.

''What do I have to do?'' she asked.

''Simply pose for a few photographs,'' Withers answered. He tried to think of a delicate way of putting it, then added apologetically, *''En dishabille,* as the French would say.''

''Huh?''

''Nude,'' Withers said, cutting to the point. ''For *Top Drawer* magazine.''

Alone, Polly thought. No friends, no home, nowhere to go, a kid on the way.

''Get away from me,'' she said.

''I have twenty-five thousand dollars in cash for you right now,'' he said. ''As a down payment.''

But I do need money, Polly thought.

''These would be like, tasteful, right?'' she asked.

''Your sweet mother would show them to her friends,'' Withers assured her.

He gallantly led her into the room.

Carmine Bascaglia watched the interview from his home in Chalmette Oaks. When Candy Landis gushed her revelation about the attempted murder and Polly Paget brushed it off as the act of a lunatic, he placed a call to San Antonio, brooking no nonsense about Joey Foglio's phone phobia.

''Joseph,'' he said when his hotheaded associate came on the line, ''I hope you haven't done anything hasty.''

''Of course not, Carmine,'' Joey answered. ''What do you mean?''

"I mean this Paget woman has just bought herself some protection," Carmine said.

"She's playing with us, Carmine. This is flat-out extortion," Joey answered. "I don't think we should stand for it."

Carmine sighed. "You don't think at all, Joseph. *I* think, and then you do what I think. I think we should proceed slowly and with great caution. Don't do anything. Do you understand?"

"Sure."

There was a long silence before Carmine said, "Joseph, tell me you haven't done anything stupid. Because if anything should happen to Miss Paget now, we would be subject to considerable unwanted attention."

Joey felt as if he was kneeling in the street munching on garbage.

He said, "She's as safe as in her mother's arms."

"See that she stays that way," Carmine said. "At least for the time being."

"We got any way of contacting Overtime?" Joey asked Harold when Carmine had finished.

"No. You know Overtime. Paranoid."

"Yeah," Joey said, praying that numbnuts Overtime didn't get it right this time.

"So who are you," Polly asked Overtime, "the photographer?"

Because he just couldn't resist it, Overtime said, "That's right. They've hired me to shoot you."

Finally, he thought.

Polly looked around the room. "This is it? No studio? No lights?"

"You're the photographer?" Withers asked. "Why didn't you—"

Overtime's pistol snaked out and clubbed Withers once and

then twice against the side of the head. Withers dropped heavily to the floor.

Overtime put the pistol against Polly's head.

It's odd, Overtime thought, hearing her on the TV and seeing her live in front of me at the same time. Live, he thought. For a moment anyway.

"That smart son of a bitch," Ed Levine said. "He beat Jack to death with Polly's performance, showed us he had Candy on his side, threatened to squeal about the attempted hit, and then made a peace offer by not going through with it."

"He's still fired," Kitteredge said. "How do you think Mr. Bascaglia will react?"

"The Banker will want to go back to the table," Ed thought out loud, "but he'll want to deal with Mrs. Landis instead of Jack, because Jack is dead meat now. He'll also want to roast Neal over a bed of coals."

You smart little SOB, Ed thought. You might just pull this off. Now, what can I do to help?

"You want me to get Bascaglia's people on the phone?" Ed asked. "Tell them three million, plus Jack's confession."

"Possibly—"

Connie was wrapping it up with, "Now you said you had one announcement you wanted to make."

Great, Ed thought. Now what?

Jack Landis was trying to get enough breath to get up from the sofa.

All that money, he thought, waiting in the Caymans . . . warm beach . . . skin like cocoa butter . . . and I can't get up off my ass to go.

He looked at the blurry images of his wife and mistress on television. Hard to hear—what was Polly saying?

"And I'm going to have a baby," Polly said. "Jack Landis's baby."

A baby, Jack thought. Jack Landis—

Then something cracked in his chest, he pitched forward, and landed face-first in the guacamole.

"You're pregnant?" Overtime said.

He held the gun on Polly, who sat on the bed, her back against the headboard. She was too scared to talk, so she nodded.

"This is a complication," Overtime said. He held the gun on her while he dialed the phone with the other hand.

"I'm not shooting a pregnant woman," he told Harold indignantly.

Polly felt a breath come into her lungs.

"Unless you pay me double," Overtime finished.

Walter Withers could just make out the man's back. Blood caked one eye and the other didn't focus terribly well. He felt as if he were listening to someone talk underwater.

But it appears, Withers thought, that this man is actually intending to kill this young lady. And I have led her to this.

"Counts as two people," he heard the man insist. "Hell, I thought you guys were Catholics. What do you mean, 'academic'?"

Walter felt as if a cold river were running through his brain as he tried to push himself onto his hands and knees. The man looked over his shoulder at him.

It's nice, Withers thought, to hear someone play a Hart tune without butchering it, but this unpleasant, amoral young man needed correcting. And the young lady needed rescuing.

"You may want to call it off, but she's seen me now," Overtime said. "I'm killing her and you are going to pay me."

As Overtime aimed the pistol, Withers pushed himself to his feet.

"See here," he said as he reached into his jacket for the revolver he had left in New York, "the game just isn't played this way."

Overtime turned around and shot him in the chest.

Oh dear, Withers thought, I've made a mess of this.

Walter Withers's last act on earth was to lunge forward on Overtime's arm, stopping him from lifting his pistol as Polly sprang from the bed and ran for the door.

Overtime dropped Walt, put a bullet into his head, and said into the telephone, "Great, now she got away. . . . What do you mean, 'Thank God'?"

Overtime was long gone by the time Polly banged on Neal's door, sobbed out her story, and brought him to Withers's room.

"Oh God," Neal said when he saw the body.

Polly went to cradle Withers in her arms.

"Don't touch him," Neal said. "Don't touch anything. You'll screw up the cops."

"He saved my life," Polly cried.

Neal looked down at the sad, crumpled corpse of Walter Withers.

"Yeah, well. He was a gentleman," Neal said.

Then he hustled Polly out of there and went back to his room to phone an anonymous tip.

26

*B*y midafternoon of that day, the court of public opinion had decided that Jack had been a good sport to have his fatal heart attack when he did. It provided a neater ending to Polly Paget's victory, spared the public the long but titillating ordeal of "The Jack and Candy Family Hour" ending in divorce, and left Jack's virtuoso "I have betrayed you" performance as a final memory.

By the evening drive time radio shows, the "Name the Baby" contests broke out on several competing stations, each, however, offering the same prize of an all-expenses-paid trip to Candyland.

Jorge became a celebrity on the evening news shows with his vivid description of finding Jack taking the long nap in his breakfast, a narrative that provided comic relief against the stark images of Candy arriving at the airport a widow, shielded from the media hordes by her grim bodyguard.

By that time, Polly Paget had risen once again, transformed from vengeful psycho female to heroic Madonna even though she remained in seclusion. Rumors that she had signed to make a porno film, or was going to be a centerfold, or had been involved in a bizarre shoot-out in a Las Vegas hotel were dismissed as idiotic and tasteless. Hollywood producers cheerfully slashed one another's throats to see who would make Polly, the movie or Polly, the miniseries. Several name actresses were said to be already signed to do the role.

Candy Landis, too, experienced a public metamorphosis—from hopelessly out-of-it suburban recipe queen to hip practical neofeminist. Scores of women ex-cons appeared on dozens of shows to tell how Candy's wisdom helped them to start a new life, and herds of sociologists went on to explain that Mrs. Landis's rural roots, keen business savvy, and courageous integrity made her a role model for thousands of women across the country.

By the time the network anchors gave their signature sign-offs, Overtime had recited his litany of complaints against Joey Foglio to Carmine Bascaglia, Joey had cleansed his soul again, and the Las Vegas police were investigating the homicide of a down-and-out New York P.I. who'd spent his last day in Pompeii.

And by the time the late news came on, a new deal was in the works.

"So everything's okay now, right?" Polly asked the group assembled in Candy Landis's living room.

"No," Neal answered coldly. "Everything is not okay, America's Sweetheart. A man is dead."

"Two men," Candy corrected.

"Right," Graham said. "One man died and another man was murdered."

"The mob is still entrenched in our business," Whiting added.

"And it's business as usual," Karen said.

"I'm sorry," Polly said. "I never meant for any of this to happen."

Neal looked at her to see whether she was using the sincerity he had taught her or whether it was real.

Damned if it didn't look real.

"Bascaglia wins; Hathaway wins; Joey Beans wins. . . ." Karen mused.

Candy said, "It doesn't seem fair."

"Well," Neal said, "at the end of the day, you do what you can do."

"So do you want to do it?" Graham asked.

Neal thought about it. He could walk away now, go back to Nevada with Karen, forget about the whole stupid thing, or . . .

"Yeah, I do," he said.

"I think we've taken a lot of shit from these people and it's time to give some back," Karen said.

Chuck nodded.

Culver grinned.

"At the end of the day," Candy said, "I guess I just can't accept being a partner with criminals."

Everyone looked at Polly.

"I'll ask St. Anthony," she said, "to help us turn the tables on these . . . these . . . these dirty . . . penises."

"She needs work," Graham said to Neal.

"I know."

But don't we all.

At the offices of AAA Trucking and Hauling, Harold held the phone away from his mouth as he said, "Joey, you ain't gonna believe who's on the phone."

Harold had developed a small tic under his left eye. It started shortly after Carmine called to warn them that they'd better not be thinking about whacking Polly Paget, had gotten a little worse after the news that Jack was on his way to that big fish fry in the sky, and was now quivering away with every fresh turn and dip on the roller-coaster ride that was life with Joey Foglio.

"I dunno," Joey answered, looking like none of this even bothered him. "Who?"

"Jack's wife. Uhhh, widow."

Joey smiled and held up his hands as an "I told you so" gesture and boasted, "See? What did I tell you? Jack ain't even cold and his old lady is scrambling to make a deal. I hope the bitch don't think it's going to be easy. This should be funny— put it on speaker."

This was his legitimate business number, so it didn't matter as long as he discussed legitimate business.

"Hello, Mrs. Landis," Joey said. "Sorry to hear about Jack. So young, so vital."

So stupid.

"Mr. Foglio?" Candy asked in a tone that gave credence to her nickname, Canned-Ice.

"The *g* is silent," Joey corrected her.

"I see," Candice said. "Well, however you pronounce your name, I'm just calling to let you know that you're fired. I'm canceling all contracts as of today. Please be so kind as to have all your equipment off of Candyland within the next forty-eight hours. Thank you."

That wiped the smile off Joey's face. He had an audience to play for, so he replaced the smile with a smirk and said, "You can't just cancel contracts, Mrs. Landis. I'd have to sue you."

"While I can picture you in a courtroom, Mr. Foglio," Candy answered, "it's easier to imagine you in handcuffs."

Say what?

"Are you threatening me?" Joey asked. He couldn't believe it. This cracker twat was threatening to drop a dime on him!

"I'm giving you a break," Candy answered. "I'm not going

to press charges against you for fraud, theft, extortion, and blackmail, but I do want you out of my hair. It's my final offer, Mr. Foglio. I suggest you accept it."

"Oh, is that what you suggest, you——"

"Careful, Joey," Harold warned. Joey's face was the color of an overripe tomato and his own eye was quivering like crazy.

"Shut up," Joey answered. "Hey, lady! You don't know who you're messing with!"

"Joey . . ." Harold moaned.

"I know precisely with whom I am messing," Candy answered, "and I don't care. Forty-eight hours, Mr. Beans."

The loud hum of the dial tone filled the room as she hung up.

"You killed Jack, you know!" Joey screamed. "Murdered your own husband like you stuck a knife in his back, you witch! Forty-eight hours! I'll give you forty-eight hours hanging upside down on a meat hook, you tight-ass Texas——"

"Joey, she hung up," Harold said.

"Goddamn it!" Joey yelled. He slammed his fist on his desk.

"This is troublesome," Peter Hathaway said.

He had come to San Antonio for Jack's funeral and to make new arrangements with Joey Foglio. Now Candy's unexpected fortitude seemed to threaten those arrangements. And without the rake-off money coming in from Foglio, he'd be nothing more than Marc Merolla's beard for the rest of his pathetic life.

Something had to be done.

"Something has to be done," Hathaway said.

Harold warned, "Joey, we can't be involved in any——"

"You got any suggestions?" Joey asked Hathaway.

"Joey . . ." Harold moaned.

"Yes," Hathaway answered. "Actually, I do."

Joey smiled at Harold and said, "Actually, he does."

"I have an old friend," Hathaway said, "who handles just this sort of thing."

Harold thought his eye might just rattle out of his head.

Joe Graham held the phone away from his ear as Carmine Bascaglia yelled dire threats about killing him, Neal Carey, Polly Paget, Candy Landis, all of their families, friends, and pets.

Then Graham said, "You're not going to do shit, Mr. Bascaglia. Let me tell you why."

After he told him, Carmine Bascaglia swept all the paper off his desk, smashed the window with his chair, and had his boys go fetch Overtime.

Overtime left Bascaglia's office a happy man.

Work found for work lost, he thought. Fair enough. One last hit and a long retirement overseas.

There was a message for him when he got back to his room. He dialed the San Antonio number and was surprised to hear the voice from the past.

"It's been a long time," he said.

"Last time I saw you was in a boat under a bridge," Hathaway said.

"That's right."

"Although you've heard from me from time to time," Hathaway added.

It's true, Overtime thought. His old roomie had been very clever about sneaking his money out of the States. He would never have been able to hide for so long if it hadn't been for Hathaway's ingenuity.

"Now I need a favor," Hathaway said.

"I can give you a discount," Overtime answered.

Hathaway agreed to his price and gave him the setup.

"Hello," Candy crooned into the phone.

"Mrs. Landis, it's Peter Hathaway. This has all gone on long enough, don't you think?"

"Tomorrow afternoon, after the funeral," Candy told the group in the room. "Hathaway, Polly, and I will meet at Candyland to inspect the property and discuss an arrangement."

"It's for you, Joey," Harold said.

"Take a message."

"Who is this?" Harold asked. "Holy shit."

"What?"

Harold whispered, "It's Stumpy."

Joey grabbed the phone. "What do you want, you bastard?"

"Hey, Joey Beans!" Graham warbled. "We have some unfinished business."

"We do?"

"Yeah," Graham said. "Unfinished business named Walter Withers."

"What about him?"

"I'm going to kill you, that's what about him."

"Anywhere, anyplace, anytime," Foglio said.

"Somewhere we won't be disturbed, clown," answered Graham.

"Candyland, tomorrow afternoon," Graham said to the group in the room. He dialed the phone again. "Ed? Let me ask you something about Marc Merolla."

Marc Merolla listened to what Ed Levine had to tell him about Peter Hathaway.

"I'm shocked, Ed," he said. "What can I say? What can I do?"

Ethan Kitteredge came to the door of his house and was surprised to see Marc Merolla standing there.

"Won't you come in?" Kitteredge asked.

"I won't be a minute," Marc said in the hallway. "I came for a favor."

"Do you think this is going to work?" Karen asked Neal late that night.

"You know," Neal said, "I really think it is."

There are only thirty thousand things that can go wrong, Neal thought, but at some point you just have to have some faith.

27

$\mathcal{M}$usashi Watanabe could see everything from the top of the water slide.

He could see the entirety of Candyland, from the vast parking lot to the condominiums. He could see the Circle of Life Ferris Wheel, The History of the American Family Tunnel of Love, The Richard Milhous Nixon Roller-Coaster Ride, the petting-zoo pens, the concession stands, and even the Journey Through the Holy Land Putt-Putt Golf Course, for which he had personally designed the Parting of the Red Sea Water Hazard.

If he looked past Candyland to the south, he could see the downtown San Antonio skyline with its distinctive Space Tower. Just to the east, in the rolling hills, he could see the long procession of cars snaking out to Jack Landis's funeral.

None of these sights interested Musashi Watanabe. What interested him was his pride and joy, the work of his life, his masterpiece—the tallest, longest, fastest water slide in the world, which, thanks to that stupid contest, had yet to be named. Musashi didn't care what they named it. To him, the designer, it would always have one name and one name only: Banzai!

Because this was a water slide for samurai. Starting one hundred feet in the air, it flumed at an eighty-degree angle straight down to build up speed, then wrapped into a double corkscrew turn before plunging down another steep straight-away, which curved into a high-banked right turn, then bent back to the left into an even higher bank to give the rider the illusion he was about to be launched over the top of the rim into space. But then the rider would plunge down to the right into another corkscrew and then into a fifty-foot shallow straight-away and then splash into a pool.

This is where things got interesting.

The truly ingenious Watanabe touch went into action here, as the rider would be sucked sideways across the pool by a powerful current and into a tube that ran virtually straight down for thirty feet to a twenty-foot open-air drop into a deeper pool, where lifeguards, flotation devices, and emergency medi-cal personnel would be standing by if needed.

This was not a game for children, Watanabe thought with satisfaction. This was the device with which he hoped to realize a lifelong dream of seeing aqua gliding take its rightful place as an Olympic event. After all, the luge was merely a frozen water slide.

Of course, it would require a spectacular televised fatality to truly popularize the sport . . .

He dismissed this pleasant thought and concentrated on the task at hand, lugging a 150-pound sandbag into the starting chamber for the safety test. Mrs. Landis had vetoed his idea—which Jack had heartily approved—of using volunteer convicts, which would have given them a much more aquadynamically accurate test. It wasn't that Watanabe had any doubts about his engineering—it was meticulous—but he did have some con-cerns about the cheaper materials that Mr. Foglio had insisted on using.

Watanabe flipped the starter switch and water gushed up into the chamber. He waited two minutes for the slide to get nicely wet, then gave the sandbag a kick.

"Banzai!" he yelled as the bag plunged down the long drop,

swept around the double corkscrew, swooshed down the next straightaway, negotiated the first high turn, zoomed along the edge of the second big bank, double corkscrewed again, then drifted down the last straightaway and into the first pool.

The suction dragged the bag across the pool and into the tube. Four seconds later, the bag dropped out of the tube, dropped twenty feet, and exploded on the bottom of the empty receiving pool.

Goddamn cheap American sandbags, Watanabe thought. Now he'd have to vacuum the sand out again.

But Banzai worked like a Swiss watch.

Then the world went black.

Overtime finished duct-taping the Japanese guy's mouth shut and made sure he was firmly lashed to the ladder.

Quite a view, Overtime thought. You can see everything from here, the Ferris wheel, the roller-coaster, the putt-putt golf course with the statue of Moses on the sand trap. When he looked through the scope, he could even see Joey Beans and his idiot Sancho la Bonza a good three hundred yards away on the vast Jack and Candy Plaza.

And coming from the other side . . . Candy Landis in the company of a tall silver-haired guy and . . . is that Peter? He's put on the odd pound.

And . . . could it be? Yes! Walking behind them is none other than America's Sweetheart, the girl with the nation's most precious little bun in the oven. . . . Ladies and gentlemen . . . let's hear it for . . . Miss Polly Paget!

I have to hand it to you, Joey. When you set up a shot, you set up a shot. Mr. Magoo couldn't miss from here.

Problem: A target-rich environment demands prioritization.

Analysis: Targets are standing in a big open square.

Solution: One shot at a time.

* * *

Neal and Karen watched through binoculars from the terrace. Foglio has that cocky wise guy rolling gait, Neal thought, although his bodyguard looks nervous as hell. Candy's walking with her no-nonsense stride, stopping here and there to point something out to Hathaway, who seems to have a special interest in the water slide. And Polly has her head down. Probably terrified to face Joey Beans.

"What do you think?" Karen said.

"I think I wish you hadn't come," Neal answered.

"I think it's going to be fun."

"What if Joey Beans goes berserk?" Neal asked.

"Then I think it's going to be more fun."

But what the hell does Hathaway find so interesting on top of the damn water slide? His eyes are flicking up there like he's expecting . . .

"He's up there," Neal murmured.

"Who's up where?" Karen asked.

"Overtime," Neal answered.

All right, think for a change and think fast. Even if you can run down from the terrace, you'd never make it across the plaza. He'd see you, make his shot, and then gun you down. He's waiting for a better shot or he'd have already done it. So see if you can get behind him.

Behind him, you dickhead? He's on top of a tower. How can you get behind him?

"Stay here," he said to Karen. "Please, for once just do what I ask without a discussion and stay here. Please."

"Where are you going?"

"Just for a walk up the water slide. Now promise."

"You think the killer's up there?" Karen asked.

"Karen, we don't have time."

"We can shout and warn them!"

"They wouldn't understand and he'd start shooting," Neal said. "Think on the bright side: It's probably just my paranoia."

Neal started running for the base of the water slide.

Then he heard the voice—*that voice*—booming across the PA system.

"Joey! Joey Beans! It's Stumpy the Clown!"

Overtime peeked up from his hiding place.

This is different, he thought as he watched Joey freeze in place. Harold pulled his pistol. But that damn Candy Landis just kept walking. She didn't look surprised at all.

"We have some unfinished business, Joey!"

"Where are you, you rat bastard?" Joey yelled.

Overtime saw Candy Landis walk to within about five feet of Joey. He should have shot then, but it was just so damn interesting.

"Hey, Joey! Carmine Bascaglia heard this tape last night. It goes something like . . ."

This is a nightmare, Joey thought. I'm going to wake up any second beside some luscious broad and laugh and—

"You didn't leave us with any choice," Candy Landis was saying. "We tried to tell you nicely, but you just wouldn't listen."

The PA system played a scratchy leader for a few seconds and then boomed: "BLESS ME, FATHER, FOR I HAVE SINNED. IT HAS BEEN ONE DAY SINCE MY LAST CONFESSION."

Joey turned white.

"It sounds good," Joe Graham said to John Culver, who was operating the system.

"A little more treble, perhaps," Culver suggested. He tweaked a dial. "Primo system. Very tasty."

"Keep playing it," Graham said. Then he went out to enjoy the look on Joey Beans's face.

Neal reached the first pool and was pleased to see that the water was running.

Of course. God would never let you climb a dry water slide. That would be too easy.

He grabbed the sides of the slide and started to pull himself up.

I'm wrong, he thought. There's no one up here. They wouldn't dare take another shot at Polly, not now, not when Bascaglia called them off.

He slipped and landed on his face as he heard:

I HAVE COMMITTED ONE ATTEMPTED MURDER . . . TWICE. . . . MAY BE PLANNING ANOTHER. . . . IS PLANNING A MORTAL OR VENIAL SIN? THE HELL AM I ASKING? YOU DON'T SPEAK ENGLISH. . . .

"You tapped a man's confessional?" Joey croaked. "You came between a man and his God? What kind of people are you!"

"DEA," Chuck answered.

"Baptists," Candy said.

THERE WAS FIVE FORNICATIONS . . . OKAY, THREE . . . TWENTY-EIGHT IMPURE THOUGHTS . . . AND I THINK AN EXTORTION. MAYBE IT'S BLACKMAIL. HARD TO SAY. . . .

"You had it coming, Joey," Polly said.

"You should talk, you whore," answered Joey.

THEN, OF COURSE, THERE WAS THE DAY'S PROTECTION MONEY, BUT THAT SKINFLINT CARMINE GETS A BIG PIECE OF THAT. . . .

"For God's sake, Joey," Harold moaned. "Did you think this was a priest or dear fucking Abby?"

"Shut up."

Graham arrived on the scene.

"Carmine heard this last night, Joey," he said. "But I told

him we wanted to surprise you. I figure you got maybe a three-hour start if you get going now. Unless Carmine's already talked to Harold here."

Joey looked wildly around.

"Harold, shoot somebody," he said.

Harold's eye was sending telegrams.

"Sorry, boss," he said.

"Leave now, Mr. Foglio," Candy said. "There has been more than enough dying."

Foglio straightened himself up and looked her dead in the eye. "You'll get yours, you bitch."

Any second now.

The high-banked curves were tough because he kept slipping and getting water in his mouth. Neal found he could dig one foot into the curved side and push while he pulled himself up with his hands. It was taking time, though, and he was running out of time.

Karen tried to stay on the terrace. She really did. But she saw her friends down there, people she loved: Candy Landis, the flawed but somehow lovable—and pregnant—Polly Paget, and Joe Graham.

Dear, dear Joe Graham.

She ran down the stairs and started across the terrace, waving her arms and yelling.

NOW THERE WAS ONE MURDER MAYBE I HAD SOMETHING TO DO WITH, BUT IT WAS REALLY THAT MUTT OVERTIME.

Excuse me, Overtime thought. I think we've all heard about enough.

He leaned out of the starting chamber and raised the rifle. He caught some movement from the corner of his eye and shifted the scope.

Oh, this is too good, he thought. There she is, running like a deer across a meadow. And no baseball bat. No dog.

Decisions, decisions.

Problem: So many targets, so little time.

Analysis: If you shoot her first, you'll spook the money targets.

Consideration: Always shoot for the money. When they start dropping, she'll freeze and you can drop her where she stands.

Decision: Get to work. Shoot for the money first, then protection, then pleasure.

Just in, just out. Professional.

Of course, there are two money targets.

ONE JERK-OFF, TWO PETTY THEFTS, ONE ASSAULT . . . I PRAYED FOR CARMINE TO DIE. IS THAT A SIN?

"I ain't going down alone, Hathaway," Joey said pointedly.

"What's that supposed to mean?" Hathaway asked.

"It's all on the tape, Mr. Hathaway," Chuck said as he pulled his revolver and pointed it at Hathaway's chest, "but we do thank you for coming today."

"You set me up," Hathaway accused Candy.

Graham saw his eyes glance up at the water slide.

I MEAN, CARMINE'S WHACKED MORE GUYS THAN CARTER HAS PILLS. . . .

Neal was winded by the time he hit the last long slope to the top. He had to lie on his stomach and pull himself up, and his hands kept slipping.

And he heard Karen yelling. Then his hands slipped and he slid backward.

"Get down!" Karen yelled.

"What's she saying?" asked Candy.

"Bye-bye," Joey Beans answered.

OKAY, ONTO VULGARITIES . . .

Overtime centered the crosshairs on Foglio's square forehead. He had worked out his priorities: Make Carmine happy first, then Peter, then take Polly out, then the bitch from Nevada, then maybe the one-armed dwarf who'd set him up, the gray-haired cop . . .

As they say, Idle hands are the devil's playground.

He started to apply that gentle persuasion to the trigger.

Or . . . do Candy first, which will make Joey think he's safe, then whack the bitch from Nevada, then the one-armed dwarf, then . . .

Neal grabbed onto the side and caught himself. He threw one foot out and managed to get straight and start pulling up again. Water streamed into his face. He had his mouth clamped shut, but the water was coming into his nose and he started to choke.

He craned his neck and saw Overtime's back and the rifle come up to his cheek.

The killer was just out of reach.

Neal opened his mouth to scream.

No . . . do the bitch first before she spooks everyone, then Joey, then Candy, then . . .

One thing at a time.

He was drawing the lead on Karen when he heard a drowning voice yell, "NOOOO!"

He squeezed the trigger just as the hand grabbed his arm.

Chuck heard the crack of the rifle, knocked Candy down, and lay on top of her.

TWELVE *F*-WORDS, TWENTY OR THIRTY *SHITS* . . .

Karen felt the rush of wind over her head and dived for cover.

Joe Graham crawled toward her.

Polly stood in the middle of the plaza, asking, "What the hell is this?"

TOO MANY *GODDAMNS*, FOR WHICH I'M SORRY, OKAY?

Hathaway ran.

Harold looked at Joey and said, "Get outta here, Joey."

"The hell difference it makes?" Joey asked. "If Carmine wants me . . ."

"A day at a time, huh?" Harold said. "Go on . . . before I don't have an excuse not to whack you."

Another rifle shot went off.

THAT'S ABOUT IT, FATHER. TAKE IT EASY ON THE ACTS OF CONTRITION, HUH?

"You're okay, Harold," Joey said.

"Long life, boss."

Joey Beans ran for the relative safety of the putt-putt golf course.

The second shot went off as Neal pulled back on Overtime's arm and tried to haul him out of the starting chamber. Overtime rammed the stock back and hit Neal on the collarbone. Neal kept his grip on Overtime's arm, braced his feet against the side of the slide, and jerked. He reached his left hand around, grabbed the killer under the chin, and pulled.

Overtime pushed his rifle hand out and probed with the barrel until he felt it touch a body.

Neal felt the barrel against him, rolled back, and pulled the man onto the slide with him as the gun went off. He was lying sideways across the slide now, with his feet braced on the edge and Overtime lying on top of him.

Neal felt as if he was drowning. Jets of water were shooting into his face and he couldn't get his head up high enough to get a real breath. Add exhaustion, terror, and the thought that a bullet was going to blow his head off any second and it was not a happy situation.

Then why are you holding on? he asked himself.

He was considering this question when Overtime's elbow crashed into his rib cage and he let go.

He felt the killer slide away from him as he dug his feet back into the side, reached over his head, and gripped the edge.

This isn't as bad as the Newport Bridge, Overtime thought as he careened down the long straightaway.

Problem: Escape.

Analysis: You're moving at high speed away from your adversaries. You still have your weapon. You can still make it out of here.

Solution: Go with the flow.

Overtime lay back to increase his speed, slid around the double corkscrew, built up tremendous velocity on the next straightaway, and flew around the first high bank. The problem came when his two hundred pounds hit the next bank a little roughly and one of Joey's cheap sections gave way and he crashed through it like a rocket and was launched fifty feet into the warm Texas sky.

Witnesses later said that his screams were truly unsettling.

The water in the pool below got pretty hard when he hit it at the speed he was going, so he was probably already pretty banged up when the current sucked his unconscious body into the tube, plummeted him thirty feet, and shot him out like a bullet into the final pool.

There were no flotation devices, lifeguards, or emergency personnel there to meet him. There was no water, either—just the rock-hard pool bottom, a busted canvas bag, and some sand—so the twenty foot high-speed dash headfirst into the concrete is what killed him.

"Was that the man who shot Mr. Withers?" Charles asked Polly a few minutes later as they looked into the dry pool.

Polly looked at Overtime's shattered remains and said, "Hard to tell."

Joe Graham held on to Karen as she crawled out and grabbed Neal's hand, but they couldn't get enough leverage to pull him out.

"Mmmmmmm," Watanabe said behind the duct tape.

"What's he saying?" Graham asked.

"He's probably telling you to shut it off!" Neal hollered. "In any case, shut it off!!"

"Oh." Graham found the switch and the flow of water stopped.

Graham yanked the tape off Watanabe's mouth.

Karen pulled Neal up.

"Ready to go home?" Neal huffed.

"I think so," answered Karen.

"I am," Neal said.

"By the way, I forgot to tell you that you're fired," Graham said.

"That's good," Neal answered as he put his arm around Karen. "That's very good, Dad."

Then he and Karen walked down the water slide.

Epilogue

Neal lined up the putt perfectly, gave it a gentle stroke, and bounced the ball off King Herod's lip for the third time.

"You're awful at golf," Karen said.

"The only thing that could improve golf," Neal said, "are snipers."

"Not funny."

It was a beautiful spring day in San Antonio. Both the bluebells and Candyland were in full bloom, and Neal and Karen had flown down for a long weekend.

Brogan snored away on a chaise lounge as Brezhnev watched the one-sided match and wagged his tail when Karen hit her shot. The old bartender and the dog had a free lifetime condo at Candyland and used it frequently.

"You want to go on the water slide?" Polly asked Neal. She held six-week-old Karrie Landis—the reason for Neal and Karen's visit—in her arms.

"No thank you," Neal said. He lined up the ball again and this time got it past Herod's molars. A moment later, Herod's tongue spat it back out.

"Where's Graham?" he asked.

"Three holes ahead," Karen answered. "With one arm."

Graham loved miniature golf. It was so tidy.

A lot had happened over the fall and winter.

Marc Merolla cashed in his marker with Ethan Kitteredge and

ended up with 50 percent of the Family Cable Network in his own name. His grandfather died in prison shortly afterward.

Ed Levine bought a house down the street from Marc Merolla and became the managing director of Friends of the Family. Ethan Kitteredge stayed on as director emeritus but spent most of his time on his boat. One of Ed's first official acts was to confirm the termination of Neal Carey with the brusque message: Get a life.

"The Polly and Candy Family Hour" became a huge hit on FCN, barely skipping a beat. They gained a lot of new viewers, lost some old ones, but most of the audience stayed for the recipes. And the show took a slightly new direction—it still stressed family but broadened the definition to include just about any combination of people living together and caring for one another, including the big house that Candy, Polly, and Karrie shared. The day that Candy endorsed gay adoptions cost her a few thousand viewers and half a dozen sponsors, but most of the audience still stayed for the recipes and new advertisers signed on.

Karrie Landis's first appearance on the show became the highest-rated hour in the history of cable television.

Chuck Whiting stayed on as head of security, stayed married to his wife, and stayed distantly in love with Candy Landis.

Harold opened a dry-cleaning business in Chalmette Oaks.

Joey Foglio was never heard from again.

Once a month, cemetery workers in Queens would see a one-armed man sit beside a headstone marked WALTER WITHERS—HE PLAYED THE GAME," turn on a cassette of Blossom Dearie, and let it run for an hour or so.

Neal transferred his credits from Columbia to Nevada and rented a small apartment in Reno, where he stayed a couple of nights a week. The severance pay, pension check, and disability (mental) that Ed sent were more than enough to cover expenses. Neal's thesis title, "Tobias Smollett: The Image of the